Deeply Bound
C.R. Misty

Deeply Bound
C.R. Misty

Deeply Bound

C.R. Misty

Cover Design by Lady Maverick Publishing

Published by Lady Maverick Publishing

The International Boundaries Series | Book 2

Chapter 1
My Assumptions

Here we are you the reader and I the storyteller. Since you are reading this, my assumption is that you can see where I am coming from or that this story is like looking at a train wreck where you cannot turn away.

Well, I promise you this that I have succeeded in gaining everything I wanted with keeping two lovers. One is a secret from the other. Devon gave me a fair chance in getting me pregnant without compromising our lives. I am over the morning sickness faze and I am no longer as tired as I found myself in the beginning. I plan to tell the family soon since I am now passed that delicate stage and I couldn't be happier.

I always knew that Josh was in my corner rooting for me. I admit that he struggled with the fact that he couldn't contribute in the way that a husband should to this pregnancy. It took some time and he was always there by my side attending the doctor appointments until finally it worked. He doesn't know that I went to another for help. He has no knowledge of Devon, nobody does and I plan to keep it that way.

You already know my thoughts on the matter. You are probably wondering what has gone on in the last three months, let me fill you in.

Josh and I are doing great. Our relationship is on good solid ground. It took some work but I am happy to say that we are now enjoying our time that we have together. Josh is still working lots of overtime but in the time that we do have we make the effort not to fight and work on making the effort to do things together. We put our phones down and pay attention to one another. We play video games, watch movies, cook and clean. I have to admit that the sex has become amazing. We try different things; new positions and he has even started going down on me. It had been something that he had stopped doing for years. I love Josh and I know in my heart that he has fallen in love with me all over again.

In terms of my career, work is work, what can I say. The department that I work for is currently downsizing its staff, which means they have cut back on the temporary staff. I don't need to worry as my job is secure. I am permanent but with the reduction in staff, the workload has increased significantly. Everyone that I work with is feeling the extra burden and office life has been a challenge. Colleagues, including myself have been unhappy and it is hard to stay positive when being dumped on with crap in every direction. I know that I need to keep my chin up for the months that I have left before I go on maturity leave and I hope when after

I return from the leave the atmosphere will be better. I have learned not to dwell on the negative and instead hope for the positive, which is easier said than done.

I still haven't caught that break on my published book. It is getting steady viewings, downloads and purchases but I haven't seen that upswing when a book takes off and launches an author into stardom. I am still hopeful that my time will come because I am steadily receiving good reviews from complete strangers, which always does bring a smile to my face when I read them. I believe that things come in time and I trust that good things will come.

Devon, my secret is back at his home in Texas doing great. He is one funny guy I tell yah. He wanted to know if I did get pregnant and you already know that I told him. Even though he is just a friend, he couldn't be more thrilled and he is confident that it was his own that made it work. It's nice to know that I have him in my corner and I am happy to have shared time with such an awesome man. I feel the same with it being his but I won't know for sure until I see the baby because of that small chance that the donor sperm worked.

We are still the best of friends and talk pretty well every day and today is no different every time I have something that I am itching to share Devon is the first to know and today is no different.

Chapter 2
New Things

It is early, about mid-morning and I have settled at my office desk. The computer is on. I have opened up multiple applications and I have organized my work pile for the day. I have returned from the water cooler in the hallway with a glass to sip at my desk. I have just been given some news that affects me and in a good way and I am about to explode. I need to share and who else to share with than my secret friend Devon.

I send a message to him, "Hey you know what? Today all my wishes are coming true. Hear me out this is whacked. I was hoping for a change at work and this morning I found out that I've been assigned to work with a new boss without even asking. I was also wishing to have an office with a window and now I am getting one. I was also wishing for more reviews on my book and I received two more emails this morning from people telling me that they are reading my book!

Devon answers back within moments with my phone screen lighting up on my desk. He says, "There you go. The universe is working for you."

I reply, "It is just nuts how it all works. A woman from New York is doing a review for me.

Actually, we are exchanging reviews and the other is a friend. How is your day going?"

Devon says, "Going meh. I'm working on creating an x server to host a calendar server."

I reply, "Bugs aren't very fun. I am just happy that I have a couple of tech people that I can go to here and they help me with my own stuff." I pause for a second and then send another text to Devon, "Since all my wishes are coming true, I wish for another Devon Chambers porn to be delivered to my inbox. Do you think the universe will deliver?"

Devon writes, "Yep, I recorded one this morning and will send to you later. It's nothing fancy but you will like hopefully."

I smile to myself then say, "I'm sure that I will thank you." I don't know why I say and ask for weird things but I do and I make the demand, "I also want a picture of you sticking your tongue out at me and flipping me the bird." I regret the text after clicking send but at this point if I try to delete the text it will delete on my end but not on his.

The office is a steady buzz of the same old things going on. There is nothing out of the ordinary except that everyone has more work to do with the office cutbacks. I have to pack my things at some point to move over to the new office space. This morning I go through my office emails, answering the requests that come in from my clients. They are all routine requests and thankfully, they are quick to complete.

As I work at my desk the odd person walks by saying good morning to me and asking the question, "So when are you moving spaces?" News always gets around quick with our group and it can be a good thing and a bad thing but this environment it is hard to keep secrets because people are chatty. I think that is why I haven't really become close friends here with anyone.

I am not too withdrawn with the group. I talk to them in the office, saying my hellos and make small chat but when it comes to doing things outside of work hours like going out for lunch or attending some event after work hours I often decline.

It's not that I hate these people, that is not true, some of them I can't stand but I do get along with the majority. The thing for me is I am already spending eight hours a day with them and that is more than enough time to spend with them. I also want to keep my family life separate from my work life and I rather leave it that way because like I said before, people are chatty here and I rather keep my family life out of the gossip that goes on in the office.

Lunch approaches and I haven't received a reply from Devon. I know that he is working so I refrain from texting right now and decide that it is time to start moving my things over to the new office. Just as I start taking down some pictures from my office wall my new boss stops in to see me.

She says in her perky upbeat and mousey voice, "Hey Jordan, so I see that you are already starting to move over to the new office space, how exciting!"

I smile politely and reply, "Yes, I am hoping to done today. I got an email from the Technician this morning. It said that he was going to stop by mid-afternoon to move my computer and telephone line over."

Her straight chin length blonde hair bounces as her petit body jumps with a clap, "Oh how exciting! Well Jordan I came over to say hello and see how you were doing with things. It sounds like you have everything under control." I nod and she continues, "This afternoon I will send you a couple of meeting requests. I think it's a good idea for us to sit down and learn how we both work and how to work together."

I say, "Yes, that sounds good."

She claps again and squeals, "Wonderful, well I am off to lunch. I guess that you are going to go for your walk?"

As I have said, nothing goes unnoticed here. Others know that I take walks on my lunch hour. I reply, "Yes, going to get a bit of exercise."

She says, "Well I love that you do that. I should do that too but I actually have to run a few errands. My son is coming in from out of town this weekend and I need to buy some things before he arrives. Anyway, we will catch up later. Enjoy your lunch."

She is already part way down the hall as she says her goodbye and I doubt she hears my response but I say it anyway, "Enjoy your lunch, bye."

I sigh, she is an older woman, maybe in her early fifties but she has a lot of spunk and is over the top. It is always as if she has guzzled ten coffees before coming to talk to me. I haven't heard what she is like to work for but so far, she seems nice. I'll need to iron out details with her about my pregnancy and maternity leave. I think that she knows about it but I'll bring it up to her anyway in case that the office gossip has not gotten to her yet. Well maybe not today but I will tell her soon.

I head out for my lunchtime walk. I need to get out. I know that it is early and it is probably my mind playing games with me but I feel bloated. Well, I always feel bloated and glance at my stomach as I walk to see if I am starting to show. I think I am. I think my clothes are starting to feel tighter but I am not at the point where I can't wear my things. I look like I have a little pouch.

I keep to the sidewalk and go through a laundry list of things in my mind with what I need to do for my novel. Marketing is always a concern and what to work on next is on the list. I glance at my phone screen to see if Devon got back to me.

There is still nothing from him so I decide to text him as I walk down the quiet sidewalk path, "I was kidding with what I said earlier. There is no need to get all shy." I press send.

Devon writes, "Ha ha, I was just working in SQL hell."

A red squirrel with a puffy tail crosses the sidewalk into the open field as I continue down the path and I write while walking, "That's why they pay you the big bucks." I send him a smiley face with my response.

"Doh" He comments.

I ask, "So how is your server coming along?"

He fails to respond right away. I know that he is hard at work and get the impression that he does truly want to chat but can't so I tuck my phone into my pocket and enjoy my walk in the late summer sun.

After work once I am home, I finally receive a message from him. I wasn't expecting to hear from him today but smile as the message lights up my phone screen.

He writes, "Meh, it's trotting along. Drink a glass for me."

"Devon you are silly. Remember there is a bun in the oven I can't. I'm like some chick who has been invited to a Super Bowl party and am asking the host to explain the game ha ha ha I know not sexy." My comment is in reference to his server problems.

Devon replies, "Laughing over here we are both silly. Well, I am finally done here so headed home. Not feeling so chipper now after the flu I just got over I am now fighting a cold too. Some co-workers came to work sick and it sucks for the rest of us here."

I know that he has forgotten the promise he made earlier so I remind him, "Hey before you forget, I want that video."

He confirms, "I will send to you when I get home. It's on my home computer."

I text him a smile and say, "Okay, well I can be patient have a good night sexy." I send him a string of kisses and hugs and write, "Rest up, no need to send tonight."

Devon explains, "I normally don't get sick but people here have kids in daycare."

I say, "It could be all that masturbating catching up on you."

"Ha!"

I say, "I am totally giving myself a full-on wax tonight. I am going to be smooth on my camel."

Devon replies. "Nice and yummy, well I need to drive so I can't think that, laughing over here. Have a great night hottie."

"Bye sexy, feel better soon and rest up." I send a smile and continue, "I miss chatting with my guy."

This conversation dragged out throughout the course of the day. I already find myself at home, diner is done and my husband still isn't home after the final message is sent. I put my phone down and decide that I should probably take a shower. Josh won't be home until later tonight.

I stand naked in front of my mirror after stepping out of the shower. I think my boobs are getting bigger. They say when you are pregnant, they do. I know I am only a few months in but I swear I look different. I feel different, a good feeling but wow I look different to myself. Anyway, I get into one of Josh's old T-shirts and a pair of pajama pants, comb my damp hair and wrap it back into a towel to let dry.

I settle back in the living room with the television turned on but not paying attention to the show that is on. Instead, I have my phone and I am browsing the social media feed and I am honored again with another unexpected text from Devon.

Devon writes, "Hey there, I sent you a quick review to your email. I am not good at the angles but oh well." He accompanies his message with a smile and uses code words to play it safe in case that Josh is nearby. Quick review means personal video.

Like the greedy horny girl that I am, I watch and then re-watch it a few more times before I reply back to him.

I write back, "I Just watched. You are so hard Mmmm and I could hear your whispers, so sexy. Thank you and now I'm soaked..."

He sends a smile and says, "That's the point. Keep that hot box of yours wet. Hope you have a great night.

"I would lick and play with that swollen head and you wouldn't be staining your carpet. I would be down on my knees eager to drink cheers!"

He replies, "Yeah. I have been cleaning floors and carpets since knowing you. Hmm wonder why." He sends me a laugh and I chuckle to myself while reading his last message.

I hear the sound of the garage door opening. Josh is home.

Chapter 3
American Smart Ass

Life is routine, I go to work during the day, chat with Devon, go home and either see Josh or don't because he has picked up extra hours. Well, it's not all routine. When I am not working or talking to Devon or spending the little time that I do get with Josh I write and edit and work on cover design.

I finally finish my new book. I know that the last time I had shared news of my writing I was still in the middle of writing it. I admit that the encounter with Devon and getting pregnant put my writing to the sidelines. Now that everything has all happened and that I am getting used to the idea of being pregnant I managed to finish the novel. Like a proud author and the fact that I am the kind of person that seeks approval from others without having Josh to turn to I seek assurance from Devon. It is not that Josh wouldn't read my work, he would if I asked him to. It is just that I am shy in sharing this book with him. Partly because I don't want him to read it and because he doesn't enjoy reading in the first place. With Devon, I can pick his brain with the business of it all since he has been a published author longer than I have.

I send Devon a text, "Hey, I just wanted to run this by you because I value your feedback. I finished

Breaking Lines and I am now working on the edits. I already started writing the second book. I'm thinking to have the trilogy completed prior to publishing the first and I'm going to stagger the release dates either by six months or a year between releases. I am also going to register myself as a publishing company. I think I am going to mark the price point at a dollar per book. I know it's low but if it's marked low, I may generate more purchases. I know that the biggest obstacle with my first book is finding the audience and I think if the price was more appealing it may generate more readers. What do you think?"

Devon answers back within moments, "That is the right approach. Sell book one for a dollar (looney) and second a little higher." Devon is such an ass at times. Really, he needs to write "looney" in brackets next to the word dollar. Sometimes I think that he thinks that because I am Canadian, I have no concept of North American terminology or that he simply likes to tease. He is an American smart ass.

I reply, "I know I have time to think but I just can't seem to ignore the price point. Okay, well it's a good idea. I am already registered as a publisher but because I want to stay discreet. I need to register a second company to change my name I'll be two publishers so free ISBNs for all! P.S. You are a goof I know what a dollar is. I think this series is going to produce me some fat stacks I'm going to buy a ranch in Texas."

Devon responds, "Gain the audience first, laughing over here and save a horse and ride a cowboy?"

I send him a smile, "Yes for sure! I realize that it wouldn't be nice to keep horses on my island so I need property where the cowboys are and live there six months less a day so that I don't lose the Canadian benefits. I have to admit that I am wondering what those cowboys taste like."

He replies, "Well there are plenty in the state of Texas. Chuckling here."

"Hey what do you take me for? I just want to taste one and grab his ass."

"Chase me."

"Hmm let's see playing hard to get, are we? Well, seeing that I know where you live and I know your schedule, I would guess a time to "run" into you and I am confident that I wouldn't need to tie you up or anything. I would do that creepy move confidant that you wouldn't turn away if you said no., I would throw a pair of panties at you and well I guess retreat defeated. You know what; I have never had to chase a guy. They have always come to me." I send him a smile and continue, "Laughing over here, boy I sound like a creeper. Reality is I would text you saying I was in town. Meet me here and we do whatever."

"So, chasing someone is new huh?" He adds in some laughs.

I admit, "I'm not about to be in the habit of chasing someone but if you turned me down, I would probably become a nun. Actually, that's a lie. I'm just hot for you." I send him a wink and continue, "I know that I could just give you the look and you would be game."

He admits, "Yeah. You got me."

"I have never ever wanted someone this bad. You drive me nuts and I have never been wet this much."

"Tongue wagging, I am honored. See are friendship is cool. We know each other's limits but know we want to fuck each other's brains out. You have me smiling over here."

"Yah I like what we have. You have made me truly happy even though you are so far away. I smile a lot more now."

Devon writes, "Good. So, can I eat you now? I'm starving again for your yummy box. I dream of entering you again and watching you get off. Want another taste of you and feel you again."

I let him know, "You can eat me whenever you visit again. I would be all smiles, eyes closing, sighs and trembling with anticipation."

Devon admits, "I want to see your chest bounce again too. Love those girls and doggy style you and go to town on you. I'm such a dirty guy. Hell, I would lick your panties dry while they are still on you. You drive me nuts. Wow I love your body features right down to every curve."

"You're my dirty guy and I can't wait to enjoy you again and P.S. Whenever the coast is clear on your side say the words and I can mail you a pair of panties with my scent on them."

"I would love that. I would enjoy that while you know what."

I smile to myself and let him know, "Thought you would."

He asks, "Can I have them drenched in your scent? I want it to last a while once I know I can get them I will let you know. I know next week Sara is going up north so I have five days available to get them. So, I am hoping after work we can FaceTime from email address, I will again let you know."

"Yah I'll make sure that they are soaked. I'll let them dry and then put them in a Ziplock (keep them fresh) and mail them to you." I continue on a second thought, "Nice. So, she goes Sunday so maybe Monday or sometime next week we can FaceTime?"

He clarifies, "She goes Sunday."

I already can't wait to get to see Devon again. I respond. "Smiling big for the FaceTime."

Devon says, "Okay, well I am off to a meeting. Talk to you later."

I put my phone away for the moment and take in my surroundings. I'm at home, its quiet and Josh isn't here. I pick up my phone to check for texts from him or anyone other than Devon. Not a single person has messaged me. Is that sad or what? I haven't announced my pregnancy yet to my family maybe tonight I should. Geez I just don't want to say it and then lose it. I decide not to say anything besides Josh and I should make the announcement together. Another time, I guess.

Chapter 4
Piece of Him

I find myself at home alone again for the evening. Josh is working late which is no surprise so I have time to let loose and unwind so to relax I decide that working on my writing is a good way to get my mind off of other things like this thing growing inside me.

I send Devon a quick message, "Hey made it home how's your work going?"

He usually takes a few moments since he has things on the go so, I just leave the window open. Our conversation time seems scheduled. He makes time during his work hours to chat with me so that his spouse Sara doesn't catch him and it's also to my own benefit because when Josh is here, he doesn't suspect. I think for the both of us we were on the path to being caught earlier on when this became more than just a friend's situation. Devon saw that and pretty well made the decision to schedule our time better. It sucked in the beginning because I craved him but over time I adjusted and I think that the relationship, well this weird relationship is stronger today because of it.

Devon is starting to succeed with his career. He has landed this amazing high paying technical job working for one of the most elite high-tech companies in the world. The book that he was working on when we first started talking, he had asked me to read a sample back then and now he finally published it. I am a little jealous to say that he made the best sellers list this past week so now our scheduled talks have been dwindling a bit as he is being pulled in every direction with people wanting a piece of him.

I have mixed feelings about all of it. Let me explain because I feel horrible with how this is coming across. You wish for your friends and family to do well and achieve all of their dreams and I am over the top happy for him. When I say the word jealous, I mean more on the level of hoping that my own books reach success. I know that it takes time and to put it simply is that my time has not arrived yet.

Where the mixed feelings come into play is I miss him. I miss the company that he provides me during the day and the fact that I know that I have a true friend on the other side of my text there to support me, love me and just simply have to talk to about anything. With him, anything goes and it is nice. I knew deep down that this day would come. Devon is one outgoing, confidant and a determined man. There was no doubt that he was going to achieve success and you know what, if our relationship takes a bit of a back seat, I just have to swallow it and support him when he needs it.

My love for him is my entire heart and with the gift that he has given me comes a love that I have never experienced. My heart craves for him but because of the entire situation that we are in I think that the time away from Devon is a good thing because it's allowing me to refocus on my pregnancy and this life that I am trying to maintain with Josh.

I look back at the chat window that I had opened to talk to Devon. Ten minutes have lapsed but there it is I received a message from Devon, "Hey, it's going really busy as usual and the media, I have no idea how they were able to get all my contact information but my phone has been ringing nonstop and my cell phone too. I have had to put it on silent because it's getting out of hand."

I answer, "That's fame for you. I still can't believe that it's happening. Let me rephrase that. I knew it would happen for you I just didn't expect it to take off so quickly."

"Yah tell me about it!"

"So have you accepted any interviews or anything like that?"

"Next week I have a couple of interviews with some major magazines and a radio show in New York City; all accommodations are paid which is awesome!"

"That is too cool. Well, I am so incredibly happy for you. I admit that I miss our chat time but you know what, seeing all this happen to you is just amazing and I am living vicariously thru you."

"Ah Jordan, thank you, it means a lot that I have your support. Please I want you to know before it becomes even more intense with interviews, traveling and promoting this book. If I am unable to talk to you, know that it is not me giving you the cold shoulder or anything. You mean the world to me and I want you to know that if you send a message, maybe I won't answer immediately but I will always answer."

"Smiling big, thanks Devon you are such a sweetheart. Well, this Canadian girl is cheering for you!"

He changes subjects, "How are you?"

"I'm good, just taking it easy at home and working on my own best seller." I send him a wink face with the sentence.

"Have you been tossing your cookies?"

"No, I seem to be passed the morning sickness which is great. The food is actually staying down. I tell yah this little thing inside me was giving me a run for my money."

"Oh, that's good to hear that you and baby are getting along." He adds a smiley face to the message. Well Jordan I hate to be the one to call it but this day has just been nuts and I am falling behind with my work. I have to get back to it. Ping me later if you need to talk."

I am sad but I knew that this was going to be a short conversation. I send a final message, "Bye, love you and giving you a butt squeeze for good luck."

"Hey no squeezing my butt, love you too!"

He is gone offline and I need to let him get back to his work. I open up my documents and get cracking on my own future best seller and just thinking it all thru I need to wish big like he did. I mean truth be told in my own personal life all of my wishes have come true up to this point. The universe has granted my wishes of publishing my own book. It has given me the love that I longed for. Maybe not in an ideal way but Devon came into my life when I needed him the most and to top it off, I am now with child and it's probably his.

Okay Jordan wish! Well first things first, I wish for a healthy, happy baby. I wish for my Devon and Josh to remain separate. I wish for myself to see success just like Devon is starting to see and with that I can have enough to provide for my family and Josh would not feel obligated to work all the time.

There we go I sent it out into the universe!

Chapter 5
Mountain Tops

Saturday evening is dinner night at my parents' home and tonight is the night that Josh and I tell them. I have kept this from them for over three months and that was a challenge in itself. I'm not always the greatest at keeping secrets and something as big as this was hard to do because I want to just scream it from the mountain tops and tell everyone. Well at least I can finally do it now.

I finish putting on a bit of makeup in front of the bathroom mirror. Satisfied with my appearance I store the makeup in a drawer, turn off the bathroom lights and meet Josh who is waiting for me in the living room. I say to him, "Okay I am ready, want to head out."

"Okay" He answers.

The fifteen-minute drive over to my mom and dad's place is more on the quiet side and Josh takes notice. He says, "So, what's on your mind?"

"Oh, not much" I say but in reality, I am thinking over how I am going to tell them the news.

It is as if he is reading my mind. He has one hand resting on the top of the steering wheel as we cruise down the highway. He glances over meeting my eyes and asks, "So are we telling them today?"

"Yes" I put on a brave smile.

We pull off the highway and are now taking the country roads on route to their home. We drive thru a small town with a combination of new and old homes as I look out the window. Then we pass by farms with cows out in the pasture, open land and then drive by spots of forested area. It's funny how when you get nervous at least when I do about something time seems to go by more quickly and this car ride soon comes to an end as we pull into the driveway.

Josh looks over at me, "Wow Jordan, breathe! Maybe we can tell them as soon as we get in the door so that I don't have to worry about you being nervous all night."

"I think I will Josh." I let a huge breath escape my lips.

"See, I am not just for looks." He smiles and gives me a kiss on the cheek. We leave the car, walk to the house and let ourselves in.

I call for them, "Mom? Dad, where are you?" I can hear them moving about they must be in the kitchen. Supper is already in the stove as the house smells like lasagna and garlic bread.

Mom has bent down with the oven door open to gauge if the food is ready as we walk into the kitchen. She is taking out the lasagna and dad is standing at the counter cutting the loaves of garlic bread. He is the first to great us as we enter the kitchen.

He gives us an enthusiastic, "Hey how is my daughter and son in law?" He puts the bread knife down to put his arm around me in sort of a half hug.

Josh answers, "We are good and you?"

"Oh, I'm good." I reply.

Dad gives me a kidding sideways glance. There is some reasoning for the expression. He says, "Jordan you are so quiet. Do you not have anything to tell your dad?"

I know that there is no way that he knows that I am pregnant. I'm not showing. His question isn't to get me to spill the beans on my news so to speak it's more of a general inquiry and I know what I am about to say will through him by surprise.

I smile at him and shyly answer in a breath, "I'm pregnant."

At this point mom stops fussing with the lasagna and turns away from the stove to face Josh, Dad and me. She blurts out, "What?"

I start to laugh, "Mom you are going to be a grandma."

"Oh, Jordan come here and as I approach her, I see Dad shake Josh's hand, which turns into a playful father son hug. She gives me a hug, "Oh sweetheart congratulations." She touches my stomach I guess that I am going to have to start getting used to this, "How far along are you?"

"Just over three months." I beam and then catch a glimpse of my dad smiling back at the two of us.

All within a second, my nerves of anticipating this entire moment have evaporated and I am standing in a room that is full of happiness and joy.

The feeling of nerves brought on by anticipation has evaporated and now it seems so silly to me that I was even nervous about this announcement.

Sitting down to my mom's amazing lasagna diner is always awesome. It's one of my favorite dishes that my mom puts together. Tonight, for some reason the food seems much tastier. Conversations are full of laughs and about the good things to come. Josh and I will be first time parents and Mom and Dad are soon to be first time grandparents.

Chapter 6
Good Son

The red eye flight to New York was okay. It was quiet. Sara dropped me off at the airport. She could have come but figured she would just get in the way. I told her that was not true. Anyway, there is no sense in arguing with her. When her mind is set it is hard to sway her the other way. I focused on clearing my mind during the time that I was in the air. It's an important interview, so I open up my email and reviewed the questions that they will ask in the morning. I read the questions but not really, because I have already gone over them a dozen times earlier and I know how I am going to answer. I put my phone back into my pocket.

There are others seated around me and the flight attendants are going from seat to seat offering drinks. I watch for a moment and aware of that airy hum that you hear when flying at a few thousand feet.

In the military, I used to fly a helicopter but one of these jets doesn't interest me so much. I appreciate the comforts of being a passenger.

My pocket vibrates and I reach in and grab my phone. I glance down seeing a message on my locked screen from my son, which says, "Hey Dad, Sara said you are already on your way and wanted to say that I'm proud you are my dad. I'll be listening tomorrow online."

He's a good son and I wish I could have been there every day for him. I was but not in person. When I divorced his mother, I was a phone call away and every other weekend I would see him. He gets it now that he is all grown up and knows that I couldn't be there in person but he knows that I love him with all of my heart.

He is an adult now, going to school and making a future for himself. I think that my divorce with his mother made him grow into the independent man that he is today. He was never one of those kids that were always asking for things. He managed a lot on his own.

I read his text over again. I write all of these books to make him proud.

I glance around to see if any flight attendants are nearby. I'm not sure if I should be using my phone. My son is important to me so I quickly text him back once the attendants have moved away.

"Hey kiddo thanks that means a lot to me. Maybe next time you can make it and we can catch up. Have a good night." I click send and tuck my phone away again. There is no sense in reviewing the notes any further to prepare for tomorrow. I already know the material and besides I need to relax.

I tilt the seat back and close my eyes. I have no clue if I have ten, twenty or thirty minutes but I feel a gentle touch on my shoulder. I open my eyes to a young, slender woman. Her blonde hair neatly tied back. She is in an airline uniform. She says, "Sir we are landing soon. The pilot has asked to tilt up your seat and buckle up."

I nod, her blue eyes twinkle in the dim light as she smiles and continues to make her way down the aisle. I stretch allow for a yawn to escape and then the message of the plane landing plays over the intercom.

Chapter 7
Wild Fire

News spreads like wild fire over the course of the week. Without me so much as hinting that I am expecting on social media or the extended family, Josh and I only told our parents and siblings and with that, I have gotten messages of congratulations and phone calls over the week. Many questions that range from the, "How are you feeling?" to, "What names do you have picked out?" Nonetheless, it comes as a surprise with all of the love that we have experienced in these past few days.

Names, wow I am not even sure where to begin? Well, that is not true I sort of do have an idea for a boy name. If I am having a boy, I want to give him two middle names, after the two men in my life. I need more time to think for picking a first name.

Hmm I wonder how Devon is doing. I haven't heard from him in a few days. I'm not worried or anything I just know that he has been very busy with interviews and promotion of that bestseller of his. He did say that he would be away but I would be lying if I said that I didn't miss his chats. I daydream for a few moments, wondering what it's like to experience the attention he is receiving as an author. I wonder how it feels to have your work get the amount of attention his is now receiving.

It is the early evening of a rather long workday. Josh is at work with his second job. He won't be home until after 10:00 PM and I am just relaxing in the living room, eating an egg salad sandwich in front of the T.V. and catching up on all my recorded shows. I finish eating and decide that the recording will have to wait. I am too destructed with thoughts of Devon so I think that it's time to head down to the office and sooth my thoughts with creeping my guy on the internet.

The nice thing with Devon reaching fame is there is usually a new article posted about him and if I am lucky, there are a few photos of him in the article.

My search doesn't fail me and I am rewarded with an exciting article that comes with highlights of Devon's interview and a couple of pictures with Devon and the Media person.

I pause on the picture and take in his smile, the spark in his eye, his masculine square jaw line and his handsome complexion. His short brown hair flicked up in the front. He is dressed in a new sharp looking black suite with a white shirt and an edgy vibrant green tie. I rest my chin in my hand as I stare. What a sexy man and now I'm wet just thinking of the time we had together. He is so loving and so passionate and his emotion not only comes through in his lovemaking but in his work to. I lift my chin from my hands to read the article. The interviewer asked if Devon had imagined his book to take off as it did. Devon's answer reads, "Yes, it's something that every author hopes for and for me I knew that my time would come in publishing this one. I spent many years as a struggling author and with every book that I published leading up to this one I knew that I was getting stronger as a writer and at the same time developing a fan base that would eventually launch me further with the publishing of this novel." I smile as I read because he had shared that thought with me in one of our many chats. I knew from the start that he would amount to something big.

I wander if his spouse Sara went with him on this trip. It's not hard for me to find that out. Sara is much older than Devon. Sara is retired and she spends a lot of her free time on Facebook. I search for her name, find her page and to my surprise it appears that she stayed home? She has a post from last night that reads, "Congratulations to my love Dev on his fantastic interview in New York City. I always believed in you and wish I was there." I close down her Facebook window. I have never met Sara or have spoken to her and she has no idea that I even exist. Her comment bothers me because it feels dishonest. She has never shown her support for his writing before. I think that she is a genuinely nice woman. I trust Devon's taste in women and believe her to have a kind heart but I know from Devon telling me that his spouse has never so much as even picked up one of his books. I'm sure that she means well and I guess that's like the tea pot calling the kettle black because Josh hasn't read my work either. Well, I guess I have no reason to be irked but I am and wish that she would read Devon's books and with that thought, I get a twinge of pain and wish that Josh would read my own.

I shake the thought and scold myself internally for creeping her wall. Sara deserves privacy and I have no right peering into her life. I close the Facebook window and switch back to Devon's interview pictures to brighten my mood again.

My mood changes back to a more neutral state and I am inspired to work on my own novel. Devon's success is fuel for my own.

Chapter 8
It Snuck Up

My first ultrasound appointment is scheduled for this morning and as weird as this sounds it sort of snuck up on me. I am happy in a way that I had been distracted because wow this morning brings loads of nerves and anticipation on what this little baby will look like. Time is passing by and I'm already at a first milestone with this first appointment.

Josh is awake before me and as I roll out of our king size bed to go to the washroom and wash up. I can hear him starting to make our breakfast in the kitchen. I hear the noise of the coffee maker brewing and smell the bacon, eggs and toast that he is putting together and their goes that blender. The sound of the blender tells me that he is making ice cappuccino's, which means that I should hurry up, get dressed because breakfast will be ready in minutes.

I put together an outfit. I am still wearing my normal and not maternity clothes, deciding on a sport a casual top and a pair or dark blue jeans. I tie my hair up, put on a bit of makeup, some eyeshadow, eyeliner and mascara and walk down the hallway into the kitchen.

He is pouring the iced cappuccinos into large cups when he looks up and smiles, "Hey Momma, how are you feeling this morning?"

I smile and before grabbing my plate and drink to take to the living room to eat. I reach up to his cheek and steel a kiss, "I am good. I can't wait to see this little thing." I say while resting a hand on my stomach."

He admits, "Yah me too. So, is today the day we find out if it's a boy or girl?"

"I'm not sure? I read online that is usually done after eighteen weeks and I am only about fourteen. I think today they are just looking to see the growth, check heartbeat and just make sure that the little one is healthy."

He nods, "Ah okay got you."

We have two recliners in our living room that are placed in front of the T.V. Josh puts on one of our recorded shows as we chow down on breakfast.

I try to keep my mind distracted while I eat but it is so hard not to think about it. This little baby, my little gift is growing inside me. I am off in la la land.

"Jordan?"

I startle and look over, "Do you need to drink water before this appointment?" Josh asks.

"Oh yes, wow I almost forgot to do that."

"We should probably leave in the next ten minutes."

"Okay" I say to him. Josh is the kind of person that likes to follow plan. He isn't one for surprises or being late or anything like that so I take his message as a hint to get moving. I finish eating, take my dishes to the dishwasher and get started on the water consumption. I hate drinking all of it at once. The first of the three glasses goes down fine but part way through the second I start to feel very full especially after downing breakfast. I finish then head to the washroom for one last pee. It's almost an hour drive to the doctor's office so that will give my bladder enough time to fill up again for this ultrasound.

The drive in feels like it is taking forever. Josh is running through all of the plans for our day. He always does this whenever we carpool together. Today we both took the morning off to see this little baby.

Josh says, "So we are going to be there in the next twenty minutes. I'll come in with you."

"Yes of course."

"After do you want to stop for lunch before going to work?"

"Sure" I say. I already know where he has in mind, his favorite coffee shop.

"We can get a couple of sandwiches and iced caps?"

"Sure, sounds good Josh." We go through this routine regularly and I just humor him. I know him reciting our plans is a way of him keeping his mind focused and at ease. Soon enough we roll into the parking lot and soon find ourselves in the waiting room.

A nurse opens the reception door that separates the appointment rooms from the reception area. She peeks her head out into the reception area and calls out, "Jordan?"

I smile and say, "That's me"

She smiles and says, "Would you follow me?"

Josh and I get up and nervously follow her back through the door and down the hall. She brings us to an area where there is a change room and a door within leads to a second room where the ultrasound will take place. She explains, "Please remove your pants, shirt and bra. You can leave your panties on." She points to some clean folded linens on the bench and says, "You can wrap one of those around you. The tops are there and you can leave your clothes in here until you are done. When you are ready just come through the door and your husband and I will be waiting on the other side."

I say, "Okay" and close the curtain after catching a glimpse of Josh following the nurse through a second door into the ultrasound room.

The lights are dim when I enter the room. There is a counter on the left and a couple of stools. The nurse is already sitting on one of them. She has a computer in front of her with ultra sound equipment on the side. There is a rather tall chair well it's a half chair half bed in the center of the room for me to lie on with a step to get up onto. Josh is sitting in a chair on the right and on the ceiling; there is a flat screen monitor.

The nurse smiles, "Jordan come lie down." She pats a hand on the cushioned surface of this chair like bed and I waddle over and scoot up managing to keep the linen wrapped around my lower half.

She helps me into a position that she wants and carefully pulls the linen down to just below where my panties are and she helps me lift the paper feeling top that they provided in the change room up.

She warns, "This is cold."

I say, "Okay"

She puts some clear gel just below my belly button. It's cold like she promised and as she prepares her equipment, I tilt my head to glance over to Josh who gives me an encouraging smile.

The nurse explains, "Today we are checking for the baby's vitals, measuring growth and making sure that everything looks normal. If you look up you can see everything on that screen."

Josh asks, "Do you take pictures?"

"Yes, we will make sure that you leave with a good picture of your little one." She smiles and continues, "Shall we see?"

We say in unison, "Yes!"

The nurse puts the wand to my stomach and presses. I can feel it on my bladder and am reminded that I have to pee but I burry the thought away as soon as I look up at the monitor.

"There's the little one's head." She slides the wand over my stomach to get a side view and I see the first image of this little one.

"There is an arm and that is the umbilical cord. There is a leg." I start to cry. I can't believe this is real.

Josh pats my shoulder and smiles, "Are you okay."

I nod and say in a breath, "I wasn't sure what we were going to see."

The nurse explains, "You're in you fourteenth week, after twelve weeks most of their critical systems are formed and after that it's growth and development."

I watch the screen as she moves the wand to produce different angles.

Josh asks, "Can you tell the gender?"

"It's too early. Your next ultrasound we will be able to have a better picture."

She pauses at different points and types stuff into her computer and then angles it one more time of a side view of the entire body. She says, "There, that is a good picture." I look up and watch the baby's arms move I can't seem to look away from the screen and then I am prompted by the nurse, "Everything looks normal. We are going to send all of the information to your doctor as a final check." She removes her wand from my stomach and hands me some paper towel so that I can wipe the gel off my stomach.

I can hear the hum of the printer as the image of our baby is printed.

The nurse says, "Dad, for you to hold onto" She reaches over and hands Josh the picture and I see him look at it.

The nurse says to me, "You can go ahead and change. You probably need to use the washroom. There is one just down the hall on the left and when you go back to reception be sure to get the date for your next appointment."

"Okay thank you" I say and exit the door that leads into the hangs room while Josh follows the nurse through the other door to reception.

I meet Josh out front and he already has the appointment card for the next visit. He smiles and says, "Ready?"

"Yes, let's go eat."

Chapter 9
It is Real

Besides the morning sickness which I am now passed today's appointment brings it all home for me. It is real. Josh handed me the photo after the appointment to keep in my purse until we get home this evening. I am back at work now and am sitting quietly at my desk after having showed my baby picture to the women here in the office.

I lean the photo against my monitor and wonder what am I going to name you? I catch a glimpse of my phone light up, it's Devon. Did I tell him that I had an appointment today? I can't remember.

I open up his text that reads, "Hey just sitting in the airport waiting for my flight home and thinking about you."

I reply back, "Hey how did everything go with you book promotions?"

"It went great, I'm just a little tired now and hate having to wait for my flight home."

"Well, that's the cost I guess of being famous."

"Yah tell me about it." He replies.

"I think I have something that will make your day." I tease.

"Please share."

"Okay sending it to your email." I take a photo of the ultrasound photo with my phone and email him the image.

I let him know, "Okay it's sent. Let me know what you think."

I know it will take a couple of minutes for him to see it so I set the phone down and start to go through my work email which is so hard to do because all I want is to know his reaction. I wish he were here. I get through one email that was just an FYI about some upcoming changes and to my relief I see my phone light up.

Devon says, "Gosh Jordan, wow that is beautiful. They already look like a little person. You made my day thank you for sharing."

"You're welcome! Glad you liked."

"Love and still happy that I was able to give you the gift."

"Smiling big, I still can't thank you enough. They are healthy and growing."

"That's what I like to hear Jordan. Well, my flight is here and they are boarding now so I'll be home in a few hours and tomorrow I have interviews with the local news. I'll be busy but please Jordan don't be afraid to drop a line and tell me how you are doing. I may not always answer but I do get the chance when I can to read them."

I rub my stomach; I feel happy about everything and then answer, "Okay Devon I wasn't sure if I should leave you be that's the only reason why I wasn't sending so many messages. I thought you wouldn't be able to get to read them and I didn't want to interfere."

"Don't be silly, you never are, anyway love you and take care of yourself and the little one I have to drop off."

"Love you to, have a safe flight."

This baby, Devon and Josh, thinking about them all at once and my emotions holy moly I am in la la land over joyed that life is good right now for everyone.

Chapter 10
A Good Friend

Hours turn to days and then to weeks. I am starting to feel like my body is no longer my own, which is okay. I wanted this for a while. Office life is good and I have no complaints.

I haven't said much of my writing and to be honest I have been so taken up with life that it has taken a bit of a back seat. I'm not completely stopped in my writing. I do still keep up with my social media daily for my first book although I am still not finished with that series. The new series that I have been working on for six months is moving along although it's not as fast as I would want. I do get some writing and editing done daily but on a good writing day, I'm only adding a few hundred words at a time when I want to at least be aiming at adding a thousand words daily.

With Devon's new found success as an Author I see the possibility of it happening to me. I feel that when this new series is complete that it will be my break through, launching my own success. I have to admit he is more disciplined than I am with this writing craft. I enjoy being self-published with the hopes that I am picked up while he has gone through the more traditional route.

It is the evening and I am home alone tonight again. It's a cool and quiet night outside. It is peaceful but at the same time I am happy to be indoors, warm and comfortable. I lit a candle earlier and the house has the aroma of chocolate chip cookie. Normally I would be sad about being alone. For tonight it is okay because I have things that I need to do, like focus on writing because hey I am a true believer in creating your own destiny and for me, I want to make my own success in writing and I have to write in order to do that.

I go downstairs to my desk and turn on the computer. My computer lights up with blue lights around the tower fans and the hum of the machine tells me that it's loading up my applications and documents. I decide to log into my social media to read my last blurb when I receive a message.

It is Devon, "Hey, Sorry for delay, have had a bad headache today."

I ask because I know it has been busy for him lately, "Did you stay home?"

"Nope"

"Poor guy" I accompany that with a sad face and continue to write, "Want me to sing you "Fluffy Kitty"?"

Devon writes the acronym for laughing out loud and says, "Just wish I could turn off the lights."

"Maybe you could put your shades on? Fluffy kitty warm kitty little ball of fur happy kitty sleepy kitty purr, purr, purr. I would probably make your headache worse if I was, they're actually singing it."

My man never fails me with saying what is on his mind. Devon asks, "Can you sing that and ride me. Ha sorry went there. I will stop, might hurt my brain today."

He is always thinking of the act and I shouldn't be surprised he went there. I admit my encounter with him was the best experience of my life. It was exciting, different and to be able to have a man with that much lust and desire is just mind blowing. His experience comes into play with being a little older. I have to remark saying, "Well, maybe if you masturbated this morning, you wouldn't have a headache."

Devon comments, "I need your attention for that." He ends the comment with a laugh.

I send him a smiley face and say, "I don't believe that you have a headache. I think you are just Horney! When I get to suck that big dick of yours again, will you let me know what you want me to do? Do you want me to do it deep and slobbery or light and fast; do you like the tip of your head licked?"

"Hell, any of that as long as you are getting what you want."

I admit to him, "Just having the chance to taste you again is everything and yah I will slobber all over it."

Devon says, "Likewise, you look so amazing and I am dying to taste your juices and feel you again. I know we talk dirty but it's true. I want to tongue fuck you and drink you, yummy. Would you let me get you beyond the point and have you squirt? Just asking as I want to stay down there for a while, too much info huh?"

Wow I chuckle to myself I could go for some right now. My dirty man never holds back. I say, "Oh boy, yes, sure you will be making me beg for it. I may beg you to just fuck me."

"I want to be deep in you when I come. I know that I am vivid with my replies but it's so true."

"Devon, I want you so bad when you take me to the edge and I squirt into your mouth I want to taste my own juices on your lips in your mouth on your tongue. I want to smell my scent on your breath. I'll be begging for your dick and I want to feel it. I want to feel the weight of you pinning me down. I want to feel the touch of your hands holding my hips in place as you fuck me."

Devon answers and I know it went from hot to heavy, "Indeed. I am going to fuck you like never before. All of your body is just hot. I want to see your lips over my shaft again as I pull out and go back in and smell your scent rise to my face. I want to drive you into the bed. You had better bring lots of water for the next time we meet. We will lose lots of sweat. I can't wait to burst in your mouth and pussy and take you over and over again. That's what I think about daily."

I type to him, "I want your juices. I want to taste you so bad. I want you to coat my throat with it."

"I will trust me I will. Soak my face."

I send him a smiley face and say, "Good and I will you have no idea."

"I can only imagine."

"The thought of you makes me wet."

"I hope that we slip and slide as I want to make you groan a lot and make your eyes roll. I hope you are wet now and playing with yourself that makes me rock hard and hungry."

"I will be soon imagining that you are here with me."

"Nice, explode lots. I'm so bad. I want to have you in public too. The thrill of that is awesome. I know not your cup of tea but I want to fuck you in a park or hallway. Just to please you girl would be heavenly. See I am a good friend to have, one that wants to bang you silly. I would love to have you in an office setting, like on desk."

"My jeans are soaked and I can feel my lips are so swollen."

"Yummy, let me at you, lucky jeans and panties."

"I just want you and I don't want to worry about any distractions of others seeing. I want my full attention on you."

Devon says, "Ok different subject. I am so hard it hurts." He accompanies his remark with a laugh and a smiley face.

"I want it all trust me I need to go finger myself right now."

"Okay, have fun. I have to wait until morning. Well, have a great night. Think of me pounding you hard."

"I want to feel your desire so bad. Wow, I'll take it all and we wonder why we have nothing to say on Face Time because all we want is each other. Are you heading home now?"

"Soon but I am so hard I have to stop or I will take an eye out and I'm dressed."

"Bet that headache is gone. Are you going to unload in your car? I hope you do."

"We need to have our way with one another again so that we can move forward with friendship and become even better friends. It is that I need to have you and I know that you got your gift but still I want you. Yeah, I am going to whack off hard over you."

I tell him, "I'll empty you. I never wanted a man's juice as bad as I want yours. I see you come in those videos and I just want to lick all of it up."

"I'm flattered, I have spilt so much over you and I have even had the pleasure of meeting you face to face. I am over active master bating for you. It is all over you in my mind."

I send him a smiley face and admit, "I am soaked here. I know I'm going to explode the moment I start touching myself so when we drop off, I'm going to master bate standing up so that it's harder to get."

"I had to go wipe up in bathroom. Wow a wet spot the size of my hand. Bad girl film it, I want it."

I make a joke to Devon, I know that he is talking to me while getting tasks done at work, "Would you rather talk about server farms?"

"I wish that you were on your knees right now sucking me. Nope, I need to wrap up here going to let you go explode."

"I'd be under your desk with my mouth wishing for those juices while drooling and not caring trying to pull you in as far as I could."

We let each other go and well I have to tend to my girl. She is foaming at the mouth with all this talk from Devon. I miss his touch, his scent and his dick so much. I have kept the toy that he made for me, the mold of himself and decide that it's time to play with it.

I head to the spare bedroom and open the top right dresser drawer of my dark wood antique dresser. I take it out of hiding my big green Devon mold and as he asked, I set up in the bathroom with the door closed. I know that it's weird to do this behind closed doors because there is no sign of Josh coming home any time soon but it is just one of those quirks, I guess. I feel more comfortable in knowing that I am in a private place.

I set up the camera on top of the antique dresser and aim it on my sweet spot as I stand in front with my green Devon toy in hand. I say little and moan as I slide the toy inside of me. I am so warm and juicy that the toy just slides in. I moan some more to that feeling. It's not Devon but its close enough that it brings me satisfaction. I speed up gradually and press in to the rhythm that I desire. I am like a teenage boy; seconds pass and I am on the edge of exploding. I say to the camera, "See how much this pussy wants you. This is what you do to me and I am about to explode."

I moan as I start to throb and more cream flows over the toy. I slowly pull out my Devon toy. If my girl could protest, it would. I tell the camera, "I got off to the feel of your big dick." I stop recording. He will certainly enjoy this one. Wow, I smile I needed that.

Chapter 11
Not Huge Bookworms

My eyes open and adjust to see the morning rays of light along the ceiling of Josh and my bedroom. I roll over and extend my arm to find that Josh is already gone. I roll onto my back looking up at the ceiling, sighing at the thought that part of my day I will be alone. Another week has gone bye and it is another weekend of solitude. Well not really, I say solitude because again like a broken record Josh is away at work but I think at this point I know longer need to mention it you can just assume that. Later today, I have plans to go to a girlfriend's home for dinner and to catch up with them.

My girlfriends are all around my age. They are in their late twenties and earlier thirties. During the day, I pass the time by catching up on the housework, doing laundry, cleaning the bathrooms. As I complete the chores, I think about tonight about seeing my friends. I am looking forward to the visit as the day rolls by and soon enough the evening comes and I find myself standing on a porch under the star filled night sky, knocking on the door. I'm greeted with a warm smile and a hug.

"Jordan, oh I am so happy that you made it!" Hailey gushes and continues, "Well come in. I take it that Josh is working tonight?" Hailey opens the door wide. Her smile is contagious and she looks great, wearing a dark skinny jean, fitted black top with a trendy large blue gemstone pendent necklace that matches her eyes.

"Yes, but this is a girl's night, isn't it?" I ask as I walk into her home.

"Yes, Matt is gone with the little one to his parents for the evening to let us girls enjoy our evening." Matt is her husband and Hailey has a little girl named Brittany.

I follow Hailey down the hallway into her open concept living room and dining room area, where the ceilings extend to the second level. The windows in this space overlook a beautiful view of the forest. I am the last one to arrive. Lucy, Maggie, Mellissa and Ophelia are already here and are sitting in the living room area with drinks in hand and I see chips, salsa and dip on the coffee table in the center.

Ophelia is sitting on the arm of the couch, sees me first and lifts her glass, "Hey Jordan!" Her dark brown hair tied neatly back and she is wearing a black pencil dress.

I walk into the room and say, "Hey Guys!"

Hailey whispers to me, "What would you like to drink?"

"Could I have a juice and carbonated water?" I want to have a fancy drink but with this little one. I need to keep it clean.

She says, "Coming right up."

Mellissa doesn't hold back and blurts, "Wow Jordan you are getting so big!" Mellissa is the kind of girl that always just says what is on her mind without putting any thought as to how it will sound or come across. She has red hair that matches that fire type personality. Sometimes she can come off as being a bit of a bitch and well that is because she can be one at times but in this situation, I know that she wasn't being deliberately mean.

I rub my belly and smile, "Yep the little one is growing and I think I can actually see myself get bigger by the day."

Hailey hands me my drink and joins the conversation by chiming in, "When I was pregnant with Brittany, I felt the same way. Jordan just don't look at the scale you just got to give your body what it needs and if you want to eat then eat."

"Yah I do. I have been craving olives lately and just food that I normally wouldn't want."

Hailey admits, "For me it was watermelon I couldn't get enough and for diner I always wanted a side of fries."

Hailey and I find a seat on the larger part of the L-shaped couch in the room and Mellissa adds, "Wow fries for dinner every night isn't good for you. If I was pregnant, I would try to stay away from greasy food all together."

Hailey gives her a look, "Melissa you have no clue. When you are pregnant you crave things and they are intense you will see one day. You may want that but trust me junk food does come into play."

Maggie is the mediator of our group of friends and she steps in before the conversation starts to take a turn from light hearted to debate, "I think as long as whatever it is you crave is in moderation then its fine to indulge the craving. Eat when you are hungry and stop the moment you are full. Lucy backs Maggie with a nod and a "yes" and everyone follows suit.

The conversation segments from there with a few conversations taking off between the friends; our group of girls have known each other for many years but with life and families and work and such we don't get to see each other very often like this so there is a whole lot of catching up when we do all meet up.

I soon find myself sharing a conversation with Lucy and Hailey. Lucy is a petit woman with straight long brown hair and a fair complexion. She fills us in on her work life. She explains, "I am still in the same position as I was the last time we talked. It is like this, I like my job, the event planning side of it but some of the drama that goes on I just can't handle. I know that it doesn't make sense but I am torn and you know what I do look for other jobs but everything that has come up just hasn't gotten my interest."

Lucy works as a civilian member for the department of defense and her office focuses on planning events for military staff and their families.

The events range from diners, to fairs for the kids, dances, Halloween and Christmas parties. I know that Lucy loves organizing the events but for the people that she organizes for some of these people have been thru a lot and well sometimes, she has to deal with very difficult situations at these events.

I say, "I get it. I remember you telling me the last time we had talked you had organized a summer dance and at the event, you had to deal with that woman. She was afraid that her husband was going to cause a scene because of some sort of affair that she had with one of the other soldiers and apparently her husband had found out about it."

Lucy leans in and nods, "Yes, exactly! I know these people are good and that is why I love planning the events because it is a small way of giving back but I am not qualified to deal with some of the heavier situations that arise. I feel that I am helpless at times and I can't do anything and all I wanted was to plan a great day or evening for them and I get caught having to deal with some type of emotional mess during the event."

Hailey says, "These are things that are out of your control. I think for event planning, even if you were to switch to like, planning weddings you would still perhaps run into issues at those kinds of events also. I think any large groups of people there are bound to have a few that are going to cause trouble."

Lucy says, "Yah I know and maybe that is why I haven't been looking as hard as I maybe should if I really don't like this. I do love most aspects of my work just not all."

I say, "Well I think that is true for any job."

Hailey adds, "Yes, I agree. If the good outweighs the bad then maybe stick it out or see at least if you can find a better solution to deal with those weird situations."

Lucy agrees, "Yah I just need to maybe think about it and talk with the others that I work with. I can't be the only one that feels this way." She shrugs and continues, "Anyway enough about me. Jordan how about you we know that you have been busy making a baby besides that how is work and life?"

I smile and shrug, "Everything is good. Work is pretty well the same. I am still at the same place, there is no gossip, it's pretty boring but it's a paycheck so I guess that is good."

Lucy chuckles, "Yes no gossip means no drama so that's good in my books. Say I remember the last party you had mentioned that you were writing a novel did anything come up with that?"

Hailey chimes in, "Oh you don't know, she published it. I read it and it's pretty good."

I feel my cheeks turn red and I say, "Thanks Hailey, yes I published it last summer and it is doing good. I am making a few sales. I am also promoting and have learned a lot when it comes to the business side of things. This entire experience has been eye opening. Not just the writing a book part but learning and essentially doing everything else that is involved with becoming an Author."

Lucy says, "That's really great. Maybe one day you will make it like that new D. Chambers guy?"

I never have talked to my girlfriends let alone anyone about me having an affair with him. I haven't even boasted that I know him and talk to this famous Author on a regular basis and kind of startle with her mentioning Devon.

Lucy says, "You know who D. Chambers is right; the guy who wrote that new thriller, "Trial" that topped the best seller charts."

Hailey says, "I just finished his book and loved it. I just passed it over to Matt to read."

I sip my drink and answer, "Yah I read his book and it is really good. I'm hoping one day to make it like him. I just had to think for a second who D. Chambers was. Blame it on my baby brain I guess." The last thing that they need to know is that I know him. I just don't want to give anything away and then let something slip that could lead to more questions. I can't believe it; I am not upset or anything but amazed at the fact that my girlfriends know of Devon and his work. Yes, he is famous I knew that, but for my girlfriends to know of him, this is crazy. I know that some of my girlfriends like to read but they are not huge bookworms so the fact that two of them know of him just speaks volumes to Devon's growing celebrity status. Anyway, Lucy and Hailey seem to accept the baby brain comment and continue with the conversation.

Hailey says to me, "Jordan you should write a book on your pregnancy."

I chuckle, "My mom suggested that. I could and I have written a bit but I don't think it will be something that will catch because there are others who have written about the entire IUI treatment process. My book wouldn't be an original."

Hailey says, "Well, just a suggestion. I know that when I was pregnant, I purchased so many pregnancy books just to know what to expect. I am sure that there is a market for it."

"Oh, I don't doubt that there is; well, I did start putting words to paper. I'll see how it goes and flows and decide later if it's something that I want to publish."

Lucy says, "There you go!"

Hailey gets up, "I am just going to check on the finger food that is in the oven." She excuses herself from the conversation and returns moments later with a large tray of hot food for the group to devour.

The rest of the night continues with laughs and more conversation and before I know it, it is late in the night and then I am on route back home. I am driving home along a quiet, dark, straight county road. The blue light on my dashboard lighting up my odometer is a comforting feeling. I don't know why but I guess it's just that I like the color. Normally I would be listening to the radio but for now, I enjoy just the sound of the car humming as it carries me home.

It is funny how we can never quite turn our thoughts off and my thoughts are on that conversation that the girls had tonight. I mean it is one thing to read about Devon becoming successful and famous but another thing when you see that the people in your life know who your secret lover is. The silly thing with all of this is if I was drunk at the party, I know I am pregnant and I would never put the baby at risk. All I am saying is if I wasn't pregnant and hypothetically speaking let's say that I am drunk. If I was to spill the beans on the affair that I am having and say that I am having it with D. Chambers I think the girls would have thought I was out of my mind and start laughing saying, "Good one!".

It's like my two worlds have sort of just aligned in light of this evening's conversations. The thing is I have to continue to be me, Jordan, the girl that has lived in this city, has had the same group of friends and is just a normal woman who is happily married to her loving husband; and who is very likely pregnant with a millionaire's baby.

Chapter 12
Not so Farfetched

I am not going to bore you with my workweek this time because well it was quiet for me. This week I took an evening to shop for maternity clothes because most of my shirts still fit that's not the problem but my stomach is starting to stick out. I got a nice simple pair of black dress pants with cotton stretch material around the stomach the sales woman said that I could expect to wear them right to the end of my pregnancy, which is nice. I also picked up a couple of pairs of casual pants for around the house and a pair of jeans with the same stretch material around the stomach. Happy with my purchases I decide to call it a night. Jumping ahead to the weekend I have the day to myself, which means, housework, writing and I'll send Devon a text.

I know Devon has been busy with his success; I get it and know that this isn't the cold shoulder that I feel like I'm getting. He has told me to message him anytime but the thing is when the conversations start it is always by me. I can't help but have the feeling that I am bothering him. I know it's ridiculous for me to feel this way but I do. However, with the weekend upon me and no Josh around my mind wonders to my amazing friend Devon.

I exhale and murmur to myself, "Jordan your inner voice is being stupid just send him a text and be done with it. You know that you want to."

I open up the social media this morning on my computer in my office downstairs. I plan to take time to work on writing and send Devon a quick message, "Hey Devon missed talking to you all week. I hope that you are doing well and I am sending you some virtual hugs and kisses anyway have a great day if we don't get to chat."

As soon as I click send, I end up rereading my message and think that, it sounds needy. I don't think I am a needy girl and, in the end, I don't regret my text because that is how I feel.

About an hour or so passes without me realizing; I found my writing groove this morning and the words are flowing. I startle to the sound on the computer alerting me. I pause to have a look to see that I have a message.

Happiness fills my heart to see that it's Devon.

He writes, "Ah you are such a sweetie. I will gladly take those hugs and kisses and just to let you know I am having for the most part a good weekend."

I ask, "Do you have time now to chat for a bit?"

"Yes, but you know that you can message me any time. So, what's up?"

I tilt my head as I think to myself, what's up with me? I want to know what has been going on with him. Anyway, I reply, "This week was pretty quiet although earlier in the week I did some shopping for maternity clothes other than that it's been the usual."

"Oh, you must look so hot. There is something about a woman who is with child that is just gorgeous anyway you must be looking yummy these days."

I send him some laughs on the screen then write, "Well I feel okay. I think that I look okay just sporting a bit of a pot and happy to be well passed that awful puking stage."

"Oh, stop you are one hottie and soon to be a hot mama."

I laugh as I read his message and ask, "So what has my sexy man been up to this week?"

There is no delay and receive his response, "Well my publisher wrote me a check earlier this week."

"Wow Devon that is so exciting! Look at how well the two of us are doing we are both achieving our dreams. I bet it was a big check with all that media attention you have been getting."

"Thank you, I am happy that you picked me to give you that gift. Well, yah let us just say the check was more than six figures. It didn't feel real. I mean none of this feels real."

I say to him, "Trust me it is real! I forgot to mention this and it has to do with you. I was at a girlfriend's home the other night for a girl's night and well conversations led to me talking about my writing and then to books in general. Others talked about what they were reading and I have to tell you that two of my girlfriends have read your book and their husbands have read it. That just goes to show you just how mainstream you have become."

He replies, "Did you say anything about knowing me?"

"Oh my god no way, the most I said is that I knew of you and read your book but telling them that yes I talk to a famous author regularly and oh by the way did you know that we made love and this baby growing inside me was from him. Yah I could see that going well." I send him a smiley face to show that I'm not taking my comments too seriously.

He sends a smiley face back, "You know it almost seems farfetched. They probably wouldn't believe you if you did end up telling them."

I chuckle to myself, "Devon I could only imagine that the conversations around the room would have come to a screeching halt and a bunch of eyes staring vacantly at me in shock, maybe disbelief, doubt then laughter."

He writes, "Yah well that just goes to show you how well we have kept all of this a secret."

I sigh then type, "Yes we did well, the two writers that plotted our own secret love affair. It couldn't be more perfect."

"There I disagree with you. In a perfect world this wouldn't have been a Romeo and Juliet tale."

I ask, "So Devon you never mentioned what you were up to. I know that you met with your publisher for that check and what else?"

"Well, I took the week off on all the traveling and promotions and stayed in town with Sara."

I smile; he is so good to his spouse and I ask, "Did you two do anything to celebrate this new life of yours?"

"We did some house hunting."

"Wow really but you just did all those renovations with the place you have now."

"It is even more reason to sell. We were happy with the place but we were looking for something a little more private and secure."

"Is it all of those crazy fans?" I was sort of half joking with the comment.

He admits, "Sara is a little freaked out actually. While I was away some people from the press have been lingering around our place and to be frank now that I have this new income we figured why not splurge and treat ourselves."

"Wow yah I can see her being a little freaked out I would be too. So have you two found anything that you liked?"

"Yes, yesterday we put an offer on a property in a gated community south of Austin."

I'm happy for him and Sara really, I am but to be honest I am feeling a little left out with him just telling me after the fact. I know it is silly because let's face it he just put an offer in yesterday but I guess I am just a little surprised that I had no idea he was house hunting and it never came up in any of our conversations. We haven't spoke for a bit. I shouldn't feel this way but I sort of feel sad about it, not because he is treating himself but more with the grander fact that this is a clear sign that time and distance is working its way into this friendship and with Devon's success we are no longer talking as much anymore. At least with text he can't see my emotion and I am not going to rain on his parade he doesn't deserve to be subject to my weird emotions and besides I need to put them in check because this is life and we are still the best of friends even though we can't talk every day.

I say to him, "Wow Devon a gated community you must have put an offer on a beautiful home. So, when do you know if your offer was accepted?"

He answers, "Yes it's just over 8000 square feet. I picked the neighborhood and Sara has an eye for a well put together home. She was the one that picked this one. We won't know until Monday morning if the offer was accepted."

"Holy shit Devon that is huge all that space for just the two of you. Well, my fingers are crossed that you get it."

"Thanks hottie. Well, I have a feeling we will get it. According to the realtor it's been on the market for about six months not because it isn't a desirable lot or anything but it's just that there is a smaller market for larger homes and the owners are eager to get this one off their plate soon."

"Yah, that makes sense. Once you move in you will need to give me the grand tour during a video chat."

"Will do, I promise." Devon accompanies his reply with a smiley face and continues, "Well hottie I have to go for now. Sara has us doing some shopping for new furniture."

"Okay love. Well good luck with your shopping."

"Thanks, I really don't have a say in the matter but luckily Sara has a style that I like. She has me to drive her around and bring the cash."

I chuckle at my desk, "Well sending you some kisses and hope that the two of you have fun."

Devon answers, "Thanks hottie love you."

"Love you too Devon."

Chapter 13
A Decent Hour

Wednesday night is well, interesting, let us just put it that way. Josh isn't working his second job this evening but he decided to take his boss up on the request to work some extra hours in an attempt to speed up the release date of some software that he is testing. He comes home at a decent hour. I say decent because I am not in bed. He is home just a little after dinner. To be exact just after 7:00 PM, this is a nice change.

This last weekend I had done up a stew in the crockpot so it's nothing for me to take some out and heat it up for him.

"Thanks Jordan." I hand him a bowl of the beef stew.

I ask, "How is it?"

"It's good, thanks lovey." He takes a seat in one of our recliners in front of the television with his dinner. I let him choose a show for us to watch and of course, he picks one of those crime investigation type shows.

I used to love watching those shows and every now and then, I get into an episode but for the most part, let's face it there are so many to choose from these days. There has to be at least twenty different crime shows on television and the annoying thing is that Josh likes to watch all of them.

I don't put up a fuss although if I was given the choice, I would want to watch some good old fashion reality television. Ah well, I just lay back into my own leather recliner and decide to play with my phone during his show.

I think to myself, being an author and keeping up this social media image his work. I know that its free advertising but sometimes I feel like a robot posting and forcing myself to share something every single day. I mean I know that my effort is paying off because if I was doing nothing, I would have at most just family making the purchases but at least with these outlets my reach is far greater.

I send out my messages on three social media sites and then browse the news feeds to see what others are doing. For a Wednesday night, it is dead. I am at the age where many of my friends have kids and there are a few overly proud parents on my feed.

I take a second and rub my belly and think, Jordan if you become like one of those overly proud parents, I think I will need to shoot myself. Like, come on there is one couple on my news feed that posts videos of their child doing stuff. In the beginning, I used to watch but after the tenth video, I stopped all together. Seriously, they just post videos of the child picking their nose or terrorizing the family cat or just screaming at the top of their lungs. Like why even bother? I make a promise to myself; I will never be that type of parent.

I know I am going on a bit of a rant here; I can appreciate those first steps and first words videos or a video of the child doing something silly but come on a video every single day. Sometimes I just want to unfollow them but then I think, wow Jordan that would be shallow if you did that so instead, I just ignore the video post and continue scrolling down the feed.

Josh looks over to me and asks, "Is everything okay? You have a look on your face and you're rubbing your stomach."

"Yah I am fine, just a habit I guess."

"What is with the look?" He focuses on me while his show continues to play.

"Oh, I am just looking at the news feed and I don't get how some people post boring videos of their kid daily. I hope that I never become one of those over proud parents that do that. It's annoying as hell."

Josh smiles at me, "Why don't you trying getting off your phone and spending some time with me."

We have this conversation regularly, "I am and you know I'm not a huge fan of your crime shows."

He says, "Just put your phone down."

I set the phone down on the coffee table next to my recliner and think of something else to keep busy. Well, I stare at the television pretending to pay attention to the show and I start thinking about my book stuff. I have to look into doing some sort of print on-demand book. My first novel is only available to purchase in e-book format and Devon had mentioned something in conversation that has sort of been lingering on my mind. Now he has two books published with his publisher and he said that even though e-book format is picking up, the bulk of his sales are still in his printed books.

"Jordan?" Josh startles me out of my train of thought.

"Yes?"

"I'm heading to bed." His crime show had ended and I had not even noticed.

"Okay love, I'll join you."

I settle under the feather duvet on our king size bed moments later and grab my phone to read for a bit as a way to help drift off to sleep. Josh comes out of the washroom after brushing his teeth, crawls into bed and takes out his phone.

We are creatures of habit. I enjoy reading my e-books and Josh loves to browse the online store flyers. If he is not shopping online, he is investigating some little gadget that he supposedly needs and after all the shopping, a purchase will happen. He always has some new toy lined up to buy. Well, I guess tonight is the first time in history that he has nothing to shop for.

He nestles up to me, peeking over my shoulder to get a look at my phones screen. He asks, "What are you reading?" Josh never takes interest in the books I read. Sometimes, when I am desperate to chat with him, I will talk to him about the books I read but he often will just tease me later about the stories that I enjoy. Lately, I have been reading Devon's books. Devon has two series. I finished his first book to his first series not long ago and then jumped into and finished his breakout novel, which is the first book to his second series and I am now in the middle of his second book to his first series.

I calmly answer honestly, "Oh this one is called, Infinite Danger"

I am mistaken in thinking that by answering his question, that it will satisfy his curiosity. He rests his head on my pillow. I think he is reading some of the words on the page. Josh follows up with another question, "What's it about?"

"It's a crime thriller about a secret agent trying to fulfill orders and not get killed." I tilt my head a tad to get a glimpse of Josh's face. He looks interested but also fatigued. His workweek is catching up to him.

I look back and continue to read a line when another question escapes his lips, "Who is the Author?"

I can't dwell on it and just answer, "D. Chambers"

He is quiet for a few seconds. For me it feels like moments and I catch myself holding my breath. What is he thinking? Has he heard of D. Chambers? I mean Jordan pull yourself together Devon has become a household name.

Josh's next words he says with a sly emphasis in his words, "D. Chambers what kind of name is that? Sounds made up."

I glance at him raising an eyebrow and say, "It's probably just a pen name."

He rolls back over to his side of the bed, "It's a stupid name if you ask me."

I say, "When I am finished, I could let you read it if you would like?"

He yawns, "No thanks, you know I'm not into reading books. Well, I am going to sleep are you staying up to read or do you want to cuddle?" Josh, when he isn't cranky and tired from being overworked can be a kind-hearted man and he does enjoy holding me in his arms as we go to sleep. I enjoy it too. Something about having his warm body next to mine is comforting.

"I think I'll read for a bit longer, good night lovey." I am still not at the point where I want to close my eyes.

"Good night." He rolls over so that his back is to me and pulls the comforter over his head.

Chapter 14
His Notice

It's the middle of the afternoon and nearing the end to a pretty good week in the office. I am at my desk, all caught up with work and decide to take a bit of a breather and chat up my sexy man. He mentioned that he was getting over a cold from the last time we had talked. All of that travelling around and promoting himself has caught up to him.

I type, "Just wanted to say hello and check in how you were feeling? Also, for the draft to your next novel I have some comments and questions." I click send. Devon and I have a bit of a system that works for us with keeping each other secret from our spouses. Besides only chatting during work hours or when we know that the coast is clear, we always start up the conversations with a clean hello, just in case other eyes may see.

Devon responds, "Hey there, I'm getting better slowly. Sure, fire away."

"The issues that I am seeing are there is a lot of repetition of topics. As a reader I am thinking, yes, I already know that, get on with it. There is also some miss used words and I sent you an email with the words that I was able to catch."

"Yeah, I'm listening also to the audio version. I agree there is too much repetition of words and grammar errors and word usage. But it's a good tool to find errors." He is referring to audio software that he is using. As writers, we know how we want our words to flow. With reading drafts after a while, the eyes tend to see what you had intended to write instead of what was actually written. With an audio version, you can listen to the text and it makes editing easier.

I say, "There were a couple things that I wasn't sure on the first is that you talk about your main characters cell phone being super crappy and the thing is that you are naming brand names. I don't think that's a good idea to do. Maybe you can leave out the brand. The second is I am not sure with copyright laws but the scene where you had the cab driver singing the words to a known song. I don't think you are allowed to do that. I would suggest leaving the words to the song out."

Devon answers, "What, not mentioning reference to it? The song yeah will remove lyrics but talking about a smartphone is no big deal."

I explain, "Well I would keep the fact that your character has a crappy phone but maybe use a made-up brand name or just leave the brand out altogether."

"No, it is just one user's experience and the device I am referring to is an old out of service phone. The time frame of this novel is 2003."

I say, "Okay, well it's your call. Another thing that I have been thinking about is the harbor of your opening scene. You know that the main ferries that are used have their own harbor. They don't dock at Victoria Harbor." I feel like I am drilling him a bit with my feedback but with the setting that he has placed his novel, I have been there and I know he has some inaccuracies that I am not sure that he knows about.

He replies, "I will look into harbor docking but it is fiction and stretching a bit could be allowed, but yeah. The main ferries I do see have their own dock. The fictional ferry doesn't. Good suggestions, thanks."

I am relieved that he seems receptive to everything that I brought up and continue, "No problem, I know other books have dropped brand names in their writing but in truth I have no idea what the rules are for naming real products in a novel?"

Devon answers, "For things that are out of service there are no problems with mentioning them but if it was a product in service than perhaps." Devon continues on a different thought back to the cab driver scene I had brought up, "You didn't like my Indian guy?" He ends the text with a laughing acronym.

I say, "Okay and don't put words in my mouth I didn't say that I was just concerned about the song lyrics." I end the comment with a smiley face.

"Ah that scene with the taxi driver was to make the ride for Alexis a little more interesting instead of saying she got into taxi as then went to airport. I thought about it that if I needed to cut words that scene would be it but I kept it for now."

I decide to change subjects because I have no more feedback for him. I don't know why, maybe because I look back and find it funny but decide to share with Devon the conversation, I had last night with Josh with regards to having Devon's book open in bed.

He answers, "Don't get in trouble and just tell him we are distant author friends."

"Wow, no way! If I said what you had suggested he would ask more questions."

Devon suggests, "We better cool it then for a bit."

Hold on what, Devon is taking my seemingly lighthearted conversation on what happened completely in a direction that I had not anticipated.

I explain to him, "Devon, I am always reading a story in bed. There is absolutely nothing to worry about; to him you are just some random author that I happen to be reading his work. I don't even think that he recognized your name as a household one even though you have already achieved that status." I look up for a moment. The noise of the coffee machine humming on the other side of my cubicle wall as it makes a cup of coffee for a co-worker startles me for a moment with my conversation with Devon. The office is quiet today so the machine seems louder than usual however; I don't need to focus back on appearing like I am working. My attention is back to Devon's reply as it appears on my phone screen.

He answers, "Ah, I meant not give him a reason to suspect. Oh, ok then, I just don't need to see you get caught or fight with him."

"Its fine Devon I just brought up the conversation because it was your pen name that he was poking fun at. Anyway, you are just a random to him that is all. So, there are no worries."

"Good, the more random I am the better." He adds some laughs after his reply.

I need to change subject again. I don't want him to dwell on him being found out because I won't let that happen. I say to him, "Speaking of names you know what, I have gotten so used to calling you Sexy instead of Devon. I know if we were to meet again, I would probably just call you Sexy."

"You are just too sweet but that works too. You are silly but I hear you."

"So, what else has been going on?"

"Right now, I'm just waiting for a response from the Publisher on the next books for the series and I am already thinking about the plot to another book. At work there have also been a lot of high cases today." I shake my head upon receipt of his text talking about his work. He was just given a huge paycheck the other day from his publisher, enough to leave his job but for some reason he hasn't given his notice. It probably doesn't feel real yet. Devon is a hard worker and even though he is under the weather, he still shows up to work.

I admit, "Sometimes I do feel like I am bugging you. If you are too busy just let me know and I can leave you be."

"Oh, it is ok. I don't mind. You know that."

I read my southern gentleman's last comment and it makes me smile. I say to him, "You know what? We actually had a normal conversation today. Usually, our talks are hot and heavy."

"There is more to this friendship than just talking about sex stuff, silly." He continues on the thought of a clean conversation, "Tell me how you as a person are doing?"

I send him a picture of me sticking my tongue out at him. Oh my, his last comment sounds like he is some doctor from one of those afternoon medical talk shows.

Devon replies, "Hey stop with the tongue I actually got a woody. Silly girl, you are looking hot as always."

"Thanks, Sexy. I am doing well. Work is normal which is good and I am still working on edits with my own book."

"It sounds like you are on top of things. Well, have a great night. I see you're close to leaving or gone already." He is right our conversation that you see was sort of strung out throughout the course of the afternoon as I would talk to him between the replies, I would do a little work to keep busy until his next message came in and now it is now time to head home.

"I'm still at work but yes just shutting the computer down and getting ready to head home. Bye my sexy man."

"Later hottie"

Chapter 15
At the Gates

I am starting to look less frumpy and more a baby bump but my appearance does not stop me from the things that I like to do.

It's Saturday morning and it is a nice summer day, which could not have worked out more perfectly because today I have a date with my girlfriends at the water park. I know that I can't go on some of the slides because of the pregnancy but I can still enjoy the pools and he lazy rivers and also get my tan on. I don't care about my pot and actually, I know that it sounds a little silly but I am sort of proud of it.

I have a few bathing suits but with my stomach, I will stretch them out so the alternative is wearing a bikini. There is no sense in hiding it. I put it on to wear to the park and put a little sundress over top. My doorbell rings and it's Hailey she is parking her car at my place and we are going to drive to the park together and meet Lucy and Maggie at the entrance.

I open the door and say, "Hey how are you?"

She is all smiles and looks great with golden blonde hair tied in a ponytail and she is sporting some swim shorts and a white tank top over a violet bikini. She greets me with, "My gosh Jordan look at you! When was my party, a couple weeks ago?"

"Yes, about that, have I changed that much?"

She explains, "You have. I mean you're not huge or anything it's just that little tummy of yours is starting to look like you are carrying a ball under your dress."

We both look down at my stomach and start to laugh.

I say, "I am starting to notice. I had to buy some new pants just the other day."

"Well Jordan you look good and you're carrying that little baby well."

I smile, "Thanks Hailey. Well, are you ready to go?"

"Yep"

I leave a note for Josh on the table in case he returns home and I am still away at the park. I mentioned to him that I was going but I leave it anyway in case he forgot.

It is a short ten-minute drive to the water park and as we drive closer to the park, the traffic increases a bit more. I turn into the park entrance, pay for my parking pass and I am guided in by the parks, parking lot staff. Lucy and Maggie are already at the gates as we walk up. The ticket stands next to the gates are a bustle of people with sun bags, towels and coolers. There are people of all ages.

Maggie waves us over and says, "Hey you two!"

We both answer, "Hey" and greet them with quick hugs.

I ask, "How come Melissa and Ophelia didn't want to come?"

Lucy says, "I invited them but you know how Melissa is. If it's not her idea on the activity she doesn't want to go and well Ophelia declined. She admitted to not being a fan of fast rides."

I say, "Okay, well Melissa's loss and as for Ophelia well I can understand but I'll be hanging out poolside when you guys do the water slides. Well, that's too bad it would have been nice to have her to hang out with."

Hailey says, "I'm sure someone will hang back with you."

I answer, "Oh don't be silly. I can take a nap in the sun while you guys brave the slides." I shrug and smile, "Just saying anyway I have already braved all of the slides last year and it's your turn now."

It is about mid-morning as we walk into the park and despite the gorgeous weather, the park isn't too busy. I guess the only reason is because they were calling for thunderstorms today but I look up at the sky and there is not a cloud in sight.

I pick my favorite spot in the park in front of the wave pool where the recliners are but up high on the hill so that we have quick access to the picnic tables.

The girls set their bags down and are discussing which slides to go on first, Maggie suggests, "Do you want to go in the pool first? That way Jordan can join us."

Before anyone answers I say, "No don't be silly. You are best to go on the slides now while the lineups are short. Go on, I don't mind hanging back and relaxing."

Lucy asks, "You sure Jordan?"

I smile and nod, "Go ahead I insist. I can work on my tan."

I spread my beach towel down on a lounge chair and take a seat. I reach into my bag and lather my body with sun lotion as I burn quickly. I try reaching to cover my shoulders and upper back and then from behind I hear a voice that I recognize, "I can help you with that?"

Surprised, I turn around and see him, "Devon?"

He is in some board shorts and is scouting some aviator shades a beige canvas cowboy hat and a large green beach towel hung over his shoulder as he comes over to take a seat next to me on the lounge chair.

My bottom lip must be hanging open as he smiles and says, "Don't act all surprised that I'm here. When you were telling me about the baby bump starting to show I wanted to see this hot momma in person and besides you mentioned that you would be here today." He tilts his shades down to let me glimpse his gorgeous brown eyes and gives me a wink. He takes the bottle of sun lotion from my hand and nudges me to turn the other way. He starts messaging it into my back. His hands are so soothing that I think my own eyes are rolling back in my head and for a second, I drift off, wait a second no I need to know why he is here. I tilt my head over my shoulder to talk to him.

"Devon, really why are you here? I thought you were in the middle of buying a home?"

"I am but can't a man take a break and visit the mother of his un-born child."

"Devon, you know that I always happy to see you it's just I am very surprise that's all."

"Well, you said that Josh was working and that you would spend the bulk of today lounging as your friends went on the rides. I thought it would be the perfect opportunity." It must be a freeing feeling to be able to jump on a plane and go where your heart desires. I am happy to see him especially with having endured the every now and then text messaging chats.

I am full of questions, "So you never did tell me if you won the bid."

He smiles, "I did and Sara is taking care of all the details today."

I ask, "She didn't need you there to sign stuff?"

He shakes his head, "No she's got it covered."

"Well, geez I'm rude, congratulations that's great so you are starting to live the life of a famous author now."

"I am and I get to enjoy the best of both worlds that much more. I get to enjoy my secret life with my best friend and what it is to be a famous author."

I turn to face him and say, "So you never explained what you are doing here. How did you get away without Sara asking any questions?"

He takes my hand into his, "A book convention here in town this weekend and I'm making a couple of appearances at the big book stores in town this evening. Come with me I actually had set up for a day in another spot."

With my hand still in his, I hesitate, "What about my girlfriends?"

"They are fine besides they are so distracted they won't even notice you're gone."

I decide, "Okay, but I'm going to leave a note in case they return while I'm with you."

I dig into my bag and find a pen but I have no paper, instead I have a napkin and leave the message,

Hey,

I just went for some iced cream and a swim in the lazy river.

-Jordan

I tuck the note in the lip of the lid of Lucy's cooler and follow Devon.

I ask him as we walk through the park, passed some of the pools and thru the concession stands, "So how are you not being recognized? I mean I am sure that if we look, we will catch a few reading your book on the lounge chairs."

He chuckles, "Jordan you are so silly sometimes. Look at me. Do you think someone will recognize me in this get up?"

I giggle, "Yes, you are right." The aviators and hat pretty well disguise him."

He leads me up the steps to the VIP tents. These lounge tents come with their own balconies that overlook the park and that have their own loungers. Each tent is a private tent for the person that rents the space it holds a group of six comfortably.

The silly sarcastic side of me makes its appearance and I say, "Devon what's with all of this? You know I am an easy-going girl and would have been happy spending time with you in the public area of the park."

He opens the curtain of the tent gesturing me to go in before him and he says once inside, "I do, but I also know that you don't like being intimate in public." I see a glimpse of that fire in his eye as he closes the curtain and sets the cushioned loungers so that they are flat and removes his aviators and hat and says, "Gosh girl, do you know just how fucking hot you are?"

I say, "I see what this is all about. You come to visit me for a booty call."

He approaches me and says, "No not just that. I came here to spend time with someone that I love."

His words are sincere and he puts his lips to mine kissing me with those sexy lips and his adventurous tongue tasting mine. He slips his hand to my back pulling the string to my bikini top. The knot unraveling and the top falls to the floor as my round breasts are exposed for his hands to play with.

I moan but try to keep my sighs quiet as I realize where we are.

He says, "I love it when you make noise to my touch."

I whisper to him, "I want you inside me."

He goes in for one more kiss; his tongue isn't shy. He ends the kiss with a playful bite on my lips. His goatee tickles my face and he smiles at me and asks, "You want me. Just how much do you want me?"

"I want your big dick inside me. I want your juices. I want you. I want your love." I'm already breathing heavily. This man drives me nuts like no other and he has me practically begging for him.

He turns me around bends me over the lounge bed, slides my bikini bottom over to one side exposing my puffy, wet little clamshell and with ease pushes his big thick shaft into my wet warmth and I feel him shiver and hear him sigh as he pushes in.

He whispers, "Oh Jordan you feel so good." He takes a moment to gain his composure and find a rhythm for me to get mine. He starts slow and hard, holding my hips in place with his hands, sliding in deep with his man and pulling partway out. He feels amazing and he is so incredibly hard. He speeds up a little faster for me and I sigh with total enjoyment.

He says in a whisper, "You will explode for me and then I want you down on your knees."

"Okay" I answer. To my surprise, he pulls out, takes a seat on the lounger and then sits me down with my back facing him. He holds me in place with his hands. He puts his big man back inside me and then he reaches over with his hand to message my sweet swollen button as he rocks me back and forth. My legs are open for him to touch. He leans me back slightly with his lips close to my ear so that I feel his breath on my neck and says, "Vibrate for me."

He presses down on my button and thrusts deep, which sets me off. I drip all over him and shiver with every pulse that my body lets out.

As I finish, he tilts my head and kisses me then says, "My good girl getting hers when I say so."

I slide off him and happy to give him what he traveled all this way for I take his soaked shaft from all my juices and start sucking and licking it all up. I like my taste. It is sweet and I clean him off with my tongue, licking the side of his shaft and putting his head in my mouth and then letting him go in deep allowing him to touch the back of my throat.

I hear him say, "Oh Jordan" I know that I am doing good as he is already pre-ejaculating on my tongue. His salty taste is warm and it makes me start to get aroused all over again. I feel one of his hands run through my hair. I know that he wants me to keep doing what I am which is deep, in and out and I drip as I pleasure him and his grunts and sighs tell me he is about to go and half a second later I feel the hot juices coat my throat as I ease up on him and swallow it all.

I come up and lie next to him on the lounger and ask, "How was that?"

"Jordan, you know how to impress your cowboy."

I smile, "Good." I get up and reach for my bikini top when he stops me with gently grabbing my arm. I turn to face Devon and he says, "I'm not done yet. Lie down."

He tugs my bikini bottoms down and starts to munch away on my hot pocket. Nibbling my lips and hot button and then following up with sticking his tongue deep inside. I am so sensitive after already getting mine and I wiggle and squirm with each nibble and lick. He starts to take notice of me moving and he comes up. I look at him and his lips and goatee are glistening with my clear juices. He playfully says, "Did you think some cowboy would go muff diving in you at the water park today?"

I answer while trying to catch my breath, "No this was a nice surprise my sexy cowboy."

"I make you squirm, don't I?"

"You do"

"I am going to make you explode in my mouth but first I'm going to do something and you are going to lie there and let me."

I give him a quizzical look. He winks at me and then goes back down on me licking and bringing me to the edge and I do my best to stay still.

Then he does the something. He brings his tongue down and circles my other opening, licking the opening and then inserting a finger. I lay back and let him, enjoying the pleasure that he is giving me. He keeps me on the edge for a while, teasing and he knows it.

Finally, he goes back to my pocket with a finger inside my girl and a second in the back. Devon licks hard with his tongue and wiggles his finger back and forth and I explode at the sudden surge.

He slows after I start to relax and he has that look that he still isn't done. Without me asking what now he says, "Jordan, you know that I have never done anyone by the back but I would like to try with you."

My mind is on overdrive with the pleasure that he has given me so far and there is nothing more that I want to do then make my cowboy happy I say, "Okay"

I back up further onto the lounger and he gets comfortable and he takes his wood in his hand and slowly pushes into the tight opening. I am soaked with my own juices and with him licking me clean and even though it is tight, he is able to slide in with a little extra force.

I watch his face and his expression makes me smile. I catch his eyes roll as he pushes in and his eyes close, he sighs as he moves in. The expression is bliss, not realizing what he had been missing out all the years of his life. He opens his eyes and kisses me. He focuses, determined to take control of his pleasure. His pushing in and rubbing up on my yummy spot, gets me once more and my pleasure makes him shoot inside my other spot. He moans as if I have stolen it from him and the sweat rolling off his temple is just hot. We have steamed up this tent but we don't care and he gently pulls out and lays next to me on the recliner.

We lie together for a moment and the sounds of the waterpark, splashing, the sounds of play in the air and the tropical theme music on the park's intercom come into focus as we relax. I lean in and kiss him and touch his face, his damp brown hair and he touches mine and he can't resist and touches my tummy.

"You look fantastic Jordan. You are one hot Momma and I am happy to be the man to have done that for you."

His hand is warm and gentle on my stomach. Normally I feel weird with people touching my bump but I don't mind with Devon. It is comforting and I know that he cares for the two of us even though his part was a donation but still I know that this man has a place in his heart for this child.

The tent flaps to the rhythm of the light warm breeze that carries with it the constant sounds of the park as we lie there for a few moments. People laughing, screaming, shouting and talking, the smell of sunscreen, salt water, chips stands and park food.

I sigh and say, "We should go for a dip and wash the sex off of us."

He pouts, "What if I don't want to."

I glance at him, "Devon, don't be silly. We are drenched head to toe in sweat and smell as if we have been busy. Besides, my girlfriends are probably starting to wonder where I am. Come on let's go for a dip and freshen up."

He sighs, "Okay, but promise me one thing?"

"What's that?"

"Promise me that you will come back to my tent for a drink." The VIP tent that he has rented for the day is somewhat separate from the entire park. In addition to the private tents, deck and lounge chairs it also has its own bar that is inclusive to the VIP section only.

I nod, "Okay sexy."

We do our best to dry the sweat from our bodies with the towels in the tent. Devon fixes the curtains of the tent opening it so that the smell of our lovemaking airs out before we descend to the water.

He takes my arm, "Shall we?"

"Yes, but Devon?"

"If my friends see me here with you...?"

He smiles, "Just tell them that you recognized me and that I had you for company."

"Devon!"

He chuckles and says, "What? It's the truth and besides you're knocked up anyway so I know and they know that you are off the market."

"Devon, don't say it like that."

"Jordan, you worry too much. Just relax and enjoy this time with your cowboy."

Chapter 16
Guilty but Greedy

I must have been a couple of hours that I had been away from the loungers that I had picked out with the girls and I feel a little guilty but greedily I needed every moment that I had with Devon. We relax together in the lazy river amongst the sea of other park goers. We float around and around the five-kilometer stretch just talking. We are so relaxed and for a bit I forget that I even came to the park with the girls until I hear their voices.

"Jordan!" It's Maggie who is with Lucy who are both floating on a board as they catch up to Devon and I. At first, the girls take no notice of Devon even though he is at an arm's length from me. He waits as the girls talk to me.

I answer, "Hey guys, did you enjoy the slides?"

Lucy says, "We have been on just about every slide in the park."

Maggie explains, "Every few slides we would come back to the spot where we had left you but you never returned. Where have you been?"

I get a little nervous. Devon is still here and unnoticed by them. Ah well I have nothing to lose in introducing him. I just use Devon's excuse even though they will now know that I know the famous D. Chambers. I glance at Devon who smiles at me.

Maggie notices my glance and looks over her shoulder at him as we float down the stream. I say to them, "I'm sorry. Well, I sort of got side tracked, That's..."

Maggie interrupts, "D. Chambers" she continues to say to him this time turning her body and opening a circle between all of us, "I recognize you from the photo on the back of that best seller of yours."

He chuckles and extends his hand to shakes hers, "You can just call me Devon. Your friend Jordan recognized me as I was walking by her lounge chair. What started as a friendly hello opened up into a conversation on writing and since we are here at the park what better way to enjoy it then going through the lazy river?"

Devon smooths everything over with ease making me appear as a fan of his and not his little sex kitten, which is fine but the thing is do they buy it?

There is a moment of awkward silence as the girls smile at him and then study me with their eyes. They are looking at me as if I have gone out of my way to flirt with him. At least that is how I feel. Maybe it is just my guilty conscious but Devon's next comment makes me trust that gut of mine.

Devon acts as if he doesn't know much about me and changes the conversation to me, "Jordan, I know you mentioned earlier that you were sitting out for the water slides because of your delicate state but do you and your husband know what you are having?" His question seems to bring their guard down. They know that Devon knows that I am off the market and they know that I wasn't trying anything with this man.

I wade in the water and get closer to the group as we continue to be pushed along in the light currant. I answer, "Well, I am far enough along to find out but there are so little surprises in life anymore. Josh and I decided to not find out." I look into those gorgeous but curious brown eyes. He wanted to know.

He says, "Well good for you for letting it remain a mystery. My ex-wife and I did the same thing. We waited and found out once he was born. My son is twenty years old."

Lucy interjects, "Twenty? Wow, Devon, well I mean, gosh you don't seem old enough to be the father of a twenty-year-old." Her face has turned beat red and it is not from the sun. I try to hide my smile because I had said that too when I had first started talking to Devon only, I had the luxury of not being on camera or in person.

Devon chuckles, "Yes, well no insult taken. I have had that comment said to me before. My ex and I were both young and well I am forty-three now."

Maggie balances the conversation, "I hadn't pegged you in your forties; my guess would have been early to mid-thirties."

Devon smiles and says, "You are too kind." We are coming up on the final bend of the river and

Devon offers, "Say ladies, I have a tent reserved for the day in the VIP section. There is a bar there also. I'm going to go back to the tent but you girls are more than welcome to join me." There is a moment of pause, Lucy and Maggie are contemplating, I spot their glances at one another and then at me and I nod giving my approval. Devon continues, "It would make me so happy. You seem like good company and I hate to admit it but I visited the park alone." He shrugs, "Life of an author. We tend to travel to many book signings and well the wife can't take all of that time off and my agent needs to remain in his office the majority of the time."

I want to take the initiative and spend as much time as I possibly can before he leaves but my gut is telling me to leave it to the girls to decide. I want to be in his company so badly but the side of reason is telling me maybe I have to let it be and spend the rest of the day with my friends and not allow any slip-ups to occur.

Maggie breaks the silence and says, "Well it sounds like a good idea; besides we have done all the rounds with the bigger slides anyway. Can we meet you at the VIP entrance in the next ten to fifteen minutes? Our other friend Hailey was waiting back where we had left Jordan."

All of them glance over to me and I shrug, "I'm sorry, I didn't mean to get side tracked. Well, you know what I am saying; I didn't plan on running into a famous author."

Devon sneaks in a devilish smile without the other two taking notice and I sheepishly smile back at them.

Lucy says, "Well, this has all worked out so now we just got to go get Hailey and fill her in."

The exit to the lazy river is approaching as we float along the steady currant and we all step out of the water.

Devon waves "See you all in a bit."

Chapter 17
Reserved Tent

The rest of the afternoon Devon is kind enough to keep the drinks flowing for my friends and me. All of mine are non-alcoholic and the gesture is still nice and without my friends taking much notice I buy my Devon one of his favorites, a Long Island iced tea and he accepts it with that southern graciousness that he has.

There is about an hour left until the park closes for the night and the girls are ready to take one more turn at the slides and feel comfortable with leaving me alone with Devon. I rather relax.

It's soon just Devon and I on the patio and once they are out of ear shot, he asks, "How was I?"

"You were wonderful; when I came it was so intense." I smile at him.

He chuckles and says, "No silly. What I meant was how did you find me with your friends?"

"Oh!" I giggle, "You were amazing! They like you and it has nothing to do with your celebrity status. They really enjoyed your company."

He leans in towards me, "Do you think that they suspected anything between us?"

I sip my diet cola and respond, "I think at first when I glanced at you before they were about to give me a hard time for being gone for so long. You helped me get out of that."

His posture relaxes with my thought and he says, "I try, well I am happy for that. I am happy I was able to be with you and meet your friends. It just shows me another side of you and makes me love you even more."

I lean in, reaching over the table and take his hand to hold and in a voice only loud enough for him to hear, "I love you more every day. You are my best friend and secret desire. I cherish every moment that we have and secretly wish that you were mine."

He smiles and answers, "I know Jordan and ditto for me too." He gets up and leads me back to his reserved tent. He gives me one more quickly and I sit on his lap and grind up against him feeling his amazing dick inside me and in the few times that we have had to experience each other he has already picked up on the moves that makes my kitty drool all over him and he gets me to climax within minutes.

I try to muffle my moans and he says in a whisper, "Ah girl, let me hear that voice of yours." He rocks me while I vibrate.

I bite my lip and open my eyes to gaze into his, "You're a bad boy. You know there could be people close enough to hear us."

He smirks, "Do you think I care?"

I chuckle as I slide up and down his shaft gently, "You should care. They could be my friends out there."

He says, "Well in that case I'll be good when I have mine. I want you on your back."

He places my legs over his shoulders and drives me into the lounge bed, panting, eyes closed and when he gets close, he opens his eyes to see me lying there and desiring his juices. We lock eyes and he keeps his grunts quiet as he explodes for me and pumps it in as deep as he can go. It feels so good and I hold him for one last moment as he relaxes and catches his breath.

We quickly towel off and take one last dip to rinse off the scent of passion.

Chapter 18
Change of Pace

Hailey and I arrive back at my home and Josh is already home from work.

I hear Josh from downstairs call out as we walk in the door, "Hey is that you Jordan?"

I shout to him down the stairs, "Yah its Hailey and me."

I hear some rustling downstairs, a sign that he is making his way from the office up the stairs to the front entrance.

Hailey murmurs to me, "Could I use your washroom?"

"Sure" Hailey and I live closer to each other in comparison to my other friends. She is about a twenty-minute drive while Lucy and Maggie are about forty-five minutes away. Still twenty minutes is long enough to wait especially if you have to go pee.

Josh comes up the stairs, gives me a hug and a kiss and says, "Hey there, you got some color today."

I smile, "Thanks, well I spent the bulk of my day in the sun and the lazy river."

Hailey comes back around the corner to the entrance and says, "Yah and she got to hang out with a celebrity all day!"

I give her a look but it is already too late, Josh heard clear as day and asks, "Who did you hang out with?"

I try not to hesitate but I do and Hailey notices it, "Geez Jordan you seem a little star struck."

The two of them are looking at me. Hailey all in teasing smiles while Josh is confused and looking a tad bit jealous, he adds, "Yah Jordan, so do tell."

I swallow and then say, "Josh remember that book I was reading and you were asking me the name of the author?"

"Yes."

"Well, I recognized him at the water park."

My insight doesn't help. Josh knows his pen name but doesn't actually know who Devon is and for a person who never reads, it's not a big deal and I can sense Josh start to lose interest. To him an author isn't really a celebrity. Despite the fact that I know Hailey and I have lost him with the hype, he continues to say, "Well that's cool Jordan. What was his name again?"

I answer, "D. Chambers, the D stands for Devon."

Hailey is just beaming and I give a shy smile. I think Josh was expecting me to bring up some singer's name or some famous movie star. He doesn't share in the excitement, however remains polite.

Hailey adds, "Devon is doing a book signing today and tomorrow in town and he invited us to attend."

Josh looks at her then gives a glance to me, "Oh that is nice of him. Are you guys going to go?"

Hailey says, "Yah, we were going to plan to go tomorrow night. I have a copy of his book at home so I am going to bring it to get signed. Jordan, are you bringing your copy?"

I laugh, "Mine is on my e-reader so I guess not." I turn to Josh and ask, "Do you mind if I go tomorrow into town? You can come too; it would be a bit of a change of pace for us and give me the chance to see what's involved with a book signing."

I caught Josh in an upbeat mood. He is tired but he is at least in good spirits, "Well tomorrow is my only day off that I get to relax."

Hailey pushes, "Ah, it's just for a couple of hours. You guys can also do some shopping or go out to diner afterwards."

I glance at him and he glances back at me. He's weighing it in and reluctantly he answers, "Well, yah I guess we can go and make a bit of a night of it."

I think wow my friends have met my secret lover and now Josh may meet him face to face. I feel like the world is starting to get smaller on me. I am happy that I get another chance to see him but with Josh there my stomach starts to turn and it's not the baby.

Chapter 19
Green Paisley Tie

We all arrive at the Grand Book Store downtown separately. Hailey leaves her husband and daughter at home. She couldn't find a baby sitter on short notice. Josh and I arrive together. Maggie lives downtown so she took a bus and Lucy drove in on her own.

We all meet at the entrance to the bookstore ten minutes before the actual signing.

The Grand Bookstore is a hum of talk and peeking in the store window I can see that there is a line up wrapped around the entire store. There has to be a few hundred people here waiting for Devon, my Devon.

I turn to Josh and the girls and admit, "What were we thinking in only arriving moments before his signing?"

Maggie says, "We can try to get his attention I'm sure he will spot us."

Hailey says, "Should we even stand in line?" Just as she asks a store worker comes to greet us, "Hello, are you here for the D. Chambers books signing?"

We all look over at the worker and Josh answers, "Yes."

The greeter smiles and says, "Fantastic, he should be arriving at any moment please take these tickets." She hands us each a ballet ticket.

I ask, "What are these for?"

She answers, "Mr. Chambers will be doing a draw at the end of the night."

"Oh, okay." Devon never said anything about a draw so it comes as a little added surprise.

She explains while walking backwards to face us for a moment, "If you will just follow me, I'll lead you to where the line ends. We have sort of wrapped everyone around the store." She turns to walk forward and leads the way.

Josh murmurs to the girls and me, "Yah we can see that."

The energy in the room is booming with excitement in the anticipation of Devon's arrival. I see people mostly holding his latest book and others with some of his older works. Others have their phones in hand ready to get a picture of Devon. It is an amazing feeling to see so much love for someone that you care for. I feel proud of him.

The stage is set in the middle of the store and I see displays of his book, "Trial" next to the table where he is to sign.

Wow, this is a big deal. I wonder if I will ever reach Devon's level off success.

The crowd towards the front of the store starts to cheer and I can't see anything. I think Devon may be shaking the hands of his fans as he makes his way in. This is nuts. There are a couple of store workers accompanying him as he makes his way into the store and finally, I see him.

He is so hot. He is sporting fitted light khakis with a brown leather belt. The cowboy in him is wearing a silver belt buckle. He is wearing white leather dress shoes and he has a light green dress shirt with a matching light green paisley tie and a dark colored sport coat over top. I don't think I have ever seen him dressed so nicely. Let me re-phrase that. He dresses nicely and usually wears a dress pant and a golf shirt but today he looks like he has just walked off some high fashioned runway. His hair looks freshly cut and styled with a playful flip in front. Devon is clean-shaven with the exception of his goatee, which is neatly trimmed.

We are too far back in the store for him to see us but it is neat to see this side of him. He handles himself well and it is a side of him that I haven't seen. Women are swooning over him. I glance at Josh; he rolls his eyes and murmurs, "Come on"

Maggie chuckles and asks Josh, "Have you ever been to a book signing?"

He replies with a playful huff, "Maggie I don't read."

We all laugh with Josh pulling out Mr. Dead Pan humor. Maggie explains, "Well any sort of meet and greet of a celebrity you are going to see people get that excited. I have seen some even faint."

Josh shrugs, "I don't get it? He is only an author."

I scold him, "Geez Josh, he's only written a best seller. If my writing takes up like his you may need to deal with me going to signings such as these."

Josh knows better than to make a low jab at my work and he tiptoes around it, which I recognize and am thankful that he does. "Maybe one day but I just don't get all the hype for a book that's it."

Hailey says, "People like different things. Some like books however you don't. To everyone here that man is a famous author."

We outnumber Josh on the topic, "Okay well you have made your point."

The crowed continues to cheer as Devon stands behind the podium on stage. One of the store workers speaks into the mic to introduce the famous author D. Chambers and the room erupts in cheers whistles and clapping. Devon stands smiles and waves to everyone and makes his way over to the podium to speak to the crowed.

He starts off, "Hello Ottawa!" That causes more cheers and I hear him chuckle into the mic. I clap and laugh. I am so happy for him.

When the crowed quiets he says, "Thank you so much for taking time out of your day to come to my signing. Seeing you all here to support me is humbling and I will forever keep this experience with me for the rest of my life." Devon continues to say a quick short speech on writing his most recent book. Sometimes authors even read a small excerpt but given the sheer size of the crowed, the store workers have him go right into signing.

I watch from a distance as he works through his crowed of fans. Taking photos with some, signing their books and shaking hands.

The store workers make the process run smoothly. A few more came in after us and then they closed off the entrance. The store was at capacity.

A couple of workers make their way down the line and soon to us. They ask, "Do you all have something you wish for Devon to sign?"

The girls nod and I say, "I was going to purchase his book today are their copies at the desk?"

"There are but here you go." The second worker hands me Devon's latest book for him to sign.

The first worker explains, "When you meet Mr. Chambers you are allowed one question to keep the line moving. There is only one signature per person and one photo with your group of friends."

Lucy says, "Okay thank you."

A couple hours pass when we finally make it to the stage. Devon just as two hours before is still gracious and polite to the people coming up from the end of the line just as those in the beginning.

Lucy and Maggie are the first to the table. Hailey, Josh and I are just behind. Devon finishes signing the books for the people who are ahead of us and as Lucy and Maggie walk up that is when he recognizes them. I wait in line and watch as he greets my friends with warm handshakes and he glances around and then sees me. He doesn't nod at me or anything but I see it in those warm brown eyes of his. He is happy that I came.

I hear the exchange of warm hellos and he signs Lucy and Maggie's books. Hailey moves in for her book and I am the last of the girls with Josh here for company.

I walk up with Josh and Devon is sitting at the table with a pen in hand. He stands up and leans over the table extending his hand to greet me, "Hey Jordan it means so much to me that you were able to make it to my book signing."

His hand is warm to the touch. I reply, "Thanks Devon. I am happy to be here." I hand him my book. He looks over to Josh whom I can feel is a bit out of his element. Before I can make introductions Devon beats me to the punch he smiles at Josh and says to him, "You must be Josh?"

A little surprised, Josh answers, "Yes that's me."

Devon extends his hand to shake Josh's, "Jordan talked about you a lot at the park yesterday."

I can see Josh start to warm up to him and with his deadpan humor he says, "Only good things I hope?"

Devon chuckles and says, "Yes your wife loves you very much. You are one lucky man." He takes a second to sign my book and Josh agrees to take a photo of the girls and me with Devon. As I thank him and am about to step down from the stage Devon whispers in my ear, "If you don't win the raffle, I will make sure Josh and you get a matching prize." I give him a sideways glance and he winks at me.

There is about another twenty more people that Devon needs to sign for and within the half hour Devon's book signing is complete.

One of the workers approaches the podium and speaks into the mic, "Well thank you for coming out, everyone. Mr. D. Chambers has one more thing he would like to get to before his departure." The store worker looks over and Devon approaches and stands by her side.

She continues, "Everyone was given a ballot ticket. The prize is a seven-day, six-night Caribbean cruise and Mr. Chambers will now do the draw." She holds an oversized fish bowl and Devon reaches in.

This is happening in slow motion. Is the draw fixed? I wonder because of what he whispered in my ear. I suddenly feel sick and nervous. I don't like the idea of wining something so publicly and besides I'm Devon's friend first. This prize should go to his fans. I mean, I am a fan too it is just that I am more than that to him. Well, I think you know what I am trying to say.

I hold my breath as he pulls a paper out of the oversized fish bowl and hands it to the speaker. She calls the number out and there is a muffle of movement in the crowd as people check their tickets. She repeats the numbers once more. Before I can confirm mine some woman in front starts screaming that she won.

I exhale as though I just dodged a bullet. Geez Jordan how would Devon be able to fix a draw so that you would win. He had no clue that you were even here until you got to the table.

Josh nudges me, "Should we head home?"

I say back to him, "Yes sure but give me one moment to say goodbye to him."

I take Josh by the hand and maneuver my way through the crowd leading the way back to the stage.

The announcer confirms the women's ticket is a winner and Devon takes a photo with her.

The speaker announces, "Congratulations! Well, that is a wrap everyone. Thank you for coming to our store event and as a reminder everything in the store is twenty percent off today and for the entire week."

Devon leans in to speak. "Thank you everyone and have a great night!"

The crowd claps and soon they make their departure. There are a couple of lingerers wanting Devon's attention as we approach the stage. Josh and I are just steps away from him and he spots me again. Hailey, Lucy and Maggie have followed and Devon makes his way over to say one more goodbye to the girls.

Devon says, "Again it was so nice meeting you and being able to enjoy yesterday together."

The girls all agree and polite handshakes and hugs are given. I say goodbye to my girlfriends as we all arrived separately.

Once the girls are out of earshot Devon leans in to Josh and me and says, "Josh your wife has really struck a chord with me but in a good way."

Josh looks at him confused and I am sure if he had been sipping a drink that he would have spit it out just now. He says, "What?"

Devon chuckles, "Let me explain, yesterday I learned that she is also an author. You know it's a very small world. Just as she has read my book, I have actually read hers."

Josh is out of his element he hasn't even read my book even though a main character is based on him. He replies, "Was it good?" There is some truth behind his question he doesn't know because he had not read it but from the few reviews that I have received I think he knows that he would enjoy it.

Devon chuckles, "You need to read her book. It was great and this is what I would like to do. I'll be also going on the cruise that I just gave away and aside from the fans I would like you two to join me."

I have been silent this entire time while Josh and Devon talk and I finally find my voice and choke a bit as I stumble upon my words, "Devon that is so kind but we can't accept."

Josh looks at me and as I stutter the words out. Josh asks, "Jordan I know that I tease with your writing and all but I think he is giving you more than just a vacation." Josh glances back at Devon who answers, "Precisely think of it as an opportunity. This cruise will also host some of the most powerful publishers in the business and what better an opportunity would it be for me to introduce you to some of them."

The two of them backed me into a corner with those points and the two loves of my life are now working together? I look at each of them who are both smiling at me.

I say, "What about this baby and my appointments?"

Josh smooths it over, "We can check in with your doctor tomorrow and see what's due but I am sure that you are still safe to travel."

Devon asks, "What do you say Jordan? Opportunities like this come far and few between." There is a double meaning in his words that I know but Josh doesn't. This is getting too close to home but I have no choice and accept.

"Okay" I respond with part nerves and part enthusiasm.

Devon shakes my hand, "That a girl! I promise that this cruise will change your life." He gives me that glance as if he already knows how he is going to do me on that cruise ship. I feel my face flush and he gives me a kiss on the cheek and a wink. Josh shows absolutely no concern. He has no idea that Devon is moving in on his territory. Well too late for that, he has already made love to me on more than one occasion.

Devon and Josh shake hands once more and Devon says to him, "Keep in touch, your wife already has me as a friend on her social media." My heart stops again worried that may raise some flags with Josh but it doesn't.

Josh says, "Great thanks so much!"

Devon waves us off, "Bye guys!"

Josh and I answer back, "Bye!"

Josh says to me after we pay for the book at the cash and depart the store, "That was nice of him."

Chapter 20
Shadow of Stubble

I brush my teeth at the bathroom sink and get ready for bed after returning from her friend's book signing. Jordan was already lying in bed when I had walked by the bedroom moments before. It looked like she was texting someone because her thumbs were moving a mile a minute on the screen. Now standing in the bathroom I stare back at my complexion in the mirror as I wash up. I feel like I missed something. I don't know. I see my wife every day, talk to her, do activities with her but everything that surrounds her writing is unknown to me. I ask her questions about her work and she could talk for hours if I let her.

She talks about the writing or editing, the marketing and social media that she is doing. She also mentions the author friends she talks with. Jordan sometimes reads and reviews other authors work and they do the same for her writing. She has even shared her work with me. I do listen but I do cut her short and with tonight I had, no idea D. Chambers existed and that Jordan is friends with this successful man.

I should blame myself for feeling like there is a side to Jordan that I don't know. She always seemed forthcoming but I would hear her start to talk and I would start to trail off. It's just not interesting.

I wonder if I should shave. I touch my face and feel the shadow of stubble growing in but I think I'll let it go another day.

I open the lid to the bottle of mouthwash from the counter next to the sink and take a sip to gargle with and swish it around.

This D. Chambers, I get that his success was recent but something like that I would have thought Jordan would have brought that up in a conversation that started with, one of my author friends... I spit out the wash and wipe my mouth with a towel.

Well anyway, now I know of him and Jordan seems thrilled about this cruise. I know it is legit, I don't want to go but I know that it would crush her if I was honest with her. Truth is I don't want to end up getting sucked into added expenses and we don't really know these people. I bet they are the snotty kind that thinks they are better than everyone else. Anyway, that's my take on it but I'll never say that to her and let her down. I'll go with her because I don't want her going alone.

I straighten out the towel on the rack, turn off the bathroom light and head to the bedroom to go lie down.

Chapter 21
Piece of Paper

The next week I have my appointments straightened out and a second ultrasound appointment booked. It actually works out because I had read that some of the airlines prefer a doctor's note advising that it's safe for a pregnant woman to travel. I'm not clear yet on which airline Devon is to have us fly on so just to be safe I'm getting a note from my doctor.

So much is going on and Josh and I actually never found out what we were having. Josh is always working and I could book an appointment on my own but I am the type of person who trusts the doctors and if the extra ultra sounds are not required then there is no point in people poking around my stomach.

It is coming on 9:30 AM and I am sitting on a love seat in the waiting area of the doctor's office with Josh. Josh is playing some game on his phone and I have been looking at my social media feed on my own phone. To be quite honest even though I am scrolling down the news feed I am not absorbing what is there. My mind is somewhere else, on his little one. I don't talk about my pregnancy as much as a first-time expectant mom should but here is my reason why. It just doesn't seem real yet. Josh and I have been without kids for so long and have had a bit of a process with the IUI attempts so it's just I think that until I hold this little one in my arms and see that they are real it just feels like it's not really happening. Don't mistake me for one of those pregnant women that have had just the perfect pregnancy to simply feel like I am not pregnant. I for sure know that I am. The first three months were a nightmare with throwing up to just the smell of something off putting and now I have to deal with stretch marks growing on my stomach and I know there will be more fun and I say fun sarcastically. There will probably be more fun pregnancy surprises to come.

I take a moment to glance at Josh; I want to get his attention. He feels my eyes on him and looks up at me within seconds.

He asks. "What's up?"

I say in a voice that only he can hear as there are other couples in the waiting room, "You know that today they will be able to tell."

He knows what I mean. He says, "Yes I know is something wrong?"

"No, well you know how I feel about knowing."

"Jordan, I would like to know so that we can get them things that are gender appropriate, pick out names and just know for the sake of knowing."

The one thing Josh hates is surprises. Take Christmas as an example, he loves receiving gifts but there is no sense in wrapping them because he needs to know what he is getting. It drives me nuts at times. He is the only person that I know who doesn't like a good surprise. Even if I buy something for him, he needs to know that it was exactly something that he asked for.

I whisper to him, "I don't want to know."

He takes his phone and slides it in his pocket. I know that I have his attention.

He whispers back and this time a little more direct. "It's better to know. This shouldn't be up for questioning."

He doesn't get it and I explain, "There are so little surprises in life anymore and I would like this to be a surprise."

Before he can debate the nurse pokes her head out from the door into the reception room.

"Jordan and Josh?" She looks around the room at all of the couples in the waiting area for acknowledgement. The conversation stops and we each get up to follow her.

She smiles and says, "Right this way."

Down the familiar hall just as before and today's appointment ends up being the same room as the last ultrasound. I strip down then meet Josh and the nurse in the ultrasound room and climb onto the bed.

She goes thru her checklist and confirms, "Has your address or telephone number changed since the last visit?"

We answer together, "No."

She goes through a few other medical questions that I answer and then the important question is asked.

"Would you like to find out the baby's gender today?"

I say no and Josh is a yes at the same time.

The nurse looks back and forth at the two of us. Josh and I look at one another. I make a face at him and he shrugs and rolls his eyes at me and we are about to open our mouths to bicker at each other when the nurse interrupts with a resolution.

She smiles and says, "You know we do see this happen more than you would think. What I can do is when we are about to look, I will warn you so that you can look away and Josh, I will write it on a piece of paper and show you. Are you guys comfortable with that?"

I look at Josh for a moment. I am annoyed that he doesn't see the joy in waiting to be surprised and wish that even though he wants to know that he would choose to follow suite and make the decision to not find out. He is so stubborn at times and I am usually the one to give in but not this time. This is my pregnancy and I have made my choice.

Josh has already answered yes, I turn my head over to face the nurse and I nod that I am okay with it even though deep down I'm not.

As she rubs the gel on my belly Josh asks the question, "Couldn't I just tell by the image on the screen what the gender is instead of you writing it on a piece of paper?"

The nurse explains, "That's how we can tell. You don't see ultrasound images as much as I do and all too often an arm, a leg or the umbilical cord are mistaken for a penis."

She makes me smile as she explains to Josh while he falls silent. She continues, "Just to avoid the confusion I'll write it down for you."

She presses that wand onto my stomach and my eyes are staring up at the television screen on the ceiling. There they are a little person right there for me to see. Just as the first time my eyes well up but I am able to keep the water works at bay and take in the sight before me. Josh and I are quiet as we stare at our little person. She moves the want over my stomach, presses from time to time for a picture and tells me when to close my eyes when she nears the area in order to check the gender. While the nurse is still reviewing the images, the doctor steps in for a few moments to look and leaves me with the note that I had asked for to advise that I am healthy to travel. Before we know it, the appointment is wrapping up.

She says, "Everything looks normal and leaves me with some new pictures to take home. She hands Josh the envelope with the baby's gender and Josh remains quiet as we walk to the car.

I feel like he is weighing in on whether he should open the envelope. That is the only thing that could be on his mind. As the car doors close and Josh starts up the engine I have to give in and ask, "So when are you going to check?" He knows what I'm referring to and seems a bit edgy in his response, "Jordan are you sure that you really don't want to know?"

"You know that I want this to be a surprise." I fasten my seat belt.

"But the baby's room and the clothes and toys?"

I say, "We can do something that is gender neutral."

So, you want to paint our baby's room green or yellow?"

"Josh, we don't need to paint their room at all. The walls are beige. Besides I was thinking of doing those wall sticker type things like do a zoo animal theme or stars or something like that."

"What about their toys?"

"A newborn doesn't play with toys."

"How about clothing?"

"They will be in Sleepers the bulk of the time."

Josh decides it is time to pull out of the parking lot and get us moving to work.

He explains, "I really want to know what we are having."

I shrug and say, "Check, it's just that I ask that you do that when I'm not around."

"Yes, but Jordan that's not the point. I want us both to know."

"Please I don't want to know. Don't take the surprise away from me." I cross my arms and stare out the passenger side window.

A minute or two passes as we drive in silence and I glance at him. He looks bummed and just says, "Okay"

We pull into his work first and park in the round about before he gets out and I switch over to the driver's side.

I give him his hug and kiss goodbye and say to him, "It's fine, if you really want to know that bad, I'm over it you can find out just please keep it a secret from me."

He inhales and exhales and says, "I was hoping that you would change your mind, you know see the envelope with the answer and give in to the temptation. Well, I'm not sure if I'll look now."

This comes as a bit of a surprise to me but in a good way. Josh, the man who hates surprises may just let our baby's gender be a surprise after all of this. I ask him, "So what are you going to do with the envelope?"

"I'm not sure yet. I want to know but then if I find out I can't share the news with anyone because of you. I need to think about it."

I give him a gentle smile and say, "Okay" this news makes me happy and even though he is still undecided. I'm not going to push it and instead just leave it to him to ponder some more until he makes his choice.

He says, "Bye lovey. Have a great day and don't forget to pick me up after work."

"Bye love, you too and I won't forget."

Chapter 22
Digging

I am not quite sure how my mom catches wind of the fact that I am going on an all-expenses paid cruise but she has and it's not long before I get her call.

My work phone rings and the caller ID displays that it's my mom and I answer, "Hey Mom"

"Hey honey how are you?"

"Oh, I'm good."

She gets right to it, like she always does. It makes me laugh because her calls are always the same. She is digging for information and what is silly is I can see that I sometimes get like that too and have that characteristic of her. She says, "So I wanted to ask you something. I tried to call you yesterday but I ended up accidentally calling Josh."

"Mom, how did you accidentally dial Josh's number?"

She sighs and says, "Oh for some reason I have his number programmed into my phone as your cell phone number."

I laugh, "Mom, you could have just called the house phone if you wanted to reach me."

"I know but anyway Josh answered and I was able to find out the news to what I was looking for."

"What was that?"

"I knew that your second ultrasound was coming up and he just confirmed it for me so I didn't need to call you." There is a moment of pause. Funny thing is Josh will usually tell me when my parents call him. I'm not too worried about it. It must have just slipped his mind with all of the work he has been doing and the fact that we had to get all our appointments arranged prior to going on this trip.

She continues, "So, are you going to tell me how everything went today?"

"Oh, it was good and the baby is growing at a healthy rate."

"So did you find out what you are having?"

"I made the choice not to find out and the nurse gave Josh the envelope with the gender but I think that he is having second thoughts with wanting to find out. I dropped him off at his work after the appointment and he gave me the impression that he is wavering on wanting to know now because I don't want to know."

"What is he going to do?"

"I don't know mom. I don't want to bug him too much about it because it seems to be weighing on his mind. I'll let him decide."

She says, "Yes, that makes sense. So, Josh also told me of a cruise that you two are going on, is that true?"

I would have rolled my eyes at her if she were here in person standing in my office. I answer, "Yes, well it's sort of a long story but the short story is that I met a celebrity author at the water park last weekend. We started chatting; he invited Josh and me to his book signing and afterwards invited us to go on a cruise. Apparently, all the heavy weights in the writing world will be on this cruise. So, this is more than just a rest and relaxation trip for me, it's an opportunity to mingle with some of the best."

I hear her gasp on the line, "Wow that's great but what about the traveling while pregnant?"

This is my mom's first grandchild on the way so she is always showing her concern.

"Mom it's fine. I called the airline and the cruise ship to make sure that they would have me and have spoken to my doctor today about it and he gave me a doctor's note explaining that I am fit to travel in case anyone asks."

She says, "You're not worried about getting sea sick or anything?"

"Mom I'll be fine, plus I have Josh there to help if I need it."

"Alright, you know that I just worry that's all."

"There is nothing to worry about and besides this is an opportunity."

"Yes, I know. So when will you and Josh be leaving for this cruise?"

"I'm not sure exactly, Devon is just finalizing the details for us."

My mom repeats back, "Devon?"

"Yes, as in D. Chambers the author."

My mom pauses for a moment and I can almost hear the wheels turning in her head. She says, "Wait a second. Are you telling me that you got invited to go on a cruise with the author D. Chambers the same D. Chambers that wrote the book, Trial?"

I have to roll my eyes at her but then again, I never really told her the famous author's name. I confirm, "Yes the D is for Devon. Have you read Trial?"

"Jordan, I just finished it. Are you sure that Josh really wants to go on this cruise? I could take his spot if you would like?" Sheesh my sexy Devon even has my mom for a fan.

I chuckle and say, "I think Josh is looking forward to this cruise as much as I am."

She playfully answers, "Okay dear well I guess I am caught up on everything. Is there anything else that you need to fill me in on?"

"Nope I'm all out of news, is there anything going on with you?"

"Just the usual here, well, talk to you later, love you, Jordan."

"I love you too Mom."

Chapter 23
She Tagged Me

It is the morning of the cruise and I can't wait to see Jordan. This is also the first of what I hope will be many events where I get to combine showing appreciation for my fans and being able to enjoy a vacation while doing so.

Sara and I flew in last night and stayed in a hotel. I couldn't risk being delayed especially since my fans are arriving today. I woke up before my alarm going off on my phone. Sara is still asleep and I will give her that time to rest. As the coffee brews in the kitchen nook area of our suite I browse the social media feed, to see that Sara was up late posting things on her timeline. She even has something posted of me. She tagged me in her post so I click on it to open up an article. The title is, "D. Chambers a Great Author and Gift Giver". I read it. It's an interview with a few of the winners of the cruise. The interviewer asked them questions on why they love my books, what was it like to meet me in person and they talked about the cruise. I was a little concerned because the last thing that I want is to have paparazzi show up at some of the cruise destinations but fortunately, they didn't mention dates of the cruise.

I'm sure if a paparazzi was really determined they could research upcoming Author events, but it's good that this article didn't include that detail to make it easier to find.

The percolating of the coffee machine stops as the final drips fall into the white mug. The aroma of the house blend awakens me and reminds me that Jordan must be on her way to the airport now. I should send her a text.

A cheery voice from over my shoulder says, "Good morning my Great Author and Great Gift Giver" Sara looks rested she takes a seat at the table.

I smile and say, "Are you teasing me?"

She laughs and replies, "You saw the article that I tagged you in from yesterday, right?"

I pour her a cup of coffee also and bring the two mugs over to the table. I answer, "Yes, I saw."

She nods, "Then you know that I am not teasing."

"Well, if you were, I'm sure I could give your cruise to someone else."

Sara smirks, "You wouldn't dare Mister D. Chambers."

"Behave Misses D. Chambers." I smirk and then take a sip of my coffee to hide it.

I love seeing her happy. Texting Jordan will need to wait.

Chapter 24
Ignorance is Bliss

Today Josh and I get on a plane to Fort Lauderdale, Florida. I had not heard much from Devon other than him providing details of the trip and sending me the itinerary. He was so kind to give Josh and me first class seats for the flight. It was both our first time flying in first class, which was an absolute treat with the large reclining spacious seats that alone made the flight enjoyable.

Josh never ever drinks and during flight, we actually toasted to our holiday with a glass of sparkling Champaign. He was very cute because after the glass my six-foot tall husband was giddy for the rest of the flight. Before you judge me with being pregnant and drinking, it was just one glass, which is harmless to the child. I know this because the doctor has said that a glass occasionally is just fine. I was able to enjoy it without the worry of having glaring eyes on me. People are always so quick to judge and I guess that I was like that at one time.

I remember a few years ago this woman at the office where I worked, she was a very heavy smoker. She must have smoked a pack a day. Well, when she announced that she was pregnant, I wondered to myself if she would quit smoking for the sake of the baby but she never did. Maybe she cut back a bit but daily I would see her outside puffing away on one of those white cancer sticks and it was early on and right until the very end. I know that I never called her out on it or anything but, I am certain that I must have given her the disapproving glance.

It wasn't until much later when I was looking up information for my own pregnancy that I found studies that mentioned that a heavy smoker who quits cold during their pregnancy puts more added stress on their pregnancy than a smoker who simply cuts back. I know now that if I don't know the facts that I shouldn't judge and I am sure that she was fully aware that she was getting those unwanted glances. I don't smoke and only have a drink occasionally.

Anyway, focusing back on our flight it was the best flight experience that I have ever had. I don't fly often but wow I now know what I was missing out on and its sort of a shame in a way because ignorance is bliss and now, I have a taste for something that I may never be able to afford.

In no time, we touch down, get our luggage, cab over to the docks and find ourselves boarding a huge white ship.

Huge is not a big enough word to describe the grand size of this ship. It is enormous. I see rows upon rows and from here they seem like tiny windows but I am sure that they are much larger more close-up. The windows are stacked eleven floors and wrap around the ship. The length of the ship has to be over the length of four football fields. The sight of this beast is breathtaking.

There is a light warm breeze coming off the ocean with that fresh clean smell of the tropical waters. The smell brings back memories of my honeymoon years ago with Josh in Cuba. The air is rich with happy chatter from others boarding the ship, people recognizing others that they hadn't realized would be sharing this cruise with and others shuffling their way over to get checked in as we shuffle our way on board. The atmosphere is an exciting bustle of people who are anxious to find their rooms in order to off load their carryon luggage.

Josh and I don't recognize anybody and there is no sign of Devon in sight. I wonder, I never asked him if his wife would be coming.

We check in at reception on board and find our room aboard the ship. We make our way up the elevator to the seventeenth floor. This is insane. I must have a look on my face because it triggers Josh to ask, "What's up?"

"Oh, I just can't believe how many floors are on this ship. When we were on the dock, I had only counted eleven rows of windows."

"You're not counting the floors below deck."

"You are right."

The elevator alerts us with a light chime and the doors slides open to reveal a never-ending hallway of doors to all of the different rooms on this level.

Josh looks at the sign on the adjacent wall that points to the direction of the different number ranges and says, "This way"

We go take a right after exiting the elevator and walk down a quiet corridor. We pass by one other couple in the hallway before finding our room. The door beeps open after reading the card in the slot and Josh opens the door to reveal a breathtaking room.

I glance at the brass nameplate of the room before walking in, "Ocean Yard Penthouse Suite". The room has a small hall with a posh bathroom to the left with a frosted glass, standing shower and white basin sink. Dark wood cabinets, cupboards and a countertop line the right as we walk further into the room. On top of the counter is this massive flat screen television and further down there is this awesome looking stainless steel coffee machine. Straight ahead is floor to ceiling glass doors that open up to a large balcony fitted with two wicker cushioned chairs and a wicker table that overlooks the water. As we make our way into the room, a circle shaped bed is to our left that is fitted with white linen, purple velvet throw pillows and a purple and beige throw blanket. The room is done up in Japanese inspired mural artwork of birds on tree branches with flowers on an orange sky. The room is a pallet of oranges, whites, browns and golds with the accent of purples. It's stunning and not a color pallet I would ever imagine would work but this does. It's romantic and sophisticated and I still can't believe Devon gave us such a beautiful room.

Our luggage has not yet arrived to our room and for now Josh and I only have our carryon bags to work with. We rest our bags on the bed for a moment and Josh asks, "What would you like to do first?"

I smile, "I would like to slip into my bikini and sun dress and maybe we can walk around and figure where everything is."

"Have you heard anything from Devon yet?"

"No, I read my texts just before we checked in and so far, nothing. He may not be onboard yet or he may just have other obligations."

"Like what?"

"Well remember at his book signing he pretty well gave this trip as a prize to one of his fans. Perhaps he is meeting with them now or something. Who knows how many book signings that he gave away a cruise to? There could be a bunch of winners from different cities that he is meeting."

"Do you think they are all staying in suites like ours?"

I chuckle, "I was actually wondering that myself." I shrug, "Maybe, Devon has no shortage of cash. It wouldn't surprise me. Well, I'll keep my phone with me I really would like to meet up with him today to thank him for this."

We both change into more comfortable clothing from are carryon bags for the exploring of the ship and head out for our walk.

I say to Josh, "You know, seeing that he invited us here for me to meet and greet the big names in the publishing world, we should check in with reception to see what the schedule is for the Publisher & Author event. I forgot to ask the receptionist when we got the key to our room."

Josh and I walk down the hallway. He says, "Oh don't be so hard on yourself Jordan. You remembered now so it's all good, nothing is missed and we have only been here for about thirty minutes anyways."

We step into an elevator that descends to the atrium where the front desk is. This large room is furnished in elegant gold and red crushed velvet chairs and plush benches, gold carpet with a red ribbon design. There is a grand piano and this massive two-story portrait of the ship that is the focal point of the room. There are two young women at the desk smiling as we approach. The initial line up when we had checked in earlier has cleared.

One of them asks, "How can I help you?"

I start, "I was wondering if you had the schedule of the Publisher & Author event?"

She asks, "Are you a Publisher or Author?"

I kind of stumble for a moment and then answer, "Yes, well sort of. I am here as a guest." I stutter his name, "Devon Chambers guest. The two of us are." I look at Josh, he gives me a nod and I look back at the receptionist.

She smiles, "Okay great. Devon Chambers I have read his books. What a talented Author. What is he like in person?"

Conscious of Josh here I respond, "He is a great guy, friendly, generous, easy to talk to and courteous."

She says as she types into her computer, "He sounds like a wonderful guy. It's so great to hear when good people become successful." She continues to type and then says, "There we go just found the schedule for the Publisher and Author event. Do you have the map that we provided upon check in?"

I look at Josh because I don't have it and he shakes his head no. The receptionist sees and says, "No worries you two. I'll print out another copy for you."

The printer behind her hums and suddenly I remember to ask, "Are you able to tell me has Devon has checked in yet?"

She says "Let me just confirm a couple of things first. You mentioned that you were his guests."

"That's right."

She smiles and admits, "I just need to confirm in the system first. With celebrities you wouldn't believe how many hard-core fans we see who come here and try to find where they are staying and what not." Her fingers tap away at her keyboard as she verifies that we are indeed Devon's guests.

"I understand." Josh and I are quiet while she confirms that we are staying under his reservation.

"Josh and Jordan, right?" She asks. We both answer yes and she continues, "I just need to see some Identification."

I don't have my purse with me but thankfully Josh has his wallet on him and she confirms with his and says, "Yes, Mr. Chambers checked in about an hour ago he is staying on the eighteenth floor in room eighteen eleven."

She turns and grabs the printout behind her and hands it to us to look at. She glances at the paper as we lay it on the desk to check the times. She says, "You know what, if I am not mistaken Mr. Chambers has something organized in the next twenty minutes." She skims over the event schedule and finds it within seconds. "Yes, right here." She touches her index finger to the spot where it is written.

It reads, "Welcome to the cruise – Host: D. Chambers – Grand Theater" The receptionist glances up and Josh and I and asks, "Do you how to get to the Grand Theater?"

Josh says, "No"

She points, "It is just down this corridor. I would recommend that you head down there soon to get a good spot. I know with checking in the database the Publisher and Author group is one of the bigger groups onboard for the week."

I smile and take the printouts she provided and say, "Will do, thanks so much for your help."

She smiles and says, "Good luck you two and enjoy your stay."

Chapter 25
Salted Popcorn

The Grand Theater is something else. It's not the biggest theater that I have ever seen. It is about the size of a typical movie theater. The seats are done up in yellow crushed velvet and are elevated so that every seat has a good view of the stage. Towards either side there are rows of balconies and the stage is a half-moon shaped platform equipped with speakers and lighting and has a pretty, sparkly blue curtain.

I lead the way down the lighted steps to the front row only to find that the seats have reserved signs on them with names and none of them is for Josh or me. I look back at Josh and say, "Well that's a bummer."

He says, "Those could be for the winners from his signings."

"Yah that or the important Publishers." I glance back at the names but there are no business names accompanied next to them.

Josh suggests, "Why don't we take those spots there, just three isles up? I don't see any reserved signs on them."

"Okay" I'm a little disappointed that I couldn't get a front and center spot and ensure that Devon sees us in the crowed. He probably won't see us being three rows in but there isn't much we can do.

I follow Josh's lead and we take the seats and wait.

Josh asks, "Has he texted you?"

"No" I say.

"Just send him a text; I don't know why you haven't already."

I take out my phone at Josh's suggestion and write, "Hey Devon we are here, actually three rows in center of the grand theatre now. We saw the room, just beautiful. See you soon." I click send and put my phone down for a moment.

Josh says, "It's too bad that they don't serve popcorn and drinks here."

"Are you hungry?"

"Yah kind of the airplane food was the last I had and I didn't eat much."

"Yah, same here" Now that he mentions it, I am a little hungry and I'm getting the odd nudge from the little one in my belly.

It's as if they heard our plea for food that a food cart comes thru a door to the left of the stage.

"Josh, can you get me a diet coke and popcorn or chocolate bar?"

"Sure"

He is closer to the aisle and within moments we are snacking away while waiting for this thing to start. I didn't realize how hungry I was. I can't stop eating, the warm butter, salted popcorn hits the spot. The theatre steadily fills in with others.

I feel my phone buzz and have a look. It's Devon and he writes, "Hey Jordan, just caught a glimpse of you and Josh. I can't come out now but we can meet up after this is done." He keeps the message tame likely because Josh is here looking over my shoulder.

I say to Josh after finishing the popcorn in my mouth, "That was a text from Devon. He spotted us in our seats and he will meet up with us once this part is over."

"Did he say where?"

"No, but we can wait here and I am sure we can figure that out. He seems busy right now so I'll leave him be and text him after if needed."

The light sound of ambient music starts. It's a recording of an acoustic guitar and drums playing a relaxing and catchy beat. A steady stream of people is now starting to come in and I notice that reserved first row is starting to fill up.

Josh and my assumptions are correct and I recognize the woman that won the trip at the book signing in Ottawa.

I point at the woman in the first row, "Josh look."

"Yah I saw that." He confirms.

"That means that the entire row is all likely winners from all of his signings?" I say amazed.

Josh admits, "This trip between the two of us we could never afford. Maybe we could if our accommodations were in one the cheapest rooms of the ship but not the one, we have now. I couldn't imagine the bill for all of Devon's fans."

"I wonder if they have the same accommodations as us."

"They must, why would we get any special treatment over his other guests?"

It is a good thing that Josh doesn't know the truth and I just answer, "Yes, you're right."

Josh gives me a sideways glance, "Are we getting special treatment?"

I shrug, "I have no idea. I just thought because he befriended us and well, he is sort of taking me under his wing to introduce me to all the heavy weights in the writing world."

He jabs, "Should I be worried about him?"

I choke on a piece of popcorn in my mouth but manage to say, "No, he is just a friend and not my type anyway." I feel my cheeks flush.

Josh's prior remark was a joke but now he is starting to show concern and says, "Why are you blushing?"

"I'm not, it's the piece of popcorn and besides you kind of surprised me in saying that."

He seems to accept my explanation. I make a jab back at him to release what is left of the tension, "For one thing, it's not in good practice to have any sort of romance with someone who is helping your carrier rocket forward and the second thing is I am clearly off the market." I glance down at my belly.

He makes a face and sighs, "Yes dear."

I need to stop talking. The theatre is full of excited people before we know it from all walks of the writing community. There is no seat left and the lights in the aisles dim down while the ones on stage light up. The crowed falls silent as the music becomes louder to a suspense themed symphony and to the right of the stage Devon makes his appearance on stage.

He is dressed casual in a white polo shirt and khakis as he takes center stage and grabs a mic in hand.

"How is everyone today?" His amplified strong voice booms thru the speakers. Cheers, a few whistles and lots of clapping erupt.

Devon smiles as he paces a few steps back and forth near to the mic stand.

He says, "Good, well I am excited to be in the company of so many amazing people and I want to say a special thank you to my fans in the front row. I am so happy that you guys made it and without your support I wouldn't be where I am today." He looks down at them as he says his heartfelt words and the front row starts to clap then the rest of the theatre.

It takes a moment before the applause settles down again and Devon continues, "This is going to be an epic cruise with the events that are lined up for this week. Just so that you know if you haven't already received your own copy there are event schedules that are available at the front desk. We are kicking off our event this evening at the Authors

Ball. There will be a couple of guest speakers from Champaign Publishing and Tail Fin Books along with their new up and coming authors. Sunday, we have the casino reserved for our group. Monday is for all the people who love to party. We have the club to drink and dance the night away and Thursday we wine and dine at the Oriental Restaurant on board."

Oh man, Josh hasn't said anything and I never thought to bring a ball room dress. I had no idea that it was going to be full on formal. I just brought a cocktail dress.

Devon continues, "I hope to see you at all of the events and let's take a moment to look at the events that have shaped our writing community this year." Just behind him as he says that, a screen comes down from the ceiling and the lights that were on stage dim so that a movie can play.

A short movie features news from the publishers here. I learn that Devon's publisher has arranged for his book to turn into a movie for next year. There are some clips of the other up and coming Authors that explain what they have done to become successful. To be honest besides Devon's news it's sort of boring. It's a lot of ego stroking but I force myself to watch because I need to learn the names of these key contenders if I want to make an impression and mingle with these people.

At the end of each clip, the crowed claps and finally the screen goes up prompting Devon to return to the stage with a guest at his side. He says,

"Just before we depart for the afternoon, I would like to welcome my publisher, Mr. Howard Stem of Tail Fin Books." Devon shakes his hand and gives the stage to Mr. Stem.

Mr. Stem doesn't command the stage like Devon does. He isn't compelling like Devon. He doesn't seem to be shy on the stage. He is more awkward and says in a serious sounding voice, "It is my pleasure to welcome you to this event. Each year this event grows in popularity and it's a good way for all of us to come together and improve and add to the story telling world."

He pauses as the audience claps. He continues, "With that said, it's time to enjoy this cruise. See you all tonight!" The crowd claps again accompanied with a few whistles. The energy in the room is great and I look over to Josh and he seems happy too but I think he is happy because our vacation is truly starting.

He asks, "Are you ready to do something, maybe check out those water slides?" At this point, the audience is starting to move out of their seats and into the aisle. Some are having conversations in the theatre and others are departing in groups. At this point Josh is half out of his seat. I follow his lead and Devon interjects us in the aisle.

"Leaving before you say hello to me?" He says it kiddingly with that gorgeous smile on his face.

Josh shakes his hand and says, "We are just getting ready to have some fun."

Devon chuckles, "Good stuff my man." He steps closer to me and says, "So how is the beautiful mom to be?"

"I am great. I didn't think this would be such a big event."

He leans in, "This event will change your life." I smile back at him and he winks at me with those big brown eyes. He turns to Josh and says, "Hey I learned that you are quite the active guy. Perhaps you would be interested in doing some rock wall climbing with me this afternoon while the mom relaxes pool side?"

Josh is warming up to him, "Sure friend."

Devon says, "Okay great let's say we all meet at 2:00 PM by the rock wall."

Josh answers for both of us, "Yes we will be there." They shake hands again and Josh takes the queue to depart the theatre. I start to follow when Devon gently takes my hand and holds me back for a second.

He whispers in my ear, "I'm dying to pound your sweet yummy spot. I want to nibble your lips too and suck that sweet juice until you are empty." I bite my lip and smile. He continues, "Oh by the way had to rub one off this morning thinking of you. You are such a great friend letting me have you. I had better not think of you pulsating and dripping right now. Not a good time but wow that is yum."

I whisper back to him with a smirk, "You are bad."

Josh turns the moment I start walking up the aisle and he lets me catch up to him.

Chapter 26
Warm Breeze

The afternoon out on deck is nothing short of fantastic. I recommend if you ever get the opportunity to take a cruise do it. Josh and I have been here for a few hours and it is a first for both of us we have never been out in the ocean like this. The only thing that comes remotely close is our honeymoon in Cuba. We went out on a catamaran and were at most about a hundred meters off shore.

There is a light warm breeze just as when we had boarded the ship and I think its perfect weather for Josh and Devon to be doing some rock wall climbing while I relax and get my tan on.

We meet up at the Elite Beach Club area. This area is just gorgeous and geared for relaxation. Glass railings section off the area from the rest of the ship. There is a small bar in the center and surrounding it are beige wicker couches, loungers and even beds. All of the furniture is fitted with hot red cushioning and pillows and all of the sun umbrellas are the same color. There is Caribbean themed music playing and the area is about seventy percent occupied with people who have the same plans in mind, to relax. Josh and I had been waiting for a few moments when I spot Devon in a sport t-shirt and shorts, followed by a woman in an oversized straw hat, black swim suite with red floral sarong wrapped around her small waste. They are making their way over to us.

Devon says with a bit of a nervous but excited smile, "Hey there."

We both recognize Devon, "Hey Devon." We both say.

Josh gives him that signature guy hand shake and then Devon gives me a hug and whispers in my ear, "Gosh you are beautiful."

I say back to him and not at a whisper, "Thanks Devon. Are you going to go easy on my husband?"

He releases me from his polite hug and he glances over to Josh with a smile and says, "I think your wife is worried that I won't go easy on you today."

Josh chuckles, "I'm ready to do this."

The woman that had been following Devon had left for a moment to the bar and returns with two drinks in hand. They look alcoholic. As she approaches Josh and I glance over at her and as she comes within earshot Devon makes the introductions, "You are probably wondering who this beautiful creature is. This is my wife, Sara."

My heart flutters. I knew it had to be her because I recognized her from photos that Devon had shared with me over the course of our friendship. I had a feeling that I might meet her but I didn't think it would be right this moment. I had suspected in the back of my mind that if she were on board, I would have met her at the ball this evening, which I have no dress for, so I am not completely mentally ready for this and my heart starts beating fast.

Devon speaks to Sara whom is smiling back at us, "Dear this is the young talented writer I had mentioned to you."

She cuts him off and says, "Ah yes, Jordan it is so nice to meet you. I would shake your hand but you can see that my hands are full. One of these is for you so that makes up for my rudeness." She winks at me. Her eyes are a rich dark brown with smile lines that frame them.

I answer nervously to the woman that I know so much about, "It is so nice to meet the woman who supports this amazing man. You must have so many stories of Devon."

She says, "Every good man is supported by an amazing woman."

Devon chuckles and looks at Josh and says while giving a nudge, "Isn't that the truth!"

Josh replies, "I thought that was the other way around?"

I give Josh a playful glare before Devon makes his final introduction for Sara, "With that said, this young strong man is Jordan's husband Josh."

She says to me, "Jordan, I like you already. You have great taste." She looks over to Josh with those dark Italian brown eyes and nods her head, "Josh it's my pleasure to meet you."

I knew that Sara was an older woman, years older than Devon whom is in his early forties and for a woman of her age she is rather stunning. She shows age on her face but you can tell that she has taken care of herself and the beauty in her is not just her looks but also the confidence. She beams of personality. It is commanding, confidant and she is sure of herself, the opposite of me. I wonder how Devon finds me attractive. I am nothing like her but I already envy that sureness that she has in herself that I lack. I can tell in her presence that she is a strong woman. She knows exactly what she wants out of life and isn't afraid to let the world know it. She is fearless.

Devon had always told me that the two of them were opposites. His approach with life was gentler, with establishing bonds, don't get me wrong, Devon is a go getter but he has described himself to me as a laid back, go with the flow sort of guy but also work oriented at the same time. He explained that rather than fight the tides that life throws at you he focusses on adjusting to the tides in order to get the desired outcome. Sara will fight to make the tides flow her way. Devon simply grabs a surfboard and rides them.

Devon says to Josh, "Shall we head over to the wall and let our women relax?"

"Sure"

Devon teases to Sara and me "Don't get into trouble."

Sara says, "Get out of here you two." She turns to me and suggests, "Shall we take those two loungers ahead?" She nods in their direction and two that are facing glass railings that overlook the open waters.

"Yes" I answer shyly.

We take a seat and she places the two drinks she had in hand onto the little wicker table between us. I don't know why but for a moment I am distracted by her hands as she sets the drinks down. Her hands show age. The surface is wrinkled and transparent, revealing the veins beneath. Blemishes of the sun over the course of years scatter the surface. Her hands don't match the rest of her. She has the hands of an old woman. She is an old woman but her hands are her only feature that shows it. She says, "Isn't that an amazing view?"

I snap out at staring at her hands, look and her and answer, "Yes, it's breathtaking. This is the first time Josh and I have been on a cruise. Devon is so kind to have given us the opportunity." I feel silly for staring at her hands, though I don't think she noticed me doing so.

She agrees, "He is a generous man and a devoted husband." I choke on the spit in my mouth but force myself to stop. I can't help but wonder if there is more meaning behind what she just said. Sara gets comfortable in her lounger, takes a sip of her drink and says, "Wow that hit the spot. Have you tried yours yet?" I am a little reluctant and she sees it and says, "Don't worry dear, Devon mentioned that you were expecting and well there is no mistaking a little belly like yours. I got you a fruit punch; go on, that baby could use some sugar."

I relax, her comments are just friendly chat. I say, "Thank you!" The drink is amazing and I set it down back on the wicker table, following Sara's lead and get comfortable on the lounger.

Sara is a socializer and she leads our conversation, which is to my relief as it calms my nerves that I had about meeting her. "Devon has always been generous even before coming into the success that he has had. Like for instance the home that we had in Austin before upgrading into a gated community. He told you about that right?" I nod and she continues, "Devon is always making sure that I was taken care of. I'm no spring chicken and he made sure that when I quote, retired that it was for real and he worked that much harder to make sure that I wouldn't have to return to work at my age. That all happened before this success as an author."

"That is something." I look over to her as the words escape my lips. Hearing her describe Devon makes me love him more. I have to keep myself in check. I am talking to his wife.

"Yes, hard working men like him are hard to find so when you find them you make sure that you hold onto them with all that you have got." Sara places her drink next to mine and lies back on the recliner. She glances over at our two men climbing the rock wall in the area below.

Awkwardly I say, "Will do, yes Josh is the same way. Well, let me rephrase that. I'm not retired it's just that we have had a lot of expenses that have come up in the last year and he has taken it upon himself to take on a second job to pay everything down sooner while I just work my normal full-time job. I do find myself missing him a lot but I know that he has good intentions."

Sara admits, "You will always miss the ones that you love. I am happy that Devon had given me the retirement that I so needed. I have had some health issues and there was no way I could have worked while suffering through them. Now that I am healthy, I do miss Devon. Even before his success, he was working a 9:00 AM to 5:00 PM job and with the drive, he was gone for nearly ten hours a day. Being left alone for that long weighs heavy on the heart but you know what you do?"

"What?" I ask.

She glances back at me, taking her drink in her hand and says, "You go out and do the things that you love, make friends and open your home to family and friends. That is what I have done and it has helped me over the years." She takes another sip of her drink.

"That's good advice. When Josh started working at his second job that was when I started to focus on my writing. It's something that I love to do and it keeps me busy." I follow her lead and take another sip of my fruity drink.

"That's good Jordan. Do you make time for friends and family?"

"I do. I maybe go out once a month with friends and see my family every other week. I admit I should see them more. I guess there is always something that we can improve upon in our lives."

"Cheers to that." She says and raises her glass and I touch my own glass with hers.

I turn the conversation over to her, "So now with Devon reaching his celebrity status you must see him less?"

She chuckles, "I wouldn't say less, it's just different. It's a different schedule now. Before he was gone ten hours a day excluding the weekends but now it is more like this. He will go on these book-signing tours and maybe for a week straight he will work remotely while away. I won't see him but he will make up for it because the following week he will be off." She takes another sip of her drink and continues, "I miss him while he is away but at the same time he is out of my hair and I can work on projects while he is gone. I have spent so much time decorating and bringing our new home up to speed. It's funny because the weeks that he is home, towards the end I just want to tell him to go fly a kite because I am now used to my alone time."

"I get like that to with Josh. I miss him but now that I have focused on my writing, I do make a conscious effort to put the writing projects away when he is home and you know what?"

"What?" She grins, knowing I am about to let her in on a secret.

I giggle, "Sometimes that drives me nuts because, I'm sure Devon can relate. For me I am always thinking of things to add to a story and when an idea forms and Josh is home, I am just itching to add the words to the story."

She chuckles, "I can see why Devon has taken a warming to you. The two of you have a passion. I guess I am like Josh in that sense. I am always telling Devon to put his phone down or to get off his computer. Maybe we should just trade husbands?"

I choke again but this time it is on my drink and not the spit in my mouth. I do a double take and she smirks at me. I say, "Maybe one day I'll take you up on it." We both start laughing.

By this time our drinks are empty and I take it upon myself to offer the next round, "Sara what would you like?"

"I'll have a Pink Fizzy"

"I never heard of that. What is in it?"

"The bartender will know how to make it. Its White Zinfandel mixed with pink lemonade and a couple other things." She explains.

I return with our drinks and we have some quiet time in each other's company in the sun. I feel it is time to reapply the sunscreen after a while and out of nowhere she asks, "Are you ready for the ball tonight?" Shit, my dress, I need a formal dress. My emotions are already clear on my face and she notices it. She lifts her head enough for the brim of her hat to reveal those vibrant brown eyes of hers, "You are going right?"

"Yes, I planned to go but I did something stupid when packing. I only packed a cocktail dress and with me being pregnant and all I meant to do some shopping at the boutiques on board this afternoon but if I can't find anything suitable. I think I may have to drop the plans of attending the ball."

"That is too bad Jordan. I know how important this evening is with being the wife to a successful author. I know that you will do what you feel is best."

I shrug, "I had no idea that it was a formal event until it was announced earlier in the theatre. I really want to go. The last thing on my mind would be to brush aside any of the opportunities given to me."

She suggests, "You have been to the main lobby, where you checked in."

"Yes"

"I saw a dress shop not far from that massive portrait of the ship in the lobby. They should be able to help you out."

"Thank you"

She laughs, "Jordan I am certain that you are not the only woman who has forgot a dress or two. Well, these ships I tell you, they know how to make their money."

I hear the voices of our men first before seeing them approach. They are laughing and you would think that the two of them were old friends, Josh says, "Wow you look like you are enjoying yourself." He leans down so that I don't have to get out of the lounger and gives me a kiss on the cheek. Devon does the same with Sara.

Sara comments, "You two need a shower."

Devon says, "No, you think?"

Sara says to me, "There is nothing like sweaty, stinky men who are looking for affections eh Jordan?"

I laugh, crossing my arms and say to Sara, "I'm staying out of this."

Josh says, "I know that I need a shower."

Devon says, "Yes me too, will we see you tonight?"

I look at Sara and Josh and then to Devon. Sara answers for me, "Jordan needs to go dress shopping for tonight."

He smiles and says, "Okay we will leave you guys to it. See you both this evening."

Chapter 27
Pizza Pie

As we walk back down to our room Josh says, "You wanted to do some shopping for tonight right?"

"Yes, you need a suit and I need a dress." I glance up at him, not sure if he is about to complain about me spending money.

"Gotcha, I have no problem with that." He says it like that because he recognizes the worry I have about where the whole money conversation is headed. He knows that this is important to me and does approach the subject with caution. He continues, "I am feeling kind of hungry. Mind if we stopped somewhere and grabbed a bite to eat?" He deflects, I know it and that is okay because I want this trip to be full of good memories.

"Sure." I say relieved.

We walk down to one of the lower decks and spot a cute little restaurant called Pizza Pie and it is a no-brainer for us. We don't even need to ask the other and head to the entrance. We push to swing open the door there is a cute foyer that opens up into a little atrium with a tree in the middle where its canopy reaches the second level. Tables and chairs are situated around the tree focal point and passed the tree are floor to ceiling windows that overlook the deep blue waters of the Atlantic.

A young host greets us. Her long straight dark brown hair done up in a ponytail and she is wearing black pants and a simple white shirt. She asks, "For two?"

"Yes" Josh says.

"Great, right this way." She sets us up at a table for two next to the windows and gives us menus to look over.

Before she leaves, Josh pipes in, "If we know what we want, do you mind if we place the order now?"

"Not at all, what would you like?" Her long brown ponytail falls over her right shoulder as she bends down just a little to hear Josh's order, taking it to memory.

Josh gives the order, "A Hawaiian pizza and to drink I will have a diet sprite and my wife a diet coke."

"Okay sure" She takes the menus from us and departs for the kitchen.

I ask, "So how did you like the rock wall climbing?"

"It was good. I got to the top but I have to admit that I am starting to feel it in my hands and arms."

"Did Devon make it to the top?"

"Yep, he is a pretty nice guy." His eyebrows rise slightly like the tone of his voice.

"Why do you say it like that?"

He glances up at the ceiling then smiles at me and sighs, "I guess I had a pre-determined idea of what authors in general were like. I pictured introverted, self-centered, artsy and to add with the celebrity status I pictured him to be a prick." He smirks.

The host who is now waitressing our table quietly places our drinks down as we converse. I giggle, "Well you know me. Am I like that?"

"Well, no honey." He scrunches up his face and says, "Well, you are a little weird but that's about it."

"Josh!" I want to reach across the table and smack him.

"What? Who says weird is bad?" He shrugs.

"You're very funny Josh." I make a face at him.

A woman from another table approaches ours. She looks to be in her sixties and has short blonde hair, a boy cut style and she is slender. I first see her pencil skirt and airy sleeveless blouse before I see her features. She had been sitting at an adjacent table. She says, "Hey guys" We both look up at her and she continues, "I don't mean to interrupt your meal."

I say, "Not at all."

She smiles and continues, "Oh good, well I couldn't help but notice you two in the theatre earlier today." She glances at me, "I also saw you with Mrs. D. Chambers earlier?"

I say, "Yes that was us." I don't mean to but I end up showing my feelings on my face and reveal to her confusion with her question.

She explains, "My name is Barb Eaton and I work for Eaton & Hampton Publishers. We heard that along with Mr. Chambers Winners that would be attending the cruise that he would be bringing an author with a lot of promise. I don't mean to be spying on you two but I noticed him talking with you two after the presentation in the theatre. The writing community can be a rather tightly knit group and no offense but I didn't recognize you and noticed that you weren't sitting in the front row with his winners and also noticed that you were in the company of Mrs. Chambers. I can't help but ask are you the special author that Mr. Chambers brought on this cruise?"

I answer, "Yes, I am an author and Mr. Chambers was so kind to invite me on this cruise."

She says with a smile, "I knew it." She extends her hand out to shake mine and says, "It is so nice to meet you." She politely prompts me to provide her with my name with an exaggerated nod and wide eyes.

I entertain her prompts and say, "I'm Jordan Connor and this is my husband Josh."

She shakes his hand also and says, "It is so exciting to meet an up-and-coming star. Will you be attending the ball this evening?"

I answer, "Yes, that is the plan."

The host arrives with our food and with that Barb says, "Well I will leave you two to dine. Here is my business card and I look forward to picking up where we left off tonight."

I smile, "Okay sounds great see you then."

She goes back to her own table and Josh leans in and whispers, "You know what that was about, right?"

I smile, "I think Devon may have started a bit of a bidding war between the publishers. She doesn't even work for his publisher."

Chapter 28
Zippers and Buttons

Josh and I spend the rest of the afternoon shopping and we make our way to the shop that Sara had mentioned. Thankfully, they also carry a men's line so as I look for a suitable gown Josh is able to browse the men's section for a good suit.

I browse the racks as Josh looks through the jacket section, reading the sizes tag by tag. I have no idea what I want and how to find something that is flattering for my belly. What color should I even go with?

A short older woman of Asian descent approaches me, "Shopping for a gown?"

"Yes, I have a ball to attend tonight and I forgot to pack something suitable."

"Ah yes the Authors Ball, that is okay my dear, you have come to the right place. Do you have a particular style that you had in mind?"

"I was thinking a full-length gown and something that will flatter my special frame." I look down at my stomach.

She smiles and touches her hand to my tummy, "Ah yes we have dresses that flatter an expectant mummy figure. Do you have a favorite color?"

I smile, "I am undecided. Could you pick something you would think works for my skin tone?"

"Sure" The short little woman disappears amongst the racks of dresses and emerges with a few gowns in hand, a deep purple, a vibrant blue and a hot red one. They are all very different. The hot red one catches my eyes.

She says, "I think you already have a favorite, yes?"

I smile and say, "Yes, the red color is just stunning."

"Follow me. We will get you dressed." I follow the short little woman to a change room and rather than leave me to change she does something different and comes into the change room with me. She doesn't give me a chance to question it and just says, "I will help you change. Zippers and buttons can me hard."

She helps me into the red one it's a strapless red formal gown. The material around the body is layered providing texture to it. There is a three-sided mirror in here and I twirl around checking out my angles.

"You like?"

"I do"

She makes some minor adjustments and says to me, "It's beautiful and flattering, makes you look tiny. Okay let's have you try the next one. She goes to work with helping me out of the red gown and into the purple one. It is a full-length strapless formal gown. Silver stones cover the breast and rib area and from the upper waste to the floor has an abundance of ripped fabric. As she zips me up, I know that it is wrong. It's too busy for me.

She says to my reflection in the mirror, "You don't like. The red one you like." Her hands rest on my arms as she peeks around from behind me.

I say, "I like the red one more. I feel like I look bigger than I actually am in this one."

"No worries." She helps me out of this one and into the last one, which is the blue one. It is another strapless formal gown and has a beaded design just below the breast and plenty of fabric covering the stomach area that flows to the base of the gown. The fabric flows straighter whereas the purple gown made me look like a giant cupcake. It is pretty and I twirl around in the mirror, unsure.

She asks, "You like?"

"Yes, it's pretty."

She says, "I think you liked the red one more."

I glance back at the red one, "Yes I think you are right."

"I like the red one on you the best. Okay red it is."

"I smile, "Yes" She helps me out of the blue dress.

Before leaving me to change back into my clothes she asks, "Your shoe size is an eight?"

I answer, "Yes, how did you know?"

"I am good at my work." She smiles and leaves me for a few moments and returns with these beautiful gold strap shoes with a low heal which is smart or else my feet will tire. I try them on and they are perfect.

The little woman wastes no time and gets everything ready to put through the cash register.

I say, "Oh my husband is also getting a suit."

She smiles, "Yes, I know his is already in the register ready to be added to the bill." She turns around, pulls a suit in plastic from the wall and a shoebox on the counter below and drapes it over the bag that contains my shoes and gown.

I ask her, "Where is my husband?"

She points just over my shoulder to the benches outside of the store, "That's him, right?"

I turn and Josh waves at me. The little woman brings up the total. "Everything comes to $800.00"

I choke, "Excuse me?" I did let her pick out my dress. Wow, I should have checked the price.

"You and your husband have good taste. Both your outfits were close in price. Can I have your name and your method of payment?"

I look back at Josh and he gives me thumbs up. I am not used to spending this much or used to the fact that Josh appears to be cool with it. This is investing in me and I need to make a good impression on these people. I am finding it a little hard to breathe but manage to tell her, "My name is Jordan Connor and I will pay by credit."

She starts typing into her computer and smiles, "Ah no, no credit card today."

My heart stops. I don't have the cash for this and just before admitting that the little woman saves me from the embarrassment, "There is a note here for your name to bill to D. Chambers account."

I say, "Oh you must be mistaken. Josh and I are staying in a room that was reserved by Mr. Chambers, that's probably what you are seeing."

"Oh no my dear, I am not wrong, there is a special request to bill your purchase to Mr. Chambers." She smiles and continues, "You did not know right?" She glances back to her computer screen as her hands move over the keyboard typing away quickly in order to finish the transaction.

I am still in a bit of shock, "I had no idea." I am still trying to pick my jaw up off the floor.

"He is a good friend, yes?" She says and takes the handles of the bag and puts them together handing it over for me to take.

I nod, "Yes a very good friend, I will need to thank him later."

Chapter 29
Muffle the Sounds

The Author's ball is something else. This is another first for Josh and me. I feel extremely out of my element. We walk into the area where the event is through white satin curtains. The lighting is dimed just a touch. The carpet is reds and gold square patterns and the columns in the room are ivory trimmed with dark stained wood. Eight columns surround the dance floor and the ceiling opens up to a second level. The stage overlooks the dance area. The room is vast with plenty of standing room area as well as furnished with elegantly styled ivory fabric alligator print cushioned chairs trimmed with dark wood and beautifully placed tables outfitted with white tablecloths dishes and silver wear. There is a bar in the room. I spot different men and women dressed in black and white carrying gold platters with a variety of appetizers.

We both look around the room. The same people who were in the theatre earlier they are all dressed to impress. I spot the woman who had won the trip when Devon visited Ottawa for his book signing. She is with Devon's other winners and the group of them seem to be getting along like old friends. They must be staying in suites close to one another and they must have spent the day with each other.

For Josh and me we only know a few here and to be quite honest I am feeling a little nervous and shy and am just about to ask Josh if he would like to go talk to the winners when I hear a voice from behind us.

"There they are, so you made your way over." Devon comes up from behind, puts himself between us and puts his arms around our shoulders. He continues, "Josh you clean up well and wow, Josh I have to say it, your wife is simply stunning." Devon's eyes meet mine. He winks and I smirk.

Josh smiles, "If you keep saying that it will go to her head."

I nudge Josh playfully, "Can't a girl get a compliment every now and then?" I say to Devon, "You really didn't need to pay for our outfits this evening."

Devon smiles, "I know, I wanted too."

I say, "Thank you" and ask, "Is Sara coming?"

"Yes, she is here somewhere. She is a bit of a social butterfly." Devon glances around, spots her and nods for her to come over.

Sara approaches us giving Josh a hug and kiss on the cheek she says, "Jordan your husband is ruggedly handsome. I may have to steal him away for a bit."

I tell her, "That is okay with me."

Josh gives me a smirk and I say, "You will probably have more fun with her than hanging around me all night while I mingle."

Devon says to Josh, "I can take your wife and talk shop, meet the heavy hitters and in a bit, we can meet up."

Josh seems a little reluctant but Sara twists his arm saying, "Trust me Josh, being the wife of this man, I have been by his side during these events and it can get a little boring. What do you say, show this old lady a good time?" She loops her arm into his.

Sara convinces him and Josh says to me, "Okay see you in a bit."

Just before we divide up Josh whispers in my ear, "Don't commit to anything without talking it over with me?"

"Absolutely"

Devon gives me his arm and he leads the way into the crowed. I shake hands and kiss cheeks and the smell of the different colognes and perfumes fills my senses. I meet so many faces, his publisher and the woman, Barb Eaton, which introduced herself at the restaurant earlier, other successful authors and many more publishers.

Then for a moment, it is just Devon and me. He says, "I had something in mind."

I know what it is I can tell with the hunger in his eyes. I say nothing, he leads me outside on deck, not saying a word, into the darkness and he kisses me. Those warm, passionate lips, his hungry tongue, he is gentle but in command all at once. He whispers, "Jordan, you drive me nuts, you are so beautiful. I can't get enough of you and you have me sporting some wood."

I chuckle, "My bad boy, well what do you suggest?"

"I suggest that we go somewhere and take care of each other."

I trust him and trust that he knows what he is doing and we descend to the lower decks to where the cheaper rooms are. He stops at one of the doors and produces a card.

I ask, "This isn't where you and Sara are staying is it?"

He chuckles, "Gosh no, I can't have your scent on my sheets or she will suspect something."

I touch his arm and he glances down, "What babe?"

"Whose room is this?" I whisper.

"Ours silly, I got it for us." The door clicks open.

The room is tiny. Immediately to our left is a bed done up with purple, white and green bed linens and pillows. We are practically tripping over the bed as we walk in. Along the wall where the bed is, there is a giant circle shaped window where it is clear that we are below the surface. The view is deep blue waters. Maybe three steps across from the door is a vanity and to the right is a frosted glass stand up shower, floor to ceiling mirror and a closet. The flooring is dark wood and the walls are white and ivory cushioned padding, my guess is to muffle the sounds of the ocean for the occupants who stay here.

The door closes behind and he wastes no time taking me into his arms and he starts kissing groping and feeling me.

He slips his fingers under the layers of the dress to find my swollen wetness. He grins and says, "Seems like someone is hungry."

I pant and whisper in his ear, "Only you make me this way." I trace my hand down to his man and it is ready for me.

I look up at him and grin back at my own discovery. He says, "Well girl you are going to have to start playing with my wood now. You teased it."

"Did I? Hmm I thought it was you who suggested this?"

He chuckles, "Well I don't recall now, my memory is fuzzy."

We undress, clothes falling to the floor and I back him onto the bed and push him down so that he is all mine and I start to move my lips up and down his shaft.

He lets his moans out and it drives me to do more to him I lick the tip, it is so swollen that it is almost purple. He is already pre-coming into my mouth, his warm slightly sweet watery juice.

His breathing becomes more intense as he gasps for air and his moan more intense as I jerk him off. He says, "Swallow my juices."

He unloads his passion into my mouth and I gulp every drop, wanting more. His body relaxes for a moment, as I slow my pace to let him recuperate but the thing is I don't stop stroking him.

Devon doesn't soften and I know that he is ready for more and I continue licking and running my tongue up and down his shaft. His balls tighten as I continue and I have the sudden urge to suck them. Playing with his soft skin and hearing his sighs as I pleasure him it is driving me nuts.

He says, "I want your hot juice coating my shaft." I straddle him and get on for the ride. My cowboy has the thickest shaft I have ever felt and having him slide into my juicy spot is intense. I am slippery and he pushes in easily but he always causes me to gasp with the painful pleasure that he gives.

He whispers, "You like that?"

"I do" I rock back and forth with him inside to get used to the feeling. I fit him like a tight glove. He is gentle and his hands are warm as he guides me up and down. I feel safe within his grasp and I am all his in this moment.

He leans up kisses me and says, "Let it go." He holds me firm, he is deep inside, so deep that my body cramps a bit but I explode and my whimpers and sighs are loud as I throb.

"I want to muff dive you and lap up that stuff my good girl."

I catch my breath and slowly let him out of my hungry little pussy and lay down in the spot where he was on the bed. He goes down on me and he doesn't give me the chance to get used to the intensity of his busy tongue.

I gasp and squirm as he laps up the juice on my lips and nibbles on me. The pressure of his tongue and the intensity of his bites are making my eyes roll back.

He gives me a break for a split second to say, "Your smell is driving me nuts. I want to hear you moan."

He doesn't give me a second to catch my breath and I moan and gasp as he pleasures and brings me to the edge and gives me my release that I so desperately need. I cry out as my kitty vibrates and convulses.

He chuckles and I look down at him and his face around his goatee is glistening. He says, "Good girl. I got to ram your kitty and explode."

I get on my hands and knees and he enters me from behind, taking my hips into his hands as he pumps himself hard into me. There is no more play now this is just what it is, straight no bullshit fucking. He wants his own and I know that he is already close and with each powerful thrust so am I. I explode again and vibrate but he doesn't have his and doesn't slow with his own thrusts. I can barely handle it, moaning and gasping as the feeling is beyond words. He slows for a second and I hear him sigh as his shaft fills me with his seed.

He comes to a slow and then to a stop. My cowboy is satisfied and he says to me while still inside, "How did you like our late-night jam?"

"Devon, you know how to please your women."

He slowly pulls out and says, "Okay enough of that. Now back to the party."

Chapter 30
Chunkier Knot

This is what the well-off do. Jordan and I arrived at this Author Ball a short while ago. I have kept my complaining to non-existent. I know she is excited and she looks beautiful in that dress. I feel like a dick in this suit but it makes Jordan smile. I'm doing this all for her.

It is not long before Jordan and I go in different directions. I watch her from across the room and I can tell she is starting to relax. To anyone else she looks relaxed. I can just tell when she gets nervous. She will fidget with her hands and she isn't doing that which is good.

Sara is nice. To tell you the truth she is a little intimidating but in a good way. I am sure Devon had no idea what hit him when he met her because that is how I feel now. She leads me around our arms locked together as though I am hers.

Sara tells me about life in Austin. She talks about her kids that I find out are around Jordan's age and mine. She mentions that Devon has a son who is a young adult now.

I feel like I am not keeping my end up with this conversation and ask, "Do your kids live in Austin?"

She laughs, "Gosh no! They live up north in New Jersey."

"Do you visit a lot?"

Her eyes glow as I ask her about her kids. She admits, "I see them when I can. Before Devon's success, I was visiting three or four times a year, whenever I have enough money to visit them. Now that Devon is making more, I will visit more mind you I haven't recently because we have been so busy lately."

I say, "That makes sense."

She smiles and glances at my tie. I ask, "What's wrong?"

She giggles, "All men are the same, utterly hopeless." I give her a sideways glance and she reaches for the tie and pulls me to her. She continues, "There we go that is better." She loosens the knot so that it is chunkier, explaining something about a looser knot going better with the suit. I'm not sure if she made up an excuse just to get close to me but I don't argue and let her do what she wants.

The more we chat, the more I like her. She has a funny side to her that goes along with that commanding personality. She's not at all like her husband but I can see now how the both of them get along as a couple.

With Sara, I soon forget that feeling of being out of my element when I first walked into this boring party.

She has me laughing as we make our way around the room, trying different appetisers from the server's gold trays. She lets me in on a secret that I can't wait to tell Jordan.

I wonder where Jordan is now. I glance around the room but don't see her or Devon. Sara doesn't notice me looking as she talks and doesn't seem to mind that Devon is nowhere in sight. She is used to this and since she isn't worried, I won't bring up their absence.

I can smell dinner wafting from the doors to the kitchen near where we are standing and soon Sara and I take our seats at our table and wait for our spouses to arrive.

Chapter 31
The Sweet Stuff

When we find our way back to the Author's Ball, we find the crowd seated at the tables while there is someone on the stage giving a speech.

My heart stops for a second because I have no idea where our table is and I whisper to Devon, "Do you know where our table is?"

He leans down and whispers, "Just straight ahead, see Sara and Josh?"

I follow his glance and spot them. Sara and Josh have their attention on the speaker. We approach the table and I take my spot next to Josh.

Josh whispers, "Hey we were wondering where you were?"

I lean in close to him and whisper back, "Devon pulled me aside to talk privately about how to negotiate with these sharks."

"Where did you guys go?"

"Oh, we were just outside talking on the deck." I don't want him to get concerned especially on the first night of this cruise so I turn the focus back on him and whisper, "How did you make out with Sara?"

"She's great. She mentioned something about this trek that you and I should do, it's up a mountain and it would be when we arrive at St. Thomas on Tuesday."

I smile, "Sounds interesting we will have to remember that."

As the speaker continues blabbing about how great his publishing company is and reading exerts of some of their backed Author's work. Dinner arrives at our table.

The starter is a Greek Salad and the waiters go around the table offering us red or white wine. I decline and so does Josh as he isn't a fan of anything alcoholic even with the flight here it took some arm twisting to get him to drink a glass of champagne. Sara and Devon each opt for a glass of white.

Sara says to Josh, "I understand your wife declining a glass but you?"

He says, "Oh I'm not a fan of wine."

She says, "Wow that is too bad. You know way back when, Devon and I used to own property in wine country in upstate New York. A glass of that stuff would change your mind, I'm sure."

Devon says, "I couldn't imagine having a nice steak without a glass of wine. You are missing out my friend."

Josh chuckles, "Perhaps, well I am easy to please I guess a glass of water or any clear soft drink and I am happy."

I say, "Oh that's not true I know one beverage that you really like."

Josh turns to me and says, "What's that dear?"

"I know that you like those white Russians and anything with chocolate in it."

He answers, "Yah well I guess you have me there. I don't really drink but I have tried those drinks and I do like them."

In between chews, Devon says to Josh, "There you go buddy. I like the sweet stuff too." I do a double take at Devon's remark and when neither Sara nor Josh is looking, he winks at me.

Sara says, "Cheers to that."

The next plates of food that arrive to the table are Baked Gulf Shrimp in Scampi Butter along with roasted corn and cheddar cheese soup. It's interesting to watch Josh taste what's served to him because for starters he is a plain eater and for seconds he has vowed never to eat seafood.

He takes his fork and digs in showing no hesitation even though I know that if I made this at home he wouldn't so much as taste the food.

I ask him, "How do you like it?"

"It's good" He replies between chews. I read his body language and I think I buy it.

I say to him, "You know what you are eating right?"

He makes a joke by handing me a sarcastic reply, "Don't make this weird."

He is on his best behavior tonight and I wish I could say the same. While we eat, the speeches wrap up and the sound of orchestra music plays in the background. The hum of dinner conversations fills the room along with the aroma of food and the sounds of cutlery touching plates as people enjoy the evening. The waiters arrive with the main course which is a braised lamb shank served with mashed potatoes and five bean stew. They also replenish our drinks and this time the waiter hands Josh a mudslide.

He says to the waiter, "I didn't order this?" and tries to hand back the drink.

Devon interrupts, "I did" and he thanks the waiter then says to Josh, "Have one on me. I want you to have a good time tonight."

Josh knows not to decline the kind gesture and besides the waiter is now gone and so he politely sips his drink. Dessert is a double chocolate cheesecake with tea and coffee and it is not long before the dance floor begins to get action.

After his drink, Josh is in good spirits and feeling a little giddy, "Dance with me?" He takes my hand into his own under the table.

I smile at him, "Sure" We walk to the dance floor and Josh energetically takes me into his arms and leads the dance.

I smile, "You are in a great mood, is it the drink?"

"Maybe" he winks at me.

"What?" I smile back, "Tell me."

"You're beautiful."

I chuckle, "Whenever you give me a compliment it's usually followed by you wanting or needing something."

He shakes his head, "No dear, anyway didn't you say that you liked getting the odd compliment?" He spins us around on the dance floor.

He was paying attention earlier. I say, "I did mention something to the fact but I do have the impression that you are holding back on something."

"You are good Jordan." He dips and twirls me and then holds me close as we move to the beat of the song. Josh reveals, "I think I know something that you don't yet."

"What's that?" I ask.

"Sara was telling me this evening that Devon has been in talks with his publisher, serious talks to bring you on board."

I admit, "Yes I sort of knew that he had mentioned my name to them but that doesn't mean anything until a contract is signed."

"What you don't know is with having you here and other publishers seeing that their competition is taking some serious interest in you. Sara said that Devon is starting a bit of a bidding war on you. Remember the lady at lunch?"

"Yes"

"She is one of those heavy hitters that Devon is hoping will bite and to be honest I think she will. Why else would she go out of her say to say hello while we were dining privately?"

I say, "Well I hope that you are right. So, tell me, you have more gossip, don't you?"

Josh admits, "I do."

I smile and look into those vibrant blue eyes of his, "Tell me!"

Devon cuts in and asks, "May I Josh?"

Josh smirks and his secret will have to wait. Josh spots Sara needing a partner and takes her up for the next dance.

Devon leads the dance, just as Josh and with just as much enthusiasm but with Devon, he actually knows the steps to the dance and leads me more slowly so that I can really follow his lead.

He smiles down at me and I smile up at him, "What?" I ask.

He says, "Oh my dear your world is going to change soon and I want you to trust me throughout all of this."

I say, "I do"

We twirl around the dance floor and he explains, "Possibly tonight or else most definitely tomorrow the business behind matters is going to start and I want you to promise not to accept any offers until you speak to me."

"I promise"

He says, "You and Josh both, the moment you are offered something tell me."

I say, "You got it cowboy."

The song ends and with that he gives me back to Josh. Devon smiles and there is a look to him that says to me, don't dwindle, go back to your husband and don't ask any questions.

Josh gives me his arm, leans in and asks, "What's wrong?"

"Nothing" I reply.

"So has he told you?"

I put my arms around Josh to slow dance with him. "He told me that business will start soon, so tell me what you were going to say before we changed partners?"

"Not now, there are too many on the dance floor, when we return to our room?"

Hesitantly I say, "Sure" If he doesn't want to tell me I am not going to beg for it.

We return to our table to sip our drinks and a man with frizzy grey hair and a full beard walks over to us he catches both our eyes and we glance at him when he says in a light raspy voice, "Hello, you're Jordan Connor?" I nod to confirm and he extends his hand and says, "Peach, first name Steven, I'm an Author of the Rosaline Battle Series."

I have never heard of his books. I say, "It's nice to meet you this is my husband Josh." They shake hands.

Steven leads the conversation, "So how do you like this Author's cruise so far?"

It is a typical conversation starter and I answer, "It's wonderful, I have never been to one of these events let alone a cruise so Josh and I are both over the moon."

"Good, I have been attending these events for years; you're here with Devon, right?"

I reply, "Yes, Josh and I are his guests."

He says, "Devon is a pretty sly guy."

Devon and Sara arrive back to our table and Devon startles this Peach guy, leaning around him and says to Josh and me, "So you have met my old partner in crime."

"Yes" I am a little confused but play along. I am not sure how Devon knows this man.

Devon says, "Did he tell you me and him go way back."

Peach gives a forced chuckle and says, "I was just about to tell them."

Devon looks him in the eye, "Well I guess I beat you to it."

Sara shuffles around Steven and Devon taking her seat at the table with us. The atmosphere feels weird now and Peach says to Josh and me, "Well, I think it is time to keep mingling catch you two later."

Josh and I look at each other and shrug, not sure what that was about and not sure that I liked it. I am feeling full, tired and my body or I should say that this baby is telling me that it is time to turn in.

One glance from Josh and he knows and has no objections. After seven years of marriage, we are good at reading the others mind.

I say to Devon and Sara, "I think it's time that I turn in for the night. It's been a long day; blame it on this baby."

We say our good byes for the evening and Josh and I make our way back to our room. Just before we enter the elevator, Peach approaches us.

"Guys, I wanted to say again that it was nice meeting you and please take this." He hands us a business card and says, "This is my publishers' information. I recommend that you keep your options open and don't let Devon suffocate you." Before either of us can defend Devon, he nods and leaves, heading back towards the direction of the ball.

I am left holding his card in my hand and the elevator dings with its arrival.

Chapter 32
A Horse Shoe

Morning comes so quickly and for once I wake before Josh. My guess is the few drinks that he had made him rest a little longer. He is always the one to wake first when we are home. I glance over at him under the soft linen sheets. He looks so peaceful when he sleeps.

Our bed in the room is facing the balcony and there is just a sliver of sunlight peeking through the curtain. My curiosity takes over and I feel the need to ever so get up and check out the view. I carefully slide out from underneath the covers and my toes find the floor. I look back at Josh and his breathing has changed. I hold my breath because I want him to get the rest that he needs and not disturb his slumber. I wait and I think that I am in the clear.

I tip toe across the floor over to the balcony window and look through. It is very sunny and the ocean appears to be calm. I turn around at the sound of the ruffling of the sheets and find Josh laying there relaxed and watching me.

I say with a sigh, "Good morning" I wanted to let him sleep.

His voice is groggy but he is in good spirits, "Good morning, babes."

"It is crazy that I woke before you. You slept well?"

"Yes." He is relaxing and I know that he is awake for the day. He is not one to go back to sleep after his eyes open which is unlike me who will sometimes try to sleep as much as I can. I admit that I can be lazy at times.

I open the curtain to reveal the sunlight and slide the door open to let in that fresh ocean breeze. I return to the bed but not before turning on the coffee machine and grabbing the remote to the television.

"So about last night how confidant did Sara seem about this news she gave you?"

Josh says, "Well, to me she seemed certain that Devon was going to start arranging for a bidding war for your publishing deal and she said that he was certain that he could get the bidding into the millions."

I lean back on one of the plush pillows and flip the channels to be pleasantly surprised that the ship has access to the American stations. He just said millions as in plural. I do a double take.

I confirm what I just heard from Josh because I don't think that I believe it, "Millions as in more than one?"

Josh smiles, "That's what she said."

I look back at the television and let it process, millions? My god, I say to Josh, "That makes more sense now as to why Devon was so insistent that we don't accept any offers and to talk to him first." I smile at him and continue, "It also makes sense now as to why you were so giddy last night. I mean I knew that you were on your best behavior for me but I had a feeling there was more to it than just a couple of drinks."

He kids, "Now you're making me sound like some money hungry guy. I really was having a great time it wasn't an act."

I give him that upwards stare like the, your full of it stare he continues, "Really, I like Devon and Sara." He shrugs and continues, "They are great, honest people and these friends are keepers no matter what happens. It's just unreal how these people came into our lives."

The hairs on the back of my neck stand on end as I feel a shiver go up my back. He takes a hand and tickles my neck, "I saw that. Was that a cold chill?"

I smile, "Yes it was. We are lucky to have everything fall into place like this it all seems like it was meant to be."

Josh laughs and shakes his head in disbelief, "Jordan out of all the people that I know you my deer, are the only one that I am convinced has a horse shoe in your ass."

"Hey!" I shove him.

"Hey back at you. You know that it is true. Everything that you have set your mind to you have gotten."

I give him another playful shove. "Don't say that, you know that that's not true."

"Name something that you wanted but never got."

"I never got that horse I always wanted."

He forces an exaggerated laugh, "Once you land that contract you know that you will have that horse."

I shrug, "Well it's true what they say about putting your mind to something and truly believing that it will happen."

Josh gives me a kiss on the cheek and gets out of bed to pee and wash up. The door to the washroom is open for us to continue our discussion. Josh says, "So I think that we are still at sea today. I wanted to go for breakfast soon; you know just to have some time with just the two of us before Devon takes you for the contract stuff. When you guys are doing your thing, I think I am going to head over to that gym and do a work out and maybe we can meet up in the afternoon before going to the next author event?"

"Sure, that sounds good to me. I'll send Devon a text to ask what time he had in mind to meet up." I create the text and click send then get out of bed. I put on some cute shorts and a loose fitted off the shoulder light green short sleeve top. I tuck my phone in my pocket and tie my hair up into a fun bun with my bang parted to the side.

Josh comes out of the washroom naked and he comes over to me for a hug.

I hug back and playfully say, "Where did your clothes go?"

He smirks and then intentionally pokes me in the leg with his man. I laugh and say, "Josh you are unreal. I just got dressed because I thought you wanted to go for breakfast."

He smiles and admits, "I am but I thought we could just have some dessert before we head out."

He hops back onto the bed and grabs the remote where I had left it on the sheets and flips stations to a porn channel. He wants a blowjob and I smile and roll my eyes at him.

He smiles and lies back on the pillow spread eagle, what a dork. He is always finding ways to make me laugh. He taps his hand on the bed, gesturing me to join him. His wood is standing tall eagerly waiting for my mouth to play with him. He says, "Come honk on bobo."

I take my clothes off and give him what he desires. I kiss his tip and then take him deep into my mouth and drool all over him. He knows my tricks and is able to hold out a little longer. I stroke him at the base of his long shaft while I hold his tip in my mouth and move my tongue back and forth over him. His breaths are quiet but I know with Josh that it means he is concentrating on holding out. I switch up my rhythm fast to slow and slow to fast and try to stuff him all in my mouth but I never can, he is too long. I don't look up at the television but judging from the sound it is two women taking turns giving some guy a blow job and I can hear their voices, sighs and slurps as I work on giving Josh his own.

He starts to push his pelvis into my mouth wanting me to take him deeper. I know that he is close.

He moans and admits, "Okay you got it Jordan."

I make sure to close my lips around him so that I swallow it all and with a few seconds of delay, he gets his and pulses into my mouth and down my throat. I ease up a bit on him but keep him in my mouth and continue with the motion but it is too much for him and now he demands, "Okay, okay, okay ease up Jordan." He is trying to pull away from my lips.

I laugh at him and say, "Was that good?"

"God yes, okay let me up." He wastes no time and soon enough he is taking care of my hungry girl. He isn't as talented as Devon is in munching but none the less, he licks and knows what spots set me off and I am soon purring like a happy little kitten.

He glances up between my legs and asks, "How was that?"

I'm still catching my breath when I answer, "It was good."

He smiles and wipes the juices that I squirted onto his face onto my thighs and then says, "Good, well want to take a shower?"

I nod, I guess I needed that after all, wow; oral in the morning is a way better start than a cup of coffee.

Chapter 33
Promise in Her

Just as plan Josh and I breakfast together just the two of us without any interruption this time. It is mid-morning and I am surprised how quiet the ship seems to be. I guess that everyone on board had the same thing in mind and stayed up late and partied to the early hours of the morning. For Josh and for me with this little baby growing inside me, it was an early night and had I been able to stay until the end of the Author's ball I am certain that I would have slept into the afternoon.

We take a walk after breakfast and stop into a few shops to pick up souvenirs for our parents and head back to our room. Josh gets his clothes ready for the gym and I am still waiting for a text from Devon.

Josh is set to go and asks, "Where are you meeting Devon?"

"Not sure, he hasn't gotten back, chances are he has slept in. I'll walk with you to the gym."

I have to admit that the gym that is on this ship is just awesome. Josh and I have our own home gym so being able to have access to this one gives Josh the opportunity to switch up his routine and try new things and different equipment. This gym could accommodate a couple hundred at once with all of the available equipment however; it looks like for now Josh has this entire area to himself.

Josh is in his element as we walk in. He pauses for a moment, likely planning what to try and glances to the long rows of treadmills, bikes, stair climbers you name it on the left and on the right, there are different weight machines. He is ready to unwind with putting his body to work. I give him a kiss good bye and he asks, "Has his text come in?"

I glance at my phone screen and reply, "Not yet."

He suggests, "Maybe text him again?" As he makes the suggestion, he starts some basic stretches with his neck and shoulders.

"Yah I think I will."

Josh smiles and says, "Do you want me to wait with you?"

I know that he wants to get started so I reply, "Oh no, go ahead and work out. I'll find something to do until I hear from Devon."

"Okay Jordan well, good luck" He heads in the direction of the weight machines first.

"Thanks"

I have my phone in hand waiting for the screen to light up but still nothing and choose to find a seat along the pool in a recliner. I send Devon a second text, "Hey just wanted to let you know that I'm hanging out by the pool. Let me know if the plans have changed?" I press send and decide to check my email and social media and find that my mom had sent a message last night to see if Josh and I made it okay. I send a reply back to her letting her know that all is well and I spoke a little about the authors' ball. I jump onto Facebook for a moment to see what is happening back home and instantly get a message from Hailey, "Hi Jordan"

"Hey"

"Are you on that cruise yet or is it next week that you go?"

"I'm on the ship now and we are out at sea somewhere in the Caribbean."

"Jordan you are one lucky girl that's for sure!"

I ask her, "How is everything?"

"Oh, you know, it's the same old here anyway I'll leave you be since you're probably racking up data charges."

I write, "Okay sounds like a plan. We can catch up when I return."

I take a moment and put the phone down to take in my surroundings. I have a full view of the ocean to my side an inviting swimming pool and rows of recliners, which are just starting to fill up with sun seekers. There are a few young families out for a morning swim with their young children. There are a couple of little boys splashing each other in the pool and a dad dipping his toes in to get used to the water. I spot a mom in a lounge chair not far from me applying sunscreen to her little girl and then to my side I look up and they say, "Why hello hottie"

I jump, "Geez Devon did you have to sneak up on me?"

He chuckles and plays innocent, "What, we can't have just a little fun?"

"Yes cowboy" I roll my eyes at him and say, "I think that you and I get more than enough fun time together."

He shakes his head no, "I don't think so. In my world you would be mine and that still wouldn't be enough."

"Cowboy you are just too kind."

He says while extending his hand to me, "Shall we?"

"Of course," I take his hand to help myself up out of the recliner.

We walk along the deck at a stroll as though we have nowhere in the world that we need to be and I am kind of chomping at the bit in anticipation of these contract negotiations. I have only ever been a self-published author and for another thing, this would be my very first negotiation period. I have never sat through any negotiations. Well, that is a lie I suppose that purchasing a home you technically negotiate but when Josh and I did that most of the negotiations were between the two realtors and we never sat down face to face with the owner.

Anyway, enough of that I am excited and am surprised that we aren't moving to the speed that my legs want to move in. I want to get started on my author career.

He says, "Jordan relax, you look like you are just about ready to run in a race. You will do just fine.

We will do just fine. Think for a second. They want you. They will be the ones working hard to make the best impression not you." We stop and he turns me to face him and says in a lower voice, almost a whisper while rubbing my shoulders, "You are merely going there to listen to his offer. You will decide on a publisher by the end of this trip along with my help. We will figure this out together which contract works the best and then you are going to make your demands to whatever it is that you don't like. Got it?"

I give a shy smile and nod and he says, "Let's hear these guys out."

He gives me his arm and we take the elevator up a few floors. We walk down a corridor with guest rooms. I ask in a whisper, "So you never said who are we meeting and are we going to their room?"

He stops at a door along the corridor and gets a key card out, "We are meeting my publisher and this is my room."

He inserts the card and the door lock clicks open. We step into a much larger room then the one Josh and I are staying in. I thought that our room was gorgeous but this one is just as beautiful but has the extra space. We come into a living room area and to our left is counter space with a bar fridge, coffee machine and a large flat screen television mounted to the wall. On the right side of the area is a living room with a couch a couple of recliners and coffee tables. Straight ahead is a large balcony with a wicker table set and an outdoor couch. I spot someone having a coffee at the table while on their laptop; it is Sara.

She hears the door click shut and she looks over to see Devon and I. This does feel a little awkward because for a moment I had thought that Devon might have been hungry for a romp. She says in a warm welcome, "Hey guys, hey Jordan are you ready for your first taste of negotiating a contract?"

I smile shyly, my nerves are starting to take over with anticipation of this, I say, "I hope so." I wonder for a moment what she had done for a living. Devon only ever explained that Sara is retired now.

She comes into the living room to talk to us instead of hollering from the balcony. She glances at Devon and then me. She catches me bite my lip and wipe my clammy hands on my side. Sara with her mother like instincts takes it upon herself to help ease my nerves. "Girl you've got this and besides you have my husband to help you along the way." She pats my shoulder and winks at me. She continues, "Speaking of husbands, where is Josh?"

"He ended up deciding on going to the gym. He is their now."

Sara looks at Devon upon me answering her and says to him, "Dear, should I go get Josh? I know at the ball last night he wanted to be here for Jordan?"

Devon shrugs, "It makes no difference. Jordan, do you want Sara to find him?"

I have mixed feelings. I want Devon to myself but I want Josh here for the support. If I have Josh here, I wonder if it will look weird to the publisher that I had my spouse with me during the negotiations. I am sort of comparing this to a job interview and we certainly don't bring family members to job interviews.

Devon says, "Jordan what's going through that pretty little head of yours?"

I look at Devon and then at Sara and say, "It would be nice to have him here but will it look weird to the publisher that I have my husband here during the conversations?"

Devon chuckles, "No you can have whomever you want."

I inhale and exhale then say, "Sara, are you planning on staying? What I mean is would you be going out of your way to find him?"

She shakes her head, "No dear, I was going to step out once the publisher arrives."

I say, "Well I do have Devon with me. Maybe you can find him and just let him know where Devon and I are and if he wants to join us, he can but I am fine here if it is just Devon and me. Just if you could let him know that we are here and let him know that we are doing well."

I know that I am rambling but I can't stop. It is another nervous trait of mine. Sara remains calm for me and says, "Sure thing, you know your husband does have good ideas. I was thinking of doing just a swim this morning but I think I may join him in the gym and do my swim after."

I chuckle, "He would probably like your company."

"Okay dear, well good luck with everything if you don't mind, I'm going to go get ready." She heads to the bedroom to dress into some workout clothes to go to the gym.

I find a seat on the couch and the little one inside of me is doing summersaults. I am gathering that he is sensing my nerves and I try to relax. The baby feels like a he today.

Devon says, "I'm going to have myself a drink; how about you can I get you something?"

"Water is fine."

He joins me and takes a seat on an adjacent recliner as we wait for the publisher to arrive. I have already forgotten who Devon's publisher is. I mean I know what he looks like. I remember him on the stage but I just can't put the name to the face even if my life depended on it. I ask Devon, "What's your guy's name?"

"Howard Stem."

I look at Devon. My lips are about to form the words to ask the name of the Publisher. Before my lips part he tells, "He is with Tail Fin Books."

I smile, "How did you know I was going to ask you the follow up?"

"Jordan sometimes you are just that predictable." He winks at me and just then, three light knocks interrupt our chat.

Sara must have heard the knocks also because she emerges from the bedroom dressed in some grey yoga pants and a light blue, short sleeve shirt and a duffle bag in hand. She says, "I got it guys."

As she opens the door, Devon and I stand up to greet Howard Stem.

Sara opens the door and says, "Hi Howard long time no see."

He chuckles and says, "Sara you are too funny, didn't we have a dance last night?"

"Howard, you know Devon is in the room."

Devon chirps in, "Ha ha Sara." He turns his focus to Howard, "Can I get you something to drink?"

"I'll have a coffee with one cream."

Devon turns on the coffee machine and says to Howard, "Come on in. Jordan and I decided the living room would be the best spot to talk shop."

He answers, "Yes that is fine." He comes in and greets me with a handshake. His small dark framed glasses are nearing the bottom of his nose as he looks through them at me and says, "Jordan it's good to see you again. We really did not get to talk much last night there were so many people there. It is good to have your time today and I am so excited to get down to it."

I say, "Thanks and I look forward to this."

Howard Stem is a very tall and rather thin man. He has salt and pepper hair that is short but is a tidy haircut and he has a trimmed short beard and small framed glasses and grey eyes. He is wearing a light beige pant, a white polo shirt and medium brown loafers. He looks like he is dressed for a casual garden party. His style is plain. I feel that if we were ever alone in a room together aside from all of the book stuff, I think that trying to maintain a conversation with this man would be like pulling teeth. He seems very dull and my take is our only common ground is books.

Devon joins us with taking a seat next to me as Howard takes Devon's original seat unknowingly. Sara gives us a wave, mouths the words good luck and carefully closes the door behind her.

Devon says, "Well shall we get down to it."

Howard replies, "Yes, well we are on a cruise after all so there is no sense in dancing around the important stuff. Okay well as you already know Jordan that Devon has recommended you. He looked at your work and mentioned to us that you are a promising prospect. A good book is in the opinions of the individual and if I were to be blunt, I thought your book wasn't that great and I will tell you the reasons why. The first thing was that your work was full of grammatical errors, poorly formed sentences and miss used words. Secondly, I think that some of your story lines within the story were too predictable and thirdly there was no structure at all. It's a funny thing because when Devon had recommended you, I had such high expectations and well I received a mediocre story."

This was the last response that I thought I would get in this meeting. I am holding my breath while Howard criticizes my writing. Devon rubs my back with one of his hands and it reminds me to breathe in. Howard continues, "Now grant you this is my job to find the flaws and if I were to take a step back and look at the story in its raw form, I see originality, dynamic characters and the elements of a love story. When I take another step backward and look at you the author, what I see is someone who has motivation and passion."

Devon gives me a reassuring smile and I look back at Howard who continues. "Tail Fin Books has to look at all of the elements. We all know that your book has flaws right now but I am certain that granted we pull you self-published book down and put a little work into it and re-publish it with Tail Fin Books backing you all the way. I know that we could make you the next D. Chambers in your genre."

I smile and answer in a gasp of relief, "Thank you"

Howard continues, "The thing with unknown authors is there is always a huge risk to just make an offer to them as there is that chance, we may never recoup that money back should your work fail. You are a risk." Howard ponders. I gather he has an offer in mind but he is waiting for a reaction in order for him to decide how to proceed.

I look at Devon for support and instead he says to him, "Howard you said so yourself that you see promise in her work. I mean you took a chance on me and it turned out. Look at this woman she has promise in her."

Howard asks, "Jordan, how many stories are you working on at the moment?"

I clear my throat, "I have two more stories that will follow my first published book and I am currently in the middle of writing a new series so I have five more stories to write in order to create two series."

He asks, "What will be the average word lengths of these books?"

"Each will be around the one hundred-thousand-word count."

Howard asks, "What is the genre of your second series?"

"Romance, erotica"

He tilts his head then says, "A completely different genre, why are you not sticking to science fiction?"

I feel myself shedding the nerves. My shoulders start to relax, my breathing is starting to become natural again and I start to open up, "I think that as a writer if I have a story to tell then I should tell it. I think that it's good to not limit yourself to one genre and besides I enjoy the fact that I am doing something that is different for me."

A glimpse of a smile crosses over Howard's face and he says, "I'm not going to lie, Tail Fin Books has already done their homework on you and we have an offer ready I just needed to talk with you first and see how you were as an individual. We need to make sure that our Authors are personable, reasonable and intelligent individuals who have goals and that this one book wasn't the end of the road for you. At the end of the day if you sum up this meeting, we are all gathered here to make money." He removes a contract from a leather folder that he had tucked under his arm and places it before me on the coffee table. I glance at Devon and he gives me the nod to go ahead and pick it up. I reach for it, picking it up and flip through the pages. I stop about four pages in and fixate on the amount, one million dollars.

Howard is not a fool and he sees my eyes fixed on the amount, "That is for you to show you that we are serious and take you and your work seriously. By accepting you would be under our wing and amongst a great list of well-known and respected authors."

My heart starts to beat fast. I knew that the offers would be big and now it is starting to sink in.

Howard stands from his seat and says, "There is a lot of information that you need to read over and for all of us I think it is best that I leave you to it and check up with you at a later time."

I look up, coming back down to reality for a second, I swallow and say, "Yes, thank you." It is all that I can say.

Howard says, "No need to get up, Jordan it was nice to talk with you again today and we will catch up later." He reaches over and shakes my hand and then Howard says to Devon, "I have a seat for you next to me at the black jack table."

Devon replies, "Yes, I'll see you tonight."

Howard lets himself out and then it is just me, Devon and an unsigned one-million-dollar contract.

I look at him and start to laugh, Devon says, "See what I told you?"

"Yes Devon."

I leaf through the contract again and Devon carefully takes my hand away from the papers and says, "Not now."

I look at him quizzically and he continues, "My girl needs a reward for being so good." He leads me to the balcony backing me up against the railing and kisses me. I pull away surprised, "What about Sara?"

He smiles and says, "She is gone for the day."

I hold him back for a moment, "Devon, think with your head for a second. She may return with Josh."

He slips his hands into my shorts and I am already dripping. He finds my spot and presses. Shivers go through my body and I fall deeper into his arms as he smiles and says, "Jordan you worry too much. I have known Sara for over fourteen years and I could tell by the tone in her voice that she wasn't planning on making a return any time soon."

He turns me around so that I'm leaning over the railing and looking out on the ocean and he pulls my shorts down and drives his length into me.

He leans in smelling my hair and makes me turn to glance at him he shows me his wet fingers and says, "This is what drives me nuts." I smile and lick my juices off his fingers. He smirks and plunges back into me so that I let out a sigh, he says, "bad girl". Then he kisses me. His warm tongue tastes me. I forget about everything and he generously gives me all of him, driving it deep. I am on the edge and he knows it. He reaches around and rubs my button and I squirt all over him he says, "That's my girl." He makes sure that he is deep to feel every throb and then he goes into his rhythm keeping me bent down and he unloads his passion into me.

His motions come to a slow and he pulls out. "You are my drug, wow I am ready to take on the rest of the day how about you?"

I grab my shorts and panties from the balcony floor and say, "Yes well you know how to relax me."

"I had a haunch that you needed it." He zips up his pant.

I roll my eyes at him, "Yes Devon but don't make it sound like only I needed it. I think you needed it too."

He raises his hands, smiles and says, "You got me."

I give him a quick kiss and say, "Where is your washroom? I need to clean up. I have your swimmers dripping down my leg."

He laughs, "Just around the corner."

Chapter 34
Play to Win

Today is passing by like nothing and we are already approaching the five o'clock hour. Devon and I have agreed to meet again this evening at the second author event on the cruise and I find my way back to Josh with my unsigned contract in hand.

As we go over the contract on the bed in our room, Josh is frozen.

He says, "So what are your thoughts about this?" His eyebrows scrunch together as he asks.

I chuckle, "I think I need to be pinched. This feels like a dream."

Josh reaches over and pinches me, "Ouch!"

He grins and says, "Guess that it's not a dream?" I push him in retaliation. He says, "So give me your real answer. What are you thinking about this contract?"

"I think that it is more than fair. I do want to sign it but Devon told me to wait for other offers."

Josh says, "So we wait, I guess. It sounds like Devon knows what he is doing." Josh kisses me on the forehead and says, "We should get ready."

Within the hour, I slip into the cocktail dress that I had packed for the trip. It is this dark pink color and has a layer of folds over the stomach like the gown but instead it has a halter-top finish. Josh wears a beige dress pant and a dark blue dress shirt with beige shoes.

Casino night is going to be interesting for Josh and me because Josh is one funny man when it comes to his money. For one thing, if it wasn't for Devon giving us this extravagant vacation Josh would have never treated us to something like this. Maybe and this is a big maybe he might have agreed to a cruise but we would be staying in the cheapest room on board whereas Devon has given us one of the better rooms on board.

I ask him before we leave, "So are you planning to play any games tonight?"

I can tell by the way that he is fidgeting he is contemplating, "Well I was thinking maybe some poker."

I ask, "Why are you saying it like you are unsure?"

He smiles knowing that I am reading him and I am right, "I'm just not sure on my skills. Like I am good when I play with my friends but I have no idea what the people will be like at the table tonight."

"Isn't that the fun of playing the game?"

He smirks and says, "The fun of playing the game is being sure that you can win."

"Josh!"

"What, it's the truth."

"You can't play to have fun?" I ask.

"I play to win and winning is what's fun." He doesn't give me the chance to bug him further and he says, "I'm ready, are you?"

"Yes" I smirk at him knowing that there is no going any further on the topic. We leave our room and head over to the cruise ships casino.

We are a bit late to the party but neither of us is worried. We are sitting pretty with a million-dollar offer. I have been intimate with my men today and I am as happy as can be and so are my men. I don't think that Josh and I missed much as all of the introductions of who is who have already been said and I gather this is just a night of fun.

A host with a tray in her hands asks, "Would you like a chocolate polar ice shooter?"

I decline and to my surprise, Josh takes one. For my man who never ever drinks he sure is proving me wrong and I give him a confused sideways glance.

He shrugs, "We only live once, cheers! He swallows it in one gulp and hands the empty back to the host.

I say, "How come I never got to see this side of you when I wasn't pregnant?"

He smiles, "Jordan everything has been perfect on this trip and it all started with a glass on the plane. I think its good luck to a good night and hoping tonight will be the same."

We walk through the casino with its deep brown carpets trimmed in gold. There are slot machines along the wall, large crystal chandeliers above, a roulette table, several blackjack, crabs and poker tables. As we pass through the crowed, there are faces from the night before that I recognize but just haven't spoken to. I see some of Devon's winners from that first row in the theatre and then recognize that woman who won at Devon's book signing. She is at one of the slot machines.

"Hey Josh?"

"Yes?"

"I'm going to go introduce myself to the lady over there. She was the one that won at Devon's book signing."

He nods, "Okay Jordan, I'll just be around the poker tables."

I ask, "Are you going to play?"

He is still eyeing the tables ahead when he answers, "I don't know yet. I want to watch first and then decide."

I give him a kiss and say, "See you in a bit."

I walk over to the woman, "Hey how is your luck going tonight?"

She looks up at me from the stool she was on and I see in her eyes the recognition of me and says, "Oh you know, well I keep wining some back but I believe that I am losing more."

I chuckle, "Yes that's how it is."

She says, "I'm Donna and you?"

"Jordan"

"Nice to meet you. Are you a fan, author or publisher?"

I giggle, "Well technically I am all three. I'm and indie author and a fan of some of the other writers here."

"I have seen you around with D. Chambers. Did you win a draw at one of his book signings?"

"No, well yes, let me explain. I didn't win from a book signing as a matter of fact I was at the same signing as you in Ottawa. I recognized you that first day in the theatre. I am here as a guest of Devon's. He is helping me out as an author by bringing me to the event. We are friends."

Her bottom lip is to the floor and she gushes, "You don't say. Wow, that is amazing. How does it feel to have a celebrity friend?"

I smile, "He is the same guy as he always was. It's just sometimes you tend to forget and it's the surprise of getting used to the fact that a lot of people love to get their time with him so you have to get used to him being away a lot. The other thing is he is the only person that has gifted such an awesome thing as a cruise. No one has ever done something this nice for me."

Donna nods, "You and me both. I got a glimpse of you in the theatre and could have sworn I had seen you before. I thought maybe it was because I saw you during boarding or perhaps on the flight but the fact that you mentioned Devon's signing, I must have remembered you from there."

"Small world" A cold shiver runs down my spine. I catch Donna's glance just behind me. I turn and there is Steven Peach. I wonder, before turning to greet him and put on my game face, why do his encounters always happen when I'm without Devon or Josh. This Peach is the last person that I want to see and after meeting him at the ball the other night, I have ill feelings of him.

He smiles and says, "Jordan it's so nice to see you again tonight. How are you?" I know that he is just going through the gestures before he gets to the real reason of talking to me.

I smile, "I am good. It was a great day, nice weather and good company, can't complain." I say the words through my teeth and glance around the casino looking for Devon or Josh.

He says, "That's good to hear. Who did you spend the day with?"

"My husband and a few friends" I suspect that he wants to know if it was Devon.

He says, "Sounds like a great day. I am alone on this cruise well that's not true. Let me rephrase that my publisher is here well they are staying in another room of course."

I hold my breath, a nervous trait of mine, I look around and I don't see Josh, Devon, Sara or even Howard Stem for heaven's sakes. Donna scoots off her bench and mouths to me, "We will catch up later" and moves on to another game. The bottom of her dress flows as she moves away. I have to get out of this.

Steven says, "I wanted to ask if I could have some time with you." He chuckles awkwardly, "It wouldn't be a date or anything. Well, it would but it would be to talk about a contract for your book between you and my publisher. What do you say?"

They always say to trust your gut. There is something about him that I don't like and there is no point in giving him the run around. Maybe he is a decent man and maybe he is not. The question is, do I want to do business with this stranger and the truth is no.

I swallow then say, "Mr. Peach I appreciate the offer but I am going to have to decline." As the words leave my lips, he is about to say some objection I can tell by his body language. Before he can get the words out, I speak over him and say, "If you would excuse me, this little baby is pushing on my bladder. Have a good night." I turn and put as much distance from him as possible. Where is the washroom? I don't have to go this moment well if I tried, I probably could go pee but that's not the point. I need to find a washroom to hide in and leave once this Peach has given up on me.

I walk through the casino further finally spotting the women's room and bolt for the door to my escape.

There is no one else in here and I stare at myself in the mirror for a moment. Okay Jordan what are you going to do next? Did I over react, he only seemed to just want some time to talk about a publishing deal? I hate my inner voice. It is always making me question my instincts. I decide that there is no hurry and since I'm here I may as well empty my bladder. I come out of the stall to wash my hands and find Sara here.

She says, "Hey Momma how are you holding up tonight?"

I fake a smile, "I'm good."

She glances at my reflection while washing her hands then tilts her head to the side to look at me, "Really, you are going to lie to me like that. Jordan, I may be a bit older than you but I'm not stupid."

I feel my cheeks warm up and I look at her and know that she won't let me leave without an answer so I admit, "Sara I think I did something stupid. I am not sure if I just over reacted."

She leans in closer and I know that I have her full attention, "Go on Hun. If I think you over reacted, I'll tell you like it is. I may live in Texas but I am from New York."

"I came here tonight with Josh and the moment that Josh left me to go check out the poker tables this man named Steven Peach approached me. Technically he said nothing that would cause me to be upset or anything." I pause for a second to gather my thoughts, "Well, that's not entirely true. Last night at the ball, Steven warned don't let Devon suffocate me. It pissed me off because he knew that we are friends. Anyways with what happened tonight I think he was waiting for Josh to leave in order to get my attention and Sara I'm not sure if I am just being too sensitive but I just have a bad vibe with him."

Sara replies, "I know the feeling. Always trust your instincts. Did he ask you anything?"

"Yes, he wants me to meet with him and his publisher to talk about getting a contract and I declined and pretty well ran away and ended up here talking to you." I smile at her only because it just sounds stupid as I explain it.

Sara says, "Jordan you know that is quite alright. I think that you did what you needed to do and besides, if you were over reacting which I know that you weren't you kept your cool."

I smile, "Thanks Sara. Could I ask you something? If I am over stepping my boundaries just say so."

She says, "You want to know what the deal is between Devon and Steven, right?" I nod and she continues, "A few years back the two of them worked together. Steven used to be a co-writer for Devon. In the early stages of editing Devon's latest book, the one that launched Devon's career to the success he is seeing now, Steven backed out. Jordan this was like infancy stages, as you know Devon just released that book in the past year. Steven dropped out and left Devon to finish the project. Devon took Steven's name off the work and copyrighted it under his pen name only. The thing is while the copyright was in process, Steven had caught wind that Devon was sitting on a potential hit and he wanted back in but at that point, Devon refused for the obvious reasons. Devon had carried the book from start to finish with barely any support from

Steven. Steven had fought back but the thing was because the final product had changed so much in the editing phases and that Devon's submission to the copyright office had the date recorded early on. The copyright office couldn't allow for Steven to be considered a co-writer. The documents that Steven could provide them they were too different from the final product. When the book had started to acquire a fan base Steven's resentment grew.

Jordan it really is a sad thing because the two of them were good friends and it's sad that it had to come to that. I stand by and support my partner in the choices that he makes and for this situation, I couldn't agree more. Why would Devon give Steven credit for not doing anything?"

I nod and say, "It makes sense."

Sara says, "Of course it makes sense. It's the right thing and Devon deserves full credit for this book. Steven is just bitter and I think that between the two of them this copyright has created such a huge wedge that they will never mend it."

I say, "Steven probably wants to work a contract with me only because he sees that Devon has interest in me and Steven wants to steal a potential success away from Devon as a way to get back at him, I take?"

Sara answers, "That is what I think. Jordan, I don't want to confuse you. You know the history between the two of them and just because they have, that history doesn't mean that you shouldn't listen to his offer. What I am trying to say is don't let us form your opinions of Steven. You need to form your own."

"Yes, I know Sara but I have already formed my own and besides your suspicion of him wanting me as a way to get back at Devon, I believe that too. I get that it all comes down to money but I would like to think that the publisher that I do choose cares about me and my work and not just the money or getting back at Devon."

She smiles, "You are absolutely right Jordan." She places her hand on my shoulder and continues, "Shall we return to the party?"

We head back into the casino and I think if Devon was completely out of the picture and I only knew Sara we would get along great as friends. It just shows that Devon picks women who have great personalities. Sara is great and I find myself warming up to her. It is times like this that I feel awful about sleeping with her spouse but then on the other hand I can't shut out the love that I have for him either.

Sara startles me, "Jordan?" I jump and she continues, "Wow girl, you were somewhere very far away just now."

I admit, "Yes I am sorry, blame it on this baby I guess." Devon's baby, I am certain of it.

She says, "Well no sign of Mr. Peach. Let's go find our men."

Chapter 35
By the Tail

Sara and I find both our men at the same table playing poker with some of the other authors. My two men side by side very much the same in some aspects and different in others.

Glancing at the two of them sitting together is weird because it forces me to compare them. Josh is serious, ridged; he has his poker face on with concentrating on the game while Devon is into the game just as much as Josh but is clearly enjoying the process of the game. Devon is smiles and laughs; he is relaxed and is in the moment.

Sara greats Devon with a kiss on the cheek and I hear him say to her, "Hey babes are you having a good time?"

I catch her say, "Absolutely, well Hun I'm going to make a trip to the bar do you want anything?"

He smiles and looks up at her, "A Long Island iced tea would be great." I am just steps behind. Sara and Devon don't see me and I decide not to disturb Josh because he's got his game face on. I'll get Josh his usual diet clear soda and so I follow Sara through the crowd.

She asks me, "So do you like to play any of these games?"

"I've played a bit of blackjack and poker with friends but never at a casino. The only other games that I have played are those slot machines but we all know how those work with taking every last penny."

"She says yah I hear you Hun."

We approach the bar, get our drinks and return to our partners sides. Josh seems to be doing well as is Devon. I just touch Josh's shoulder to get his attention and hand him his drink as he gives me a quick thank you and returns to focusing on his game. Around the table are other men. The faces are familiar to me from the other events including Howard Stem, which Devon seems to be razzing him a bit. He catches my eye and I smile back and sip my drink.

To be honest the casino isn't my thing and where others are clearly in their element, I just want to do something else.

A woman around Sara's age approaches her and whispers in her ear and then the two of them start laughing. Sara turns to me and says, "Jordan some of the women are going to start their own poker game. You are welcome to join us."

I say, "No thanks, I'm no good anyway. Go ahead without me I may stop by to see how the game is going."

Sara says, "Okay dear, you know that I don't like to see friends board."

"I'll find something Sara, don't worry about me."

The women set up a few tables over and as the game progresses at Devon and Josh's table, they become more invested. I decide to take a walk and start doing my own hand shaking without the company of Devon. I meet a couple of different publishers who tell me that Devon has already set up appointments for me to meet them later on in the week and how excited they are to get down to business with me, blah blah blah. These meets with them seem to be all the same. Well, I have to be thankful for the opportunity. I'm not in a bad mood or anything but I am tired and board.

My diet cola is empty and I hand the glass over to one of the servers walking by with a tray. I glance over at the poker tables and there is no sign of the games ending any time soon. I decide that maybe some fresh air will wake me up. I step outside into the breezy moonlight.

Out on deck I'm not alone, the smokers are out here puffing on their cancer sticks while gabbing away. Some have had a little too much to drink and I can tell this by how loud they are speaking to one another.

I take a spot downwind from the cigarette smoke and lean up to the railing looking out on the moon lit water.

I breathe in and out and close my eyes for a moment. All I have been thinking about all day is that million-dollar offer. It just doesn't seem real. Just then I feel a light tap on my shoulder, I ask, "Josh?"

I turn and my heart stops.

"Did I startle you, Jordan?"

"Yes Mr. Peach, I was just about to head back inside." I can't believe that I had just mistaken his touch for Josh's.

I start to walk and Steven holds my arm. I look into his eyes and he says to me, "Before you return to the party, which from watching you, it hadn't looked like you were enjoying I would like to say something if I could."

I shake my head and say, "Steven my mind is made already and if you would excuse me."

I try to step around him but he tightens his grip on me, "Wait Jordan." He smiles, it is forced and he continues, "You may want to reconsider. Let's just say it would be in the best interests of you and Devon if your spouses didn't know the truth."

He releases his grip and I remove my arm from his grasp and look at him in shock, hoping that I just imagined the threat. He smiles, "We will be in touch." He nods his head and walks away with a bounce in his step. I feel alone again amongst the crowed of smokers gabbing away. They are having fun and I am not.

I have no idea if Steven returned to the casino or what but I snap out of the shock that I am feeling, knowing that Steven knows and rush through the crowed of smokers to the elevators that take me back to mine and Josh's room. I cannot go back because Josh and Devon would know that something was up because I tend to wear my emotions on my sleeve.

I lock the door behind me and paranoid I check the room to make sure that I am alone. Jordan you should have stayed in the casino. Why does this shit happen? I know Josh and Devon both have their phones on them so I send them each a text to let them know that I have turned in for the night and wish them good luck on their games.

What am I going to do? I'm an author I should be able to think of something clever to get around this but right now I can't think of a single thing. Catch a tiger by the tail, Steven has me by the tail. What am I going to do? I sigh and get out of my dress, take a quick shower and then lie down in bed. I won't let this get the best of me.

Chapter 36
Some Kind of Bro-mance

I wake with a bit of a startle. I sit up in bed, forgetting where I am for a moment and then it all returns to me. I am on a cruise ship. My head hurts even though I slept. Gosh what time is it? I peek over at the clock. It is a few minutes before 7:00 AM and I check my side to see that Josh made it in okay. I hadn't even heard him come in last night. It must have been late when he returned.

Today is Monday; I reach over to the night side table for the author event schedule. I have no idea what today's schedule is. Ah yes, the club event, drink and dance the night away. Gosh, these authors like to party. Maybe it is just the pregnancy but I am having a hard time keeping up and to be honest I am feeling a little drained.

I could try to go back to sleep but there is no point I am up. I get up and start the coffee machine and turn on the television setting the volume to almost mute to let Josh sleep a bit longer.

Last night wasn't a dream. I know it. I can feel it and I have no idea what I am going to do about it? I still don't know and I haven't even told Devon yet. I am not sure if telling Devon would make the situation any better. Telling him would mess him up. He is here with his fans and I don't want it to take away from their experience.

I pick up my phone to check out what Devon has scheduled for us today. He has us meeting Champaign Publishing at 11:00 AM. We have a break in between and then have another meet set up with a smaller publisher. Devon mentioned that it is worth the meet because they have a good reputation for getting behind their authors and their track record is starting to reflect the smaller publisher's hard work.

I think that this type of cruise is great regardless of the blackmailing Steven has started. I have to put this Steven business aside for a second or else I am going to go crazy. Jordan focus. I look at the author event schedule and see that tomorrow the ship docks in St. Thomas. Maybe the change in scenery will help me think more clearly in resolving this Steven issue.

The coffee machine makes a gurgling sound, a sign that the coffee is ready. I make my way around the bed and peek out the balcony to see that the sky is grey with clouds and the furniture on the balcony is wet. It must have rained in the night.

I hear Josh stir as I pour a cup to drink. He is awake I can just tell by the sound.

I say, "Good morning do you want a cup?"

His voice is raspy like he had been screaming all night, "Sure"

I make my way back to the bed and climb in beside him I ask, "What time did you get in at?"

"A little after 2:00 AM"

"Josh, this cruise has you doing things that you don't normally do. I honestly can't remember that last time you were up that late. I am thinking maybe back when we were dating and working the night shifts in the call center?"

He rubs his eyes open, takes the cup from me and says, "You are probably right." He takes a sip and sets the cup on his bedside table."

I ask, "So, did you win some or lose some?"

He smiles and I know it was a good night for him. "I made $500.00"

"Wow, that's awesome Josh."

He smirks and shrugs, "It's just pennies in comparison to that contract you have that is waiting for your signature."

Yes, that contract that I may not be able to take because of a certain someone. I say nothing and just respond, "Until I sign something I say $500.00 is still a lot of money. I am happy that you had a good time. How did Devon do?"

"He did a bit better than me he made out with just shy of $800.00."

I smile, "Sounds like you two have things in common. So did the game go on for a while after I left?"

"After I received your text, we were maybe at the table for another forty-five minutes before people started to through in the towel. Devon didn't want to go toe to toe with me so instead we called it."

I ask, "So what did you guys do for the rest of the night?"

"We watched Sara play for a bit. I got to speak a little more with Howard Stem and then Dev invited me back to his room for drinks and we watched some DVR recording of a football game from earlier in the day."

I chuckle, "If I didn't know any better it sounds like you two are starting some kind of bro-mance."

He makes a face at me, "Jordan don't get all weird. Yes, I like Devon. He is a good guy." I smile to his reply and he continues, "So are you ready for those two meetings today?"

I shrug and say, "I think so. It will be interesting to see how these ones go, knowing that the competition is stiff."

Josh agrees, "I know that you are in good hands. I think I am going to take a nap while you are at your first one."

Yesterday my feelings were to let Josh go to the gym and not have so many people there during the meeting with Tail Fin Books but today with knowing that asshole is watching I want to keep Josh close without alarming him. I just don't want Steven to get anywhere near my husband and say something. I say to Josh, "Are you sure you don't want to come with me. You are comfortable with Devon."

"He stretches and says, "It was a late night for me. I know that you two have everything in control.

I will just stay here and nap. I won't go anywhere. You can come get me when you are done."

Think Jordan, maybe Steven doesn't know the room we are staying in and if Josh remains in his room there is no way Steven would say anything to Josh. I respond, "Okay sounds good."

He gives me a look, "Geez Jordan was it that hard?"

I took too long in answering and Josh can read me like a book. I squash his concern in saying, "I'm still waking up, I guess. No, its fine, I can get you when I am out of the first meeting."

The morning rolls bye and Josh and I relax in the room. I have to hand it to Josh because the overcast outside makes for great napping weather and I kind of envy him. 11:00 AM soon approaches and before I know it, Josh is giving me a kiss and wishing me luck.

I walk down the hallway towards Devon's room and catch myself looking over my shoulder. No one is there. I am just anxious and over reacting. Maybe what Steven had said wasn't about what I think it is? Maybe I am just being paranoid.

I tap on the door and Sara lets me in and says, "Are you ready for the next round?"

"I think so." I shrug and smile at her.

Today she is wearing a fitted black short, loose blue sleeveless shirt with a matching blue baseball cap. She has her purse over her shoulder. She is on her way out. She says, "Good girl, well I will leave you two be. There is this beauty place and I am going to get my nails done. See you guys later and good luck."

She smiles and closes the door behind. I turn to spot Devon on the couch he pats the cushion next to him and I walk over and take a seat.

"How is my girl this morning?"

"She is okay." I'm excited but it wasn't the same level of excitement that I had the first time.

"Is something wrong?" He asks.

"No, just nerves I guess."

He puts his arm around me. He is quick to believe the lie and says, "Well we should maybe deal with those nerves of yours after the meeting?" He nibbles my ear.

I laugh, "Stop you're tickling me."

"There's that smile that I love. Okay so it's the same thing as yesterday but just with another Publisher. They will go through what they are looking for and give you a contract for your review. We aren't signing today, got it?"

"Yes" He has me smiling again and he makes me forget my worries for the moment, which is exactly what I need to have this meeting, go well.

On queue there is that tap on the door and Devon gets up to answer it. Round two of contracts begin.

Chapter 37
Contingent

Talks goes well but, in this meeting, they offered me three million on the stipulation that I produce a certain number of books in a specific period. Sara ended up returning and I am thankful that she did because I wasn't feeling like getting intimate with Devon because of the stuff that Steven had hinted at and to be honest that would have been the first time saying no to him.

I return to the room to find Josh relaxing in bed he looks rested and he has his phone out texting.

"Who are you talking to?" I ask him as I put my paper down on the counter and hop up on the bed.

"Oh, just mom and dad, they are just asking how things are going." He continues to ask me, "So how was this meeting?"

"It was good but I think that I still want to go with the first publisher, Tail Fin Books."

He glances up from his phone and asks, "Why what did they offer you?"

I say, "I'm warning you, don't get all funny on me I'll explain my reasoning, okay?"

At this point, I have his full attention and he puts his phone down and listens. I explain, "They offered me three million but its contingent that I produce more novels. The thing is sure with one million or even three, I wouldn't need to work so that would free up more time to write but there are so many other factors that could come into play."

He asks, "Like what?"

"Like this baby. What if I lose my desire to write because my love and attention is taking care of a baby, I mean I know that my focus will shift, what if my desire to write takes a back seat? Also, what if I lose my imagination?"

He interrupts, "Jordan don't be ridiculous. A baby isn't going to cause you to lose that overactive imagination of yours."

"Well, no but I am afraid of losing the drive and worried about being held to a time frame on producing more books."

He asks, "Do you think that you can write more books?"

"I have five stories in the works but I can't force a time frame even if this baby wasn't on the way."

"Well three million is a lot more than one million."

"I know but I don't want to be one of those people who get stuck because they bit off more than they could chew. I mean the first offer of one million is still amazing and the thing I like about that offer is it's Devon's publisher and he knows them well and the contract is just for my one book."

He says, "Jordan, I love you and will support whatever you decide. If you have your doubts with being able to meet the demands for the three million you simply don't take it."

I rest my head on the pillow and say, "This stuff is so tiring."

He pats my head then running his fingers through my silky hair, "We will figure it out. Anyway, do you want to grab some lunch before your next meeting?"

I glance up and answer, "Sure, I don't know about you but I am dying for another pizza."

He smirks, "Sure but didn't we just have pizza yesterday?"

I answer, "No that can't be right. I'm pretty sure it was Saturday, when we first boarded. Blame it on this baby, not sure what's going on but just thinking about pizza is making my mouth water."

He gives me a kiss on the forehead and says, "It's settled then."

Lunch flies by in a heartbeat. Josh keeps me smiling and laughing He has my mind off the pressing things over lunch. He is good at noticing that stuff and before I know it, I find myself back in Devon's room ready for the last meeting of the day with this unknown but apparently promising publisher. The meeting goes well and their offer is for two million and again another contingency on producing more books but their contingency is over four years, which is an easier period for me but I still don't know. Maybe I don't like the word contingent.

After the final meeting, Devon explains that I have the vacation to decide on which to choose of the three and offers advice for the rules of each contract and what it entails.

Devon plays it safe with me today. There is no sneaking around for a secret romp or anything. Today we are just two friends hanging out together. Eventually I decide to take a breather from this contract stuff and say to Devon, "I think that I need to do something else just to get my mind off of this for a bit."

He says, "That's cool but why do I feel like you have something more to say?"

Sara is in the room so for now a lie will have to do, "I think I will have more questions but for now I need to rest my eyes from it and maybe get back to you later with some worthy questions?"

His eyes show concern and he nods, "Okay well you just let me know and we will go through it."

"Thanks." I get up, he follows my queue, stands and I give him a quick hug and a friendly wave to Sara as I head out the door.

I walk down the hallway to the elevator press the button to go down to my room and wait a moment for its arrival. I get a cold chill up my spine and there he is.

"Fancy running into you" Steven says with a grin.

"Are you following me?" I take a step back, crossing my arms and glare up at him.

"I don't need to Jordan. I already knew where you were. Authors and publishers talk so I knew that you had some meetings taking place around this time."

The elevator signals its arrival and I intentionally choose the main floor. Steven knows where Devon's room is but he may not know where mine is and I would like to try to keep it that way. The door closes behind us as we make our decent."

He asks, "So Jordan have you put some thought into when we could meet?" He asks me while revealing some incriminating photos of Devon and me kissing each other out on deck the night of the Authors ball. There is no mistaking that it is Devon and I. I look at him in disgust and he smiles and says, "These are just to give you some incentive. I didn't want to get another decline from you."

I take a step back from him, gulp and then say, "Okay, tomorrow when we arrive at our first destination. Give me a few hours to go on the excursions with my husband and afterwards we can meet at the beach?" The words escape my lips and I am already regretting it.

He smiles, "Now we are talking. I knew you were a smart girl." The lines on his face when he smiles make him look like some freakish clown.

The door opens to the lobby and I exit while Steven remains in the elevator. He hollers at me, "See you at the dance tonight." The elevator door closes and all I can think about is yes, whatever douche bag. Words and verbal threats are one thing but now photo evidence, Fuck!

Chapter 38
Two Brains

I feel numb, as I get ready in my room, putting on a pair of dark blue skinny jeans and put on a fluorescent orange tank top trimmed in lace that shows off my curves. Josh is sporting some relaxed fit denim and a black collared shirt and baseball cap.

He is mindful around me. He knows that something is on my mind but knows not to ask as he thinks that he already knows that it is about the three contracts but actually, there is a fourth.

The venue is like a club. We walk in to a dark place with colored lights on the stage, a live band, huge speakers placed around a bar and a dance floor. I have to chuckle to myself because I feel so out of place since I don't feel sexy at the moment with this bump and the fact that I am a pregnant woman at a bar. Then again, last night I was a pregnant woman at a casino. For some reason casino seems more acceptable to me than a bar. I look around the room and there are many happy, rowdy people. Some are sharing a beer together at the bar some dancing to the upbeat music, some standing on the sidelines mingling. I spot a couple of people making out. I guess this Author event isn't barred to stuff like that happening. I guess with the amount of people here and that we all have something in common there are bound to be hookups.

The three publishers that I met with stop by at different points to say hello and make small talk and soon enough Josh asks me to dance.

He asks speaking up enough so that I can hear him over the music, "Jordan, I know you have a lot to decide on but I can't help but feel like there is something more?"

I say, "Well there is, do you remember that weird guy that approached us just as we were leaving the ball the other night?"

He nods, "Yes, what's his name, Steve?"

"Yes, Steven Peach, I ran into him today and he insisted that we meet for a bit tomorrow to listen to his offer. He is working closely with his publisher."

Josh gives me a look, "Jordan if this meet is what's eating you up this much cancel it."

"I already said I would go. I made it clear that I would be busy with you so instead we are going to meet at the beach when it's closer to the time to board. It should be a short meet."

"Hun, you can cancel if you need to."

"I'll hear out Steven but his is the last offer that I'll listen to as the offers that are on the table right now are fair."

I see Josh's chest rise and fall as he sighs in response and we continue to dance. I could use a stiff drink right about now. The thought that Steven is blackmailing me into a meet just pisses me off and I don't know what I want to do or if I want to talk to Devon about it? I am going to have to eventually; two brains are better than one but when is the question. Devon's ears must have been ringing and he and Sara join Josh and me on the dance floor with their drinks in hand. They are both as happy as can be and I wish that I were to. I wish that I never met Steven Peach.

Sara circles around us to the beat of the music and lifting her drink high in the air and I try to forget for the moment.

Devon asks Josh with a shout that can be heard over the music, "May I dance with you wife?"

Josh says, "Take her."

I smile as he swirls me into his arms and leads. He murmurs in my ear, "Your husband gave me permission to take you."

I smirk, "Wise guy, he meant dance, not the other stuff."

"Oh, Jordan that is why I like you so much. You try to act all goody but you and I already know that you are a wild little fuck."

Before I can argue, he takes my hand and makes me to rest it on his shoulder. As we dance, he whispers to me, "You know that I'm hungry." As he says it, he presses his hard bulge into my leg as we step to the beat of the music. He asks, "You feel it?"

I whisper, "Yes"

"That is what you do to me. I want you now." He dips me.

I say, "What about Josh and Sara?"

He smirks, "Jordan sometimes I don't even know if you're joking. They won't even notice we are gone."

He leads me to the restrooms and gestures me to go in first so instinctively I choose the women's washroom.

I enter and I have no idea how he is going to pull this one off because just as the bar this washroom has a few people here. There is a woman at the vanity doing her makeup and I see a couple of occupied stalls.

I approach the vanity and retouch my makeup. The woman beside me looks me up and down then asks, "When are you due?"

"Oh, late January early February."

"Do you know what it is?"

"No, I want it to be a surprise."

She smiles and says, "There are so few surprises these days. Well good for you and congratulations!"

"Thank you." She puts the cap on her lipstick, slips it back into her purse and leaves the washroom.

I watch her open the door and catch a glimpse of Devon in the doorway and then he enters and I know to pick a stall. He follows me in and it begins.

He shuts the door behind us. I hear a toilet flush in one of the other stalls and know that we are not the only ones here. Thankfully, the stall doors have a few inch gaps from the floor so without someone actually bending over to check the bottom of our stall no one would know that there are two of us here.

His back is to the stall door and my back to him. He un-buttons my pant and pulls them down. He comes in from behind as I rest my hand on the back wall over the toilet.

Devon whispers in my ear, "I want to fuck you so hard." The sound of his voice makes my hot spot shudder with desire. He holds me tight and forces my hips down onto him and I bite my lip. He stays still inside allowing me to feel him. My eyes roll back, everything, the scent of his cologne mixed with his natural scent, the strength in his hands forcing my kitty to feel him and the hunger in his voice has me squirting within seconds. A whimper escapes my lips as he gives me this painful pleasure and I have to keep biting my lip to muffle the sound. He knows that he has me as my little soft spot violently throbs in orgasm and then it is his turn and he isn't gentle. He goes for what is his to take and pumps his love fast, hard and deep into my quivering kitty.

He pulls out and I am about to do up my pant when he stops me and kneels down, kissing a trail from my stomach all the way down to my wet opening.

I look down at him and give him the look that is supposed to imply that I am good and he just smiles and shakes his head to disagree. He first takes in a huge smell and I watch in curiosity and then he plunges in with his mouth and tongue to my over sensitive girl.

I practically lose my footing as he plays with me with his tongue. Devon is not shy and does what he wants licking hard and biting down to hold me still. He has me between his clamped down teeth. He gives me a second one that I didn't think I had in me, draining me of my juices and then he gets up and pulls his member out again and I know what he wants.

I kneel down and give my cowboy what he desires and I hear him sigh and whisper, "Ah Jordan." It is loud enough for me to hear inside the washroom stall.

I slurp his anticipation from the tip of his red swollen head and stroke his thick man. I know to speed up my pace and his breathing tells me he is near. I swallow his seed as he sighs in relief of the pleasure.

He whispers to me as I stand, "Jordan you know how to get me. Gosh girl you are good."

I smile, give him a kiss and exit the stall. No one else is here and I tap on the door and let him know that the coast is clear and he exits as I was at the vanity with my back to him. I glance at him through the mirror. He smirks and leaves the washroom and I follow within moments.

Back into the loud music and back to the mingling and I am somewhat already over it. More people offering to make connections with me and I have to politely pretend that I will consider their offers as I move on from group to group.

"Hey babes, where have you been?" Josh asks as he puts his arms around me.

Seeing Josh is a relief. I find meeting people and making small talk is a bit of a tedious effort and with him here I don't need to work and can be myself.

I say, "Oh you know the usual meeting and mingling."

He says, "I know that look."

"Yes, I am pretty drained." No pun intended.

He says, "Well I am good for heading back to our room. Besides, St. Martin is tomorrow. You still want to do that nature hike of the island?"

"Yes, I am missing the land and need to get my heart pumping well sort of, it's just a walk."

Josh and I say our good byes to Devon and Sara and head back up to our room. I wonder how I am going to tell Devon about tomorrow. I am still undecided on telling him. If I did tell Devon in the morning, it would be so that he could be with me when I meet up with Steven or would this make this whole Steven Peach situation worse.

Well, I just have to get through tomorrow.

Chapter 39
Caribbean Sky

In the early hours of the morning, it rained on St Marten. The ship arrives to the dew-covered island shortly after breakfast. It is a little bit on the humid side but I know with the weather it is supposed to reach a high of twenty-eight degrees Celsius, which is about eighty-three Fahrenheit give or take. The sticky humid feeling will probably dry out during the day as the sun peaks in the Caribbean sky.

All of us are out on deck, Devon, Sara, Josh and I. I spot the publishers that I met with earlier in the week and their spouses. I think that everyone is ready to touch land and do something different.

St. Marten has a busy dock. There is a pier just for cruise ships to dock at and the ship hums as it slowly approaches the dock and maneuvers to its spot. Even though I have never seen this I thought that there would be tug boats helping along the way but this cruise ship does it all on its own and seamlessly.

We are walking out on to the massive pier within moments and the feeling in the air is excitement from the hum of many conversations from the ship's passengers. They are ready to explore and enjoy the island. Some are in their swimsuits ready to enjoy a day of sand and sun.

Others are in summer attire and some are in sportswear. Josh and I are wearing some sport clothing.

I'm wearing a Capri dark grey yoga pant and a baby blue tank top and Josh is sporting a basketball short and silky t-shirt with a backpack to carry our belongings for the day.

There are a few shops for tourists on the pier. People offering horseback tours, helicopter tours, bike tours, scuba and snorkeling tours and finally we find someone that is offering a hiking tour.

Josh asks the man, "How long are your walking treks?"

The man answers him, "The walk is about two hours. We walk through Great Bay and up to Cole Bay Hill and then we loop back and return through Philipsburg."

Josh turns to me and asks, "Are you good for a two-hour hike?"

"Yes, bring it." Maybe the exercise will do me good and help me to think through this entire Steven Peach bullshit.

Josh pays the tour guide for the both of us. The guide waits until his group reaches thirty people before we start the trek.

While we are waiting to head out, I see Devon and Sara from a distance. Devon's eyes meet mine. He smiles and nods and I return the gesture. They are spending the day doing something more leisurely and I think I watch them approach the helicopter tour place, which doesn't surprise me because if you have the money why not. I eventually lose sight of them and hope that I don't see that asshole Steven but unfortunately, I do.

He has the nerve to walk up to us as soon as we lock eyes.

Steven says, "Good morning, Jordan." He nods his head and says, "Josh, how are you?"

Josh replies, "We are good and just about to head out on our tour." Josh puts his arm around my stiffened shoulders.

Steven says, "That sounds like a good way to enjoy the day." As Steven talks, my heart starts to pound. I don't want him going on the hike with us. I must have glared at him and he takes it as a queue to push a little further, "Maybe I should come with you guys. I am sure that the guide will have more. If you would excuse me for a moment I will go and find out." He walks past us and tries to make his way over to the stand to purchase a walk tour bracelet.

I whisper the words, "fuck!" They rather escape my lips.

Josh asks, "What's eating you up love?"

I mutter, "I wanted this time just with you and not with a person looking to talk contracts which I know this hike is going to become."

He rubs my shoulders in an attempt to try to relax me and says, "Want me to say something to him?"

I sigh, "No it's okay I'll go" I start to walk over to the stand where Steven is standing in line when our own tour guide calls out, "Everyone with a green bracelet come over to me. We are about to leave." People start to huddle around the guide. I look back at the stand and Steven is still in line at the counter. Ah, fuck it, I need to go back to the group if Steven gets a bracelet in time, so be it.

The guide calls out, "Okay we are thirty-two on the hike today and I can see that we are all here. Please follow me. Stay on the paths you will all get to see great views of the island today and if you have any questions, my name is Julian.

I smile to myself and think; thank God, that Steven didn't make it in time to be on our tour. I think that I would have asked for a refund. We walk down the pier and then down a road along the shore of Great Bay. There are already a few smaller boats anchored in the bay and we soon make our way into Philipsburg. There are a few narrow streets in this small town with colorful buildings and tropical tree lined streets. To my surprise, I even spot some fast-food joints along the route. The same kinds that we have at home which I think I am going to ask Josh later if he wants to eat there for lunch because just thinking about it, salty fries and some chicken nuggets sound just right even though it's still morning. I know it is getting old but I guess that I am blaming it on this baby once more.

As we pass by the different shops, we see tourists having breakfast on restaurant patios, shopkeepers opening their doors, sweeping along the sidewalk and bringing out their displays. We must be one of the first tours of the morning. Julian, our tour guide stops every so often to explain some of the history of the island and we continue on our way. Some people in our tour group snap pictures.

The trek soon takes us up hill. The sky opens up and we have a panoramic view of the island from Cole Bay Hill. We are able to view the different bays nearby and Philipsburg and off to the other side you can see and airport runway in the distance.

The group sort of spreads out while on the hill. Our tour guide Julian helps in taking some of the photos for the others in our group and Josh and me are no different with taking pictures of each other and the landscape. By this point in the morning, the dew has dried up and it is a perfect day of warm tropical sun on the island.

About half an hour later Julian gets the group back together and we make our decent back to Great Bay.

Its afternoon by the time we get back to Philipsburg and I am able to convince Josh on the fast-food place so we stop there to eat.

Josh says, "You are one silly girl. You know you are on this tropical island and prior to this vacation your like, Josh we never go anywhere and never try anything new and here we are and you default to eating cheap fast food we can get at home."

I smirk at him and say, "I thought that you liked this restaurant?"

"I do, I love burgers and fries. I'm just saying that you are a hypocrite."

"Well, if you want, we could try that restaurant over there?" I glance just passed him at the restaurant across the street.

"No, no there is no point in wasting the food we have just saying you had the opportunity so don't complain that you never have the chance to try new things."

I roll my eyes, "Yes Josh. Well, we are one for two today at least. We saw an island that we have never seen before so I count that as doing something new."

Josh replies, "I'll give you that."

We finish eating and then do a bit of shopping. Mostly just picking up little trinkets for family back home and eventually make our way to the boardwalk at Great Bay Beach.

I have the feeling that Steven had been following us from the restaurant to the boardwalk because I spot him not far behind us and decide that I need to face the music and whisper to Josh, "I better get this over with. There is Steven, can I meet you later, right here?"

"Sure love, are you sure that you don't want me to stay?"

"No, it's okay, it shouldn't take long anyways." I put on a brave smile and continue, "Hey look over there in that boardwalk bar. Is that Devon and Sara?"

Josh turns and looks, "Yes, that's them. Okay I'll keep a lookout for you. Talk to you soon." I give him a kiss on the cheek, turn and walk down the path to meet Steven Peach.

He is wearing leather thong sandals a loose khaki shirt and white linen shorts. He has round sunglasses resting on his head.

"Jordan, I was starting to worry that the young and beautiful author was going to get cold feet but then I thought again and had a feeling that you would come through and meet."

"Steven, I would like to get back to my husband as soon as I can." I cross my arms.

He glances down, "Don't you mean Devon?" I slap him across the face hard and a few people on the boardwalk turn and stare.

Steven says to the few that have taken notice, "That is what I get for telling a bad joke!" A few shake their heads and seem to return to minding their own business. Steven addresses me, "Let's take a seat over in the shade at the cafe." He points a few buildings down from where Josh, Sara and Devon are which is just out of sight from them.

I mutter, "Sure"

As we take our seat a bubbly waiter approaches our table and asks, "What would you like to drink?"

I ask, "Do you have iced cappuccinos?"

She smiles, "Well of course would you like whipped cream on top?"

"No thanks"

"Okay sweetheart and for you sir what speaks to you." She glances down at the drink menu in the center of the table as a gesture to have Steven look.

He rubs his chin as he looks at the table menu, "I will have iced coffee with milk."

The waiter replies, "Okay darling I'll be right back." I don't think the waiter takes notice to the coolness between the Steven and I or if she does, she is doing a fantastic job at hiding it.

Steven explains, "Jordan, you and I both know that this negotiation is really quite simple. I have something that you want and you have something that I want and you and I both have a shared interest in making money." He shrugs and says, "So really this entire information exchange is a no-brainer for the two of us."

The waiter sets our drinks down, "Enjoy you two." She replies, we nod and she departs.

I just glare at him not even touching my drink and waiting for him to continue. He pauses for a sip of his.

He says, "I will give you all of the evidence of infidelity in exchange that you sign this contract today for three hundred thousand to publish with my publisher who I may add is fantastic. What I get out of it is my own monitory amount for discovering and signing on new talent." He had the contract tucked under his arm. I guess that I didn't notice it there before and he lays it on the table before me and removes a pen from his shirt pocket and places it down next to the contract.

I look down at it and back up at him. I say, "You know that I have been made offers in the millions?"

He laughs, "Jordan you and I both know that you are not a good wife or soon to be Mother. What woman cheats on her husband and father of her child?"

That second part he has wrong but that is none of his business. I ask, "What if I don't sign?"

He stops laughing leans forward and says, "Then you know what happens. Just sign today and this will all go away and if we can't get there by the time this coffee is done Josh and Sara will be given some nice photos of your endeavors with Devon."

I glare back at him, "Is that all that you've got?"

His voice lowers to a murmur, "That is all that I need."

We glare at each other in silence and the bubbly waiter returns and asks, "How are your drinks love birds?" Clearly, she is disillusioned.

Without looking up at her I reply, "Fine, thank you."

She chuckles and says, "Can't keep your eyes off of one another." I hear her footsteps depart.

It's my turn to play my hand. I take a sip of my drink and say, "Now you listen to me Steven, don't take my soft-spoken manors as a sign of being timid because I am far from it. If you think you can push me around with a few photos than you are mistaken. Listen up because if it's true that you want some sort of payout for signing me on than you will give me the time that I need to review this contract properly."

He leans forward in his seat, resting his elbows on the table with his fingers now intertwined together. He smirks, "Jordan, you surprise me. What makes you think that I am going to let you have an ounce of control in this?" He leans back, crossing his arms and staring back at me.

I slurp my drink loudly. I don't care. He can't scare me or ruin this cruise. I answer, "Steven you revealed to me your only move and after that what's in it for you?" I shrug and continue without giving him the chance to respond, "I leave this table without signing and let's say you share your photos, ruining both mine and Devon's relationships and then what? I'm definitely not signing your contract after that and look there is no money for you. You did say you were in this for the money, right?"

A blood vein in his forehead starts to swell, as his face turns red. I have him by the tail and he knows. He says, "Don't for a second think that I won't. This is also for vengeance."

This time I smirk. "Well, we all know what comes first and if you want the chance of a payout than you will give me time."

We both know that he is out of moves and after a long moment he caves, "Okay, one day."

"Three days." I counter.

He argues back, "All you need is a day to review, one day."

I say, "Tomorrow is St. Thomas and I won't have the time."

"We will meet in the middle, two days."

"Steven, do you think that I am playing games?"

"You know that I am seeking money but you also know that I have nothing to lose in this. What's the saying, don't count your chickens before they hatch? I am relying on you to make the right choice and if I so much as feel that you won't I am prepared to make the move besides Devon has it coming to him after screwing me over. That in itself is priceless."

I see the crazy emerge from him and wanting it to stop, I extend my hand out to shake. "It's settled two days."

I place some change on the table and get up with haste. The contact is in my hand and I don't look back. I have two days to straighten this out.

Chapter 40
Powdery White

I meet Josh at the patio bar where I left him and he is hanging out with Devon, Sara and a few of Devon's guest winners from his book signings. They are all sitting next to each other on bar stools at the main bar that overlooks the beach.

I pause for a moment before walking over to them, trying to shake off that unsettling feeling and threat that Steven brings into my life.

I hear Devon holler, "Jordan, where have you been? We had to take care of your husband he was sulking over here."

I smile at Josh because I know that Sara has encouraged a couple of alcoholic beverages on him.

I say, "Oh, you know the life of an author. We are always wondering around and getting into trouble." I smile through a faint quivering voice which both Josh and Devon pick up on."

Josh is the one to step to the plate and as I pull up a bar stool next to him. He murmurs, "What is wrong love?"

"Oh, I am just worried that I won't make the right choice."

He presses, "Is that all?"

"Yes"

Josh says, "Do me a favor no more new contract meetings okay?"

"I won't I promise."

He rubs my back and says, "You have no reason to stress. Look where you are."

"I agree," The bartender notices me and offers a drink and I reply, "a bottle of water please."

At this point Devon and Sara are in conversation with Devon's fan guests who are sitting on the opposite side of Devon. I catch a concerned glimpse from Devon every now and then.

Josh asks, "So what did this guy offer you?"

"Nothing to make me change my mind, I am going with my first choice."

"Like I said before, I think you know what you need to do."

"Yes, you're right."

Josh makes a joke, "I'm always right. I am not just for looks." He winks.

"Yah yah." I grab his hand under the bar squeezing gently. I don't know why I do but I do. Touching his hand is comforting, I guess.

He smiles back at me, "There's that smile. I know that you want to go to the beach. I am just about ready if you are."

The bartender returns with my bottled water and Josh asks for another one for him before heading to the beach.

We wave to Devon and Sara who remain with their other guests and we walk out onto the powdery white sand.

Josh has the bag we packed from this morning so I tuck the publishing contract inside as I remove my clothes to reveal my swimsuit.

Josh asks, "Want to go in now?"

"Yes." I am trying my hardest to shake it but he still sees it's on my mind.

"Jordan, you've got nothing about the business stuff to worry about now."

"It is easier said than done." I shrug.

He shakes his head, scoops me into his arms and carries me to the water. The white sand creates turquoise water and is nothing short of perfect as we dip in and refresh ourselves. After some playtime in the water, we wade closer to the shore so that we are in around a foot of water. We sit with each other and resting our hands on the sandy bottom.

Josh ponders allowed, "What do you really think life will be like after this little one arrives?"

As I answer my eyes are fixed on the shore, watching a couple of kids with their parents working on a sandcastle, "Umm maybe hard at first with getting used to a new routine but I think we will ultimately adjust and life will be busier but in a good way."

He lays back a bit on his elbows and replies, "I think your right. I mean I have heard our parents talk about it and your friends and mine. It's just hard to believe that this is finally happening. What is silly is we haven't even decided on names. What did you have in mind?"

I have to hand it to Josh for making the effort to keep my mind off Steven and his stupid contract. Baby names are a good distraction and something that we should talk about.

"Well, I'm not decided but I liked the name, Evan for a boy and Ava for a girl."

He ponders for a moment then says, "You know, I like those. There wasn't an Evan I didn't like and I don't think that I ever met an Ava. How did you come up with those names?"

I shrug, "I think I just heard them and they just stuck with me. They aren't over used either. Anyway, what names were you thinking?"

"Maybe we could stick with names that start with J to match our names, like Jack for a boy and Jasmine for a girl."

I laugh, "Josh that is so tacky to do that."

"Well do you like my choices at least?"

"I do like Jack it is a simple but strong name. I like Jasmine but whenever I hear it, I think about Princess Jasmine in the movie Aladdin."

Josh says how about this, "If it's a boy, I have the ultimate decision on what to name him and if it's a girl the decision is yours."

"I like that but I have a question for you?"

He leans in and says, "What's up?"

"Can we still give one another suggestions?"

He smiles and gives me a kiss on the forehead and answers, "Absolutely."

I take his hand in mine under the water and admit, "I'm still not decided. I think I will only know when I see them."

"Don't worry about it. Whatever we choose I am sure it will be good."

"Well, I know that. It has to be good."

He touches the corner of my lips, "There's that smile."

The rest of the day passes in a heartbeat and we soon find ourselves boarding the ship to depart.

I have time to check my messages when we get to our room and I am not surprised to see a text from Devon. We hadn't really spoken all day and at that boardwalk bar he seemed concerned with all of his glances. The text reads, "Text me when you get this. We need to talk."

Josh asks, "Sheesh Jordan what is it now?"

I look up, "It's Devon he wants to talk."

He sighs, "Ah Jordan, I think that you need to take a break tonight. We just returned from a tropical paradise and you wouldn't know it by the look on your face."

"I know but I can't afford to screw any of this up and maybe talking it over with someone who has been there will bring me some insight that will give me peace of mind."

He asks, "Can I come?"

"If he wants me to meet him, I don't want to bore you to death. Just hang back or I can text you when I am done."

Josh replies reluctantly, "Okay"

We both get comfortable on the bed and Josh flips stations as I respond to Devon, "Hey I am here what's up?"

Devon's reply message comes through, "I saw the look on your face and noticed the papers under your arm when you were at the boardwalk bar. Who did you meet with and why was I left out?"

I text back, "Devon I was going to tell you, I am being blackmailed by Steven Peach. It just happened and I didn't want to bring you in because I thought it would make the situation worse."

A few minutes pass and I am certain that he has read my text but I don't follow up with another. I have explained it all.

A knock at the door startles Josh and I. Josh looks at me and asks, "Was Devon meeting you here?"

"We never got that far in the conversation."

Chapter 41
Rips It

I shrug as Josh looks at me and he steps towards the door, peeks through the peephole and then opens to let Devon in.

Devon says in a bit of a breathless voice, "Hey Josh how did you like the island today?" I know that recapping the day with Josh is not the real reason for Devon's visit.

Josh a bit confused replies, "It was good. Devon I'm not trying to be rude or anything, you know that you are always welcome but what are you doing here? I just thought that you were spending the evening with Sara and your other guests." Josh takes a step back letting Devon step inside and Josh closes the door.

I peek over from the bed to see Josh and Devon glances back at me and says, "Oh you know, we have to know where we are at in terms of contracts and such. Jordan texted a few minutes ago to say that she met with another publisher today and I just wanted to chat with her about it. It shouldn't take long."

Josh looks at Devon then turns to me to ask, "Jordan, if it was important for Devon to be with you during today's meet why didn't you bring him?"

"Josh, I didn't want to interfere with Devon's day at St. Marten and besides I thought I could handle it on my own seeing that I have had a few meets like it already." I look at Josh when I respond and then glance between the two of them and admit, "I'm really sorry about this."

Devon replies, "No worries, we can review quickly tonight so that we are ready for our next move." I can see the concern in his brown eyes as he pretends that he is okay with it.

Josh insists, "I'm going to be in on this discussion."

I look at Devon, who glances back at me and then says to Josh, "Josh, it really won't take long. I promise that when it comes down to deciding I recommend that you be there to support her but this will be quick. Don't let this interfere with your night and I'll have Jordan returned safe and sound."

Josh glances back at me for a feeling and I give him the nod to let him know that I will be okay to meet on my own and he says in a breath, "Okay, see you in half an hour?"

Devon gives him, his word, "I promise."

I pick up the contract that Steven Peach gave me and I leave with Devon. Without saying a word, we walk to the elevator and take it down to the floor where his secret room is and we don't talk until we are in the secret room and the door is locked shut.

He orders, "Sit down and tell me what is going on."

I take a seat on the foot of the bed, shaken I reply, "It's Steven Peach."

"Yes, you told me that much but explain." He crosses his arms, standing like a statue in front of me.

I go through everything with him. From the comment Steven first said to me in passing at the Author's Ball on the first night to the evening at the casino and the time he caught me alone in the elevator up to the time on St. Marten. I explain the photos he had of us doing stuff that we should not have done and let him read the contract. I tell Devon how I was able to get out of signing the contract today.

I have never seen Devon like this. He is not happy about it. I mean who would be happy with being blackmailed. Devon sits next to me on the bed reads the contract over again. He is deep in concentration. He is going through our options in his mind. To my surprise, he rips it up.

He says, "This is ridiculous."

Dumbfounded I ask, "You aren't worried about this?"

He shakes his head then answers, "No Jordan, you clearly put him in his place this afternoon. He won't do it. I know him. I mean look at the grudge he holds on me and really, it's not called for because it was Steven that dropped out. Yes, the man wants vengeance on me but I know that the prospect of making money out weighs it. Steven would lose respect from the writing community if he stooped to the level that he is threatening us with."

I murmur, "Devon, I think that you are mistaken. I mean his threats were clear to me. If he catches any whiff of me not wanting to sign his contract, he will blow the whistle on us."

"And what will he do, give Sara and Josh copies of us making out? So, what, all we do is tell Josh and Sara that desperate people will go to great lengths to bring others down. We deny that they are real. That's all."

"Why do I feel like you are just sweeping this under the rug?"

"Jordan, really what are we going to do? You were never going to sign that contract and you called out his move."

I look at him, "Are you going to do something that I won't agree with?"

"Like what Jordan? Do I want to throw the man off this ship? You bet, will I? No."

"So, what now?"

He asks, "How many days did he give you?"

"Two", I sigh.

"So, in those two days we lay low and accept the contract that you want. We won't do any celebratory dinners or anything that would tip him off and once we get to the two days, we face the music then."

"In two days, we will be in the Bahamas." I blurt out.

He tucks a strand of hair behind my ear and says, "One day after that we will be arriving back in Florida to go home. Jordan, he didn't think this thru. Steven was counting on scaring you into signing as soon as he could. That was his move. Time is on our side, not his and besides we are two brains to his one. Anyway, I'm glad you brought me up to speed because we can work together and put it to rest. Our move will be to make him wait until it is too late. We both need to relax and I know just the thing before sending you back to Josh."

I am in no mood for sex but somehow my cowboy gets to me. He looks at me with those hungry brown eyes. It's hard to look away and then he steals a kiss with those sexy lips of his and passionate tongue. We lie down next to each other after slipping out of our clothes. This man is standing tall and he is ready to shove himself deep into me and feel my juicy insides.

"I want to fuck you so hard. Get on top Jordan."

His dick is hard and warm from his massive swell and I close my eyes as I ease myself down onto him. He grabs my hips and forces me down quick and I let out a sigh. He wants it quick and he goes to work. He rocks me back and forth. I bite my lip as I get my release and he doesn't stop and I know that it's his turn. The rocking turns into thrusting, harder and faster and I close my eyes and enjoy the ride. His strong hands are forcing me down onto him and my kitty is just drooling all over him as he gets closer and closer. His breathing changes and I know that he is close. I feel his shaft pulsate into me as he grunts as each love explosion flows into my pussy. I feel his body relax and see a smile appear on his face.

He says to me, "There, I think we both needed that."

I'm still sitting on him, lightly rocking and reply, "bad cowboy"

"Don't you mean good cowboy?"

"Devon, I worry that's all."

"Worrying is okay but worrying until it cripples you is an entirely different matter. We stick to our plan and it will be okay. We should wash up and head back. I promised Josh to have you back in half an hour."

I dab my parts off and put my clothes back on and Devon walks me back to my room.

He murmurs, "Remember lay low for two days and we will be okay we are two and he is one."

I tap on the door and Josh opens. Devon says to him, "Just like I promised here she is back in one piece."

Josh shakes his hand and asks, "Want to come in? Do you two still need to talk?"

Devon assures, "No we got everything cleared up. Jordan can fill you in. I do need to get back to Sara and the others. Have a good night."

Chapter 42
Horseshoe Up

Our next destination is St. Thomas. I explained the contract to Josh and mentioned what Devon is going to do about it after returning to my room last night. I told Josh that I was ready to sign the contract from the publisher that Devon is working with. I explained to him Devon's and my concern with Steven Peach but all I mentioned was Steven's hatred for Devon and that Steven would go to great lengths to make people question Devon's reputation and try anything to get me to sign his shitty contract.

This morning I was out on our balcony looking over at the water. It looks a little choppy however; the waves are small enough that you don't feel it on a ship as big as this one.

The ship is still a bit of a ways out but I can see St. Thomas in the distance as we move forward to the dock in Havensight.

Josh joins me on the balcony, surprising me with a hug from behind. He gives me a kiss on the cheek.

I smile and look at him and ask, "What's that for?"

"Oh, nothing just thought you needed a kiss."

I turn and give him a kiss back. He holds me as we look out at the water and he asks to confirm, "We are meeting with Devon and the Tail Fin publisher this morning to sign that million-dollar contract, right?"

"Yes, his name is Howard Stem."

Josh asks, "This Steven Peach guy if he is as crazy as you guys make him out to be do you think he is keeping an eye on us and Devon?"

I ask, "Come inside and I will explain."

We close the door to the balcony. I have no idea if anyone in the rooms beside us can even hear our conversations out there but decide that it is best not to take any chances.

I explain, "I texted Devon this morning to confirm my decision he knows that Steven is likely watching our rooms with who goes in and out so Devon has already taken steps to get Steven off our trail. Devon reserved a room in one of the lower decks. Devon has given Howard access so he is going there first alone. Steven may have eyes on us but it is impossible for him to have eyes on every publisher on board this ship. Once Howard is in the room, we are going to get a text to meet there. If Steven happens to follow us, he will only see me, you or Devon and not Howard."

Josh says, "I understand."

"Let's head out and when I get the text we can head down."

Josh takes my hand into his and I glance into his eyes, he asks, "Are you ready for this?"

"I think so." I look into those clear blue eyes of his. They are full of anticipation.

He says, "Not the contract stuff. Are you ready for your life to change?"

I smile, "I'm excited, ready, now I'm not so sure that anyone can prepare you for everything that happens after signing a contract."

He smiles and says, "This entire turn of events is crazy. I am still scratching my head at how you just so happened to start talking to a famous author at a waterpark of all places. Jordan there is no doubt in my mind that you are talented but you have to admit that you have a horseshoe up your ass."

I giggle, "Yes I know. Well, it is what it is and everything that we dreamed of is coming true."

Josh says, "Just wild to think that we boarded this ship leading average lives and we will be leaving it with extraordinary lives."

"Don't be silly our lives were always extraordinary. Shall we head out?" I give him a playful nudge.

He gives me another kiss and says; "sure"

It is just an average morning, well average for a day on board of a cruise ship. Josh and I grab a coffee and a bagel and we are on our way, wondering around and waiting for the text from Devon. I don't see any sign of anyone following us or any sign of Steven Peach and to be honest the ship decks are pretty quiet. My guess is that people are getting ready for the day on St. Thomas.

After about half an hour the message comes in and I tell Josh it's time to head on down. I look around before entering the elevator and Josh takes notice and murmurs, "You think that guy is watching us? If he, is its no big deal, he can run his mouth off but I can run mine off too."

If only it were that easy. I know Josh is coming to my defense as any husband would. My worry is the moment that Steven starts running his mouth off about Devon and me or shows Josh his photos then what? Does Josh trust me enough to believe my lie, that they aren't real or will he believe what he sees? For now, I have to let Josh be my protective man. I have two days.

We arrive at the room where Devon and I have spent our alone time and I tap on the door and it quietly opens. You can never forget how small that room is, the bed takes up the bulk of the space but it feels much more cramped with four people in the room.

Josh closes the door with his back and as soon as I hear the click of the latch, Devon says to us, "I know it's a tight space guys but this was the best that I could do given our unique circumstance."

Josh nods, "Understood friend. So, I understand that she just needs to sign and it's done?" Josh's question is to both Howard and Steve. It's funny how guys sound different when they talk to each other. Their voices change just a tad to a lower note to make them sound manly to one another, both Josh and Devon do this and I think its subconscious.

Devon answers, "That's right" to Josh and says to me, "Jordan, Howard will help you with signing off on everything."

I look at Howard who is sitting closer to the head of the bed with his feet planted on the ground and body turned toward us. I sit next to him. I have the documents and lay them between the two of us.

Howard explains, "Okay you are going to sign here and here." He points to different lined spaces on the contract. I start to look for a pen but Howard recognizes my fidgeting and hands me his own.

"Thank you" I reply.

"My pleasure"

As I am signing and dating, he asks, "So what activity do you and your husband have planned for St. Thomas?" He is being polite while I work through signing paper after paper.

I respond for Josh and me, "I think we are going to do some diving. We wanted to look first to see if we could do it. I am not sure if you need you certification for the St. Thomas dive or if it's something that people without their certifications can do?"

I look up at Howard and he sees his queue, turns some more pages and points to more places to sign. While I work on the next round of signatures he says, "I'm not sure? I did look at that activity as something to do but I just don't recall if they required it."

Devon pipes in, "I don't think you need it."

I say as I carefully sign, "Well, I guess we just have to go there and find out but that's pretty well what we had our heart set on doing and then after I wanted to take a walk around town."

Howard flips to the final pages and directs me to more signature boxes. I spot the direct deposit information and I look to Josh. He knows what I need and provides me the bank numbers. After I finished filling in the final spaces with information Howard hands the document over to Josh to have a look over and then brings out a duplicate to have me do the same thing and complete.

I ask what Howard has planned after this as I work my way through the pages of the second document. Howard explained that he would return to his room to send all of the contract information to the head office. He said that it should take an hour and then he has the day free to explore the island. He explains that he plans to visit one of the museums, a couple of churches and then in the late afternoon he wants to take a walk down the beach.

I finish signing and adding in the banking information for a second time and hand the document over to Josh and he hands the first one back to me and I provide it to Howard.

Howard smiles and says, "That one in Josh's hand is yours and this one here is mine."

"Okay" I reply in a breath wondering what's left to do.

Howard smiles at me and explains, "We are done"

I am a little confuse and look at Devon who is grinning ear to ear and next to him is Josh, who is making sure our documents are in order.

Devon says, "Jordan you are officially a signed author and millionaire."

"I am?" I look back at Howard and he smiles and gives me a confirmation nod.

"Josh did you hear what they said?" I ask.

Josh looks first at me then Devon then Howard and asks, "Are you sure?"

"Yes!" I start to cry. They are happy tears from all of the work that I have put into this and it's finally official. I get off the bed and give Josh a hug and say, "We are millionaires!" Josh is quiet. He says nothing but holds me tight. Josh hugs and lifts me up and swings me back and forth in his embrace. I can tell that he is happy and don't need to hear the confirmation from his lips.

I look up at him and he has to confirm with Devon and Howard, "This isn't a joke, right?"

Devon chuckles saying, "No my friend, welcome to the club!" Devon shakes Josh's hand and by this time Howard has tucked the contract away and shuffles around the bed to shake Josh's hand and then mine.

Howard says to me, "Jordan I am confident that this will be a great business relationship. Congratulations and I look forward to working with you."

Devon is about to open his mouth when Howard confirms saying, "Don't worry I understand that you wish to keep this transaction discreet."

Devon says, "Thank you."

Howard says, "Alright I am going to head on out and if we don't run into each other have a great day guys." Howard shuts the door behind him.

Devon says, "We need to leave just as we came. I can leave next and you two just hang out for a few moments maybe collect your thoughts." He smiles and continues, "It's just amazing to see the energy in you two. It makes me think back to the day when I first got my contract, which wasn't that long ago but sometimes it feels like a lifetime ago." He gives Josh one of those one handed man hugs, a quick pat on the back and gives me a hug and a kiss on the cheek and whispers, "Congratulations, we may not be able to celebrate now but soon enough we will have a celebration." Devon lets himself out. Josh and I glance at each other and I start to laugh and fall backwards onto the bed, he joins me for a kiss.

"Josh, did you ever think for a second that this would be our life? I mean when we step off this ship our lives will be forever changed."

"You know Jordan that I have always believed in you. I was just always skeptical because a lot of the times even the best people don't get discovered or reach this sort of success."

I want to believe his words but I think with Josh there was always that grain of doubt and I don't hold it against him nor does it take away from this moment because he knows now and I, in my own little way have proven him wrong. I reply, "I know what you mean."

He asks, "So really when we get back what are we going to do?"

I laugh and shrug, "I guess tell our family."

He asks, "Should I quit my job? Should you quit your job?"

I smile and say, "I don't know? I can see myself going in to work for a bit longer just until things start happening and maybe decide after?"

"Do we sell our home? There are just so many what to do things I'm not even sure where to begin?" He admits.

I murmur to him, "I think that it's best that we continue to lay low and that means not texting our families while on this vacation. I just think if we tell them and they tell others and it somehow leeks to the press it will quickly come back to Steven Peach."

Josh answers, "I can do that."

"We are mid-week so it's really not a long wait."

I hug him, close my eyes and hope that everything goes to plan.

Chapter 43
Back in Fifteen

It is still morning after returning from Jordan's contract signing. I am relaxing back in bed and checking my messages on my smart phone while under the sheets. I received a couple of messages, one from my son and the other from my brother. I messaged them back which it turned into full on live conversations.

The news from them is all light hearted. They chat about the upcoming football game, work, what I have missed.

Sara was up after I returned from my meeting with Jordan, Josh and Howard. She takes a shower while I relax and by the time, she is dry, her hair done up in a loose twist and she is dressed, I am still on my phone. I look up at her, "That's a nice outfit."

She smiles, "Thanks, I picked it up in St. Marten remember?"

"Ah yes." I smile at her. I don't remember because she bought a lot of things that day.

"I am going to pick up a couple of things at the pharmacy." She grabs her purse that was resting on a chair in the corner.

I rest my phone on the bed and give her my complete attention and say, "I can come with you. It will take me two minutes to get changed."

She assures, "I won't be long; besides I saw that you were talking to your brother and son and it looked like good conversation."

I smile at her, "Thanks honey. Okay I'll wait for you here."

She says, "Be back in fifteen."

She exits and I continue to text family a bit longer. About fifteen minutes later I let them know that I need to drop off, besides Sara will be back any minute.

I get out of bed and change into something more casual. I glance at the clock on the nightstand. Twenty-five minutes has passed. Sara sometimes runs late. This is still normal for her. I tidy things up around the room to pass time and glance at my phone to see if I received a message from Sara.

I look outside on the balcony. Now the ship is docked at St. Thomas and I see on the deck below that the passengers are already leaving the ship. Where is she?

Forty minutes has passed after I tried texting her. I startle as the door opens.

Our eyes meet but it's not the same. She has a plastic bag in her hand from the pharmacy. She closes the door with her back and stares and the pharmacy bag drops to the floor.

"Sara, what's wrong?" She looks like she is sick or something. I walk over to take her into my arms but she puts her arm out.

I glance at her hand in my face and follow the length of her arm to her face.

Sara says, "Just don't"

"Sara, what?"

She can't even look me in the eye now. It's like the sight of me disgusts her. She looks away from me, down at the floor and admits, "I know Devon."

My heart starts to thump and my ears grow warm. This can only mean one thing. The words are stuck in my throat. I want to say that I didn't mean to hurt her, that I love her, that it wasn't her fault it was mine. I want to tell her that I will do everything I can to make it up to her and that it was a mistake but nothing comes out.

I look down trying to keep my tears in my lids but it doesn't work. They start to roll down my cheeks and I look back into her Italian eyes.

Sara says, "Get out." The sadness on her face turns to anger.

I don't argue or try to plead my case. I say nothing and grant her wish. I don't even grab my things. All I can do is leave.

Chapter 44
Say Nothing

The ship makes its way to the dock in St. Thomas and the deck of the ship is full of eager people waiting to visit the island. Josh and I are sporting casual beachwear. Me in a little flowing halter top style pink dress with a pair of white thongs and my hair is done up in a simple bun and Josh is sporting a light grey baseball cap, shorts and white t-shirt. He looks handsome and like the weight of the world is off his shoulders.

For all the years that I have been married to Josh, money has always been a concern for him. He is a penny pincher even though we have always done well for ourselves and he worries often about our account balance. Now with having this amazing publishing deal, I look at Josh and he is carefree which is just so beautiful to me.

The two of us watch over the railing of the main deck as the ship inches closer to the dock. I feel a light tap on my shoulder. It is Sara.

I go in for a hug, her shoulders feel stiff as I embrace her, "Hi Sara, how are things? Did Devon make it back to your room okay?"

"He did and he told me the news, congratulations to the two of you. I know this news is on the low key for now but I am happy for the both of you."

"Thanks Sara." I say and Josh gives her a quick hug and thanks her.

Sara whispers in my ear, "Can I talk to you honey?"

"Yah sure what's up?"

She says to Josh, "If you don't mind Josh, can I steal your wife for a few minutes?"

"Go right ahead. I'll wait here."

I wonder if this is about the contract that I just signed. We walk around a corner into an empty stair well. She waits for the door to close.

She gets close to me grabbing hold of the neck of my top and says in a low but sharp voice, "I ought to slap you. You are lucky that baby is in your belly because if you weren't I would kick your ass. I knew something wasn't right. I felt it in my bones. Shame on you, you have a husband and baby on the way, fucking little bitch!" She says the words through her teeth while staring me down and some sort of realization comes over her face. She says, "Devon took a trip to Ottawa a while back. How far along are you?" I freeze and say nothing. She knows by the blank look on my face and her own expression goes from anger to complete disgust. She releases her grasp of my top, shoving me away from her. The wall behind keeps me from falling back, Sara spits back, "Yes that's what I thought. You fucking little home wrecker. Now you know that I know. Get out of my sight you dirty little cunt."

I say nothing and just high tail it out of the stair well and run in the opposite direction from where Josh is waiting. I'm out of breath and stop, lean back against a wall and slide down to the ground and cry. How did she find out? Devon and I kept things secret and as far as Steven, he gave us two days.

I feel the glances of strangers as they pass, unsure whether to stop and offer to help. A woman's voice that I recognize says to me, "Jordan?"

I look up and its Devon's fan winner from Ottawa, Donna, the woman I spoke with on casino night. I say, "Yes?"

"Sweetheart what's wrong?" she kneels down before me.

"Oh, it's nothing."

She says, "Come on, I know those aren't alligator tears. Let us get you up off the ground. Tell me what's wrong."

I barely know her but share a bit of my troubles, "I just had a bit of a confrontation with someone and am letting my emotions get the best of me." I sniffle and continue, "You know, pregnant women we get worked up over little things."

Donna nods, "Ah Jordan, just breathe and whatever it was give yourself some time to cool off and when you are ready try to sort whatever it is out with that person."

She hands me a tissue, "Thanks Donna."

She stays with me a few minutes while I regain myself. She asks when my sobs start to subside, "Sweetheart, are you okay now?"

"Yah I'll be fine. I just needed to let it out, that's all." That is a part truth but really, I am falling apart inside.

She pats me on the back, "Is your husband nearby?"

"Yes, he is just near the front where they will be letting us off the ship."

She smiles, "Okay, dry those tears, I'll let you get back to him. Whatever is eating you up I know you will sort it out."

"Yes, thank you."

She heads in the direction where Josh is waiting and I give myself a pep talk in my mind. Jordan, you made your bed and need to lay in it. This probably won't be good but it's too late to fix this, Sara knows.

I return and find Sara with Josh and my jaw is on the floor. I slowly walk up to the two of them.

Sara in a caring voice asks, "Where were you honey?"

I look her in the eyes, which are full of anger and hatred, but the expression on her face is that of happy and caring. Confused I answer, "Oh I just slipped away to the rest room."

Josh asks, "Your eyes are puffy is something wrong?"

"I just had a bit of a sneezing fit. It must be something in the air that I am allergic to."

He comes over kisses me on the forehead and playfully says, "Ah my poor girl." He hugs me and I peek over his shoulder and receive Sara's dagger like glare.

I don't know what to do or say and just continue to act like nothing has happened. My man is on one of the biggest highs of his life. If I decide to tell him about my infidelity, I am not doing it in this moment.

Sara has excused herself from Josh and me with a "see you later" wave. I look back at her with my own defeated glance and wonder what she will do? Whatever her decision is I know I won't be able to stop her. Sara is a strong-minded woman to convince her differently and a complete opposite of Devon when it comes to listening to others.

The ship gate is open to my relief and we are free to visit St. Thomas. I don't know where Devon is and can imagine that he isn't with Sara, who is out of sight right now because they must have fought. I am not about to go and ask and I have no idea if Josh asked Sara while he was waiting for me.

St. Thomas is similar to St. Marten with its large bay, clear water and white sand. The island caters to the thousands of visitors that arrive daily. We aren't the only cruise ship that's docked and when we set foot on the dock there are crowds of other tourists deciding where to go and such.

I lose sight of Sara and I really don't mind. I want to forget that this morning ever happened. Maybe I dreamed it. Josh pokes me.

"Hey what's up?"

Josh says, "You looked like you were somewhere else just now."

"This morning has been something else hasn't it."

"Yes, it has. So, are we doing the Sea Trek today?"

"You bet." I smile back at him while returning to reality.

"Okay cause there is a taxi van over there taking people to that place."

We navigate the crowed and squeeze into the van that is full of other tourists like us. A few others come on after we take our seats. The taxi driver climbs in and we are on our way to the destination.

We see a bit of everything as we make our way through the island. We see parts of the port town and then we are soon outside and weaving our way uphill. Our view is full of green vegetation and I catch the odd glimpse of the ocean. Soon the taxi van makes its way down hill and we are entering the grounds to where the Sea Trek is. Everyone in this taxi gets off and a parking lot attendant walks with the group to the entrance.

This place is small, not at all what I was expecting and as we get in line at the main desk to purchase our Sea Trek. The atmosphere is full of excitement and anticipation with the constant hum of conversations as families wait in line. I gather that this is a first for many of the other tourists here. Kids are jumping up and down and laughing with their parents. There are other couples like Josh and me and a few older people enjoying an adventure in their retirement.

It's our turn to be served at the counter. The receptionist says, "Welcome to Coral Bay my name is Yvonne what are you two interested in doing today?"

Josh says, "We would like to do the Sea Trek."

Yvonne answers, "Good choice." She is about to bring up the bill, pauses and glances at me then asks, "Miss, I have to ask. Are you pregnant?"

"Yes" I bit my bottom lip. I already know what she is going to say.

"I'm afraid you won't be able to participate in that activity. It notes that in our brochure."

Josh glances at me and I say, "I'm sorry I didn't see that. Josh did you want to do the Sea Trek alone without me?" I don't mind sitting out. I need time to wrap my head around the entire Sara situation.

Josh explains, "No Jordan. We came here to do something together. It doesn't make sense for me to go out alone."

Yvonne pipes in, "Did you two see the Sea Lion Swim on our brochure?"

Josh answers, "No, what's that?"

She explains, "You two can both participate. We have South American sea lions here and allow our guests to swim with them. The program is about seventy-five minutes and it includes your check in, orientation, interaction and photo processing."

Josh looks at me and I smile, "I am good with doing that if you want to."

Josh says to Yvonne, "Okay we will do that."

She rings up the total and provides us with colored bracelets and we are guided to the change rooms and then to the Sea Lion area to meet the instructor and the animals.

The instructor explains how many Sea Lions they have, their names and what they do. He explains some of the tricks they know and soon our group of four, an older couple, Josh, me is heading into the water with the instructor.

I hold Josh's hand as we go into the water and it's just seconds when we have a sea lion swim up to us. The instructor is just steps away and says, "Go ahead and touch her. She wants a pat."

Josh and I touch her shoulder and she glides by as we pat her back and touch her tail flipper. The animal has short thick fur that I can feel as the creature swims by.

I am happy that we did this instead of the Sea Trek. It is not as though I had the choice but I never thought I would ever be able to touch one of these creatures because they only ever seem to be on display in zoos.

"Josh, can you believe this?" I am like a child all over again. For the first time on this entire trip my mind has forgotten about all of this book stuff and now Sara.

Josh is smiling just as much as I am, "Yah this is cool."

The creature swims around the pool and then back to Josh this time. The instructor says to Josh, "She wants a kiss from you. Immerse yourself up to your shoulders so that she can reach your cheek."

We are about chest deep in the water and Josh lowers his body so that it is just his head above water and the sea lion touches her nose to his cheek.

I start to laugh, "Josh you have a girlfriend." He chuckles and says to her, "Aren't you a curious creature. Do you like me?" She sticks her tongue out at him and swims to the older couple in the water.

Josh says, "Did you see that?"

"I did." I giggle.

Josh says to the sea lion, "Well, I feel the same about you too."

He splashes in her direction but not strong enough to splash the older couple. The sea lion takes notice, comes back and jumps over us.

I start laughing and Josh swims towards her he says, "Hey come back here." As he is trying to get her attention, a second sea lion swims up to me.

The instructor says to me, "If you allow yourself to float and hold on to the animal's shoulders, she will take you for a ride."

I do what he says not sure what to expect and as soon as I have both hands on the creature's shoulders, it just knows what to do and we take off around the pool. I get a mouth full of water because I can't help laughing and it makes me laugh even more at being a goof. I let go and see that Josh is getting his own ride on a sea lion when he lets go the creature gives him a high five with its fin.

He says, "Did you see that?"

"I did. Did you see when I was on the other ones back?" I ask him.

"Yes, did you swallow some water babes?"

I chuckle "Yah"

I wonder why in the world they call them sea lions because they are more like dogs, giant sea puppy dogs. They are so playful and affectionate and I can tell Josh is in love with them as am I.

Our seventy-five-minute encounter with the sea lions soon finishes and I can say that my cheeks are sore from smiling so much.

Chapter 45
Citrine

Coral Bay, where we had our sea lion encounter has its own small beach with white sand and a nice little bay to swim. Josh and I say our good byes to the sea lions and thank the instructor for such an amazing experience. We take our towels and walk over to the beach to dry off.

Josh says, "How was that?" If I could freeze this moment in time for him, I would. Deep down I hurt for him in knowing that this high from life that he is on may be short lived.

I push the thought deep down and smile, saying to him, "I think I can honestly say that was my favorite thing that I have done on this entire trip."

"It wasn't signing your contract?"

"Gosh no, I mean I am happy that I did but this memory I will hold on to for the rest of my life. I could tell you were having fun. Was this your favorite thing too?"

Josh nods, "Yah, that one sea lion stole my heart. I wasn't expecting them to be that friendly and their personalities are something else. I didn't know how smart they were."

"I didn't realize either, it was very cool."

We change out of our damp swimwear as soon as we are somewhat dry, get back into our casual wear, and take a taxi back to town.

We arrive in Charlotte Amalie and grab a bite to eat at a sidewalk shop. Nothing hits the spot like a good old sandwich. It is silly how when you get caught up in a day of activity that you don't feel your hunger creep up. I wasn't really hungry when we ordered but taking every bite, I quickly realized that I was and it hits the spot.

We walk the streets, which are rows of buildings that kind of look like old town homes converted into stores and shop fronts. Grey stone buildings with bright colorful doors and window trim. There are flags draped up over top and I see the American flag often as we explore. Lining the streets are rows of vendor tents that are full of summer clothing set up along the sidewalk. Other tents are selling trinkets and cheap jewelry. As we continue down another street, I can see and smell the beautiful flower arrangements, reds, pinks and yellows.

Josh says to me, "So did you have anything in mind to get or are you making a list and going back to buy your favorite things?"

"Oh, I don't know. There is a lot of nice stuff but I haven't seen anything that wows me."

"I understand"

"What about you? Is there anything that you wanted to pick up on the way back?"

"No, I'm good. Well maybe we can pick up some trinkets for the family. There was a stand that had some nice stuff." He pauses for a moment then Says, "You know I don't want you to get all weird or anything but you know that St. Thomas is duty free."

"Yes, I know that." I am not sure where this is going.

He continues, "Well I know I've heard that this place has some nice jewelry stores."

I chuckle, "Have you been talking to Devon?" Now I feel like I am in another dimension. Did my Josh really just mention a jewelry store?

He smiles, "What's that supposed to mean?"

"Well, you have seen all the jewelry that Sara has. I suspect that you were taking notes or something."

"Jordan don't make me change my mind. Anyway, I think the place is just down this way."

We turn down a narrow street, which is wide enough for pedestrians to walk. The buildings are old grey stone and the window sills are lined with window sill flowers and ivy and we come to a bright purple door.

"After you" he says and I walk in.

The place on the inside doesn't match the laid-back tropical feel of the outside. Inside there is deep grey carpet with swirls of black and there is a giant horseshoe shaped shiny white counter with a glass top that displays all of the store's jewelry. Large gold framed color pictures of beautiful people wearing beautiful jewelry decorate the light grey walls.

Josh and I start on the left side and look at the display. I ask, "What did you have in mind?"

He shrugs, "That's up to you."

"Are you for real? Where is my real husband?"

"Oh, Jordan you are sometimes just too funny." He lightly pinches my cheek; he is in a silly mood.

An older man wearing a grey dress pant and white button shirt smiles and approaches Josh and me. He says in a gentle raspy voice, "Are you shopping for a special occasion?"

I look at Josh who answers, "Yes, you can call it that. It's more of a gift to celebrate an achievement."

The man knows not to ask any further, nods and says, "If there is anything you like just say and we can take it out of the display for you."

Josh says, "Thank you."

This is somewhat hard for me. Don't get me wrong I love jewelry but I have no clue what to get myself. I browse the display and see many yellow and white gold chains, bracelets, watches and charms. They are all beautiful but nothing is really standing out until I come across the display of rings.

There are simple bands lined in diamonds. They catch my eye and look like my own wedding band that accompanies my engagement ring then there are these beautiful solitary diamonds, topaz, citrine, emerald, sapphire in all sorts of beautiful settings.

I stop and look at them. Wow, these are gorgeous and the old man takes out the display from under the glass and sets it before me.

He says, "These are all very unique pieces, colorful and vibrant. Please try what catches your eye."

I glance down at the gorgeous rings, what to choose? I already have plenty of diamonds, aquamarine and topaz. Emerald isn't really my color although there are some gorgeous gems here. Maybe I should pick something different, a stone that I don't already own. It will be special to mark this day. This day, gosh its funny how things work out. The best day of my life could still turn into the worst day of my life. The sea lions had distracted me from Sara. I can't be sure about her. Will she tell my husband? Is she that kind of person? I shake my head to try to get the thought of her out.

The man interrupts my day dreaming, "I think you like this one. I've seen your eyes go back to it a few times." He takes it out of its setting and places it on my right middle finger.

The ring is a white gold with a rope design along the band. It has a huge yellow citrine that is square and tiny green garnets surround it.

I say to the man, "I have never seen something quite like this."

"It is eye catching isn't it. Citrine isn't as popular as the emeralds, rubies and sapphires but nonetheless it's a stunning gem and isn't as popular as it should be."

I hold out my hand to get a good view of the ring and say, "I do love it." It's sparkle and color are what draws me in. I say to Josh, "I think this is a good choice. I like it and it's bright like the tropical sun to mark this time. Do you like it?"

Josh puts on a bit of a poker face as if he is ready to negotiate on a big-ticket item. Some things never change. He whispers to me, "It's nice I like it. Do you want it?"

I smile, "Yes this is the one and it's a perfect fit."

He whispers in my ear, "Okay go wait outside."

I nod and carefully hand the man back the ring and step out of the store and wait on a park bench. I'm left to my thoughts alone to think for a second and come back down to earth. I wonder about Devon and Sara and about how Sara found out. How is this going to affect our relationships? I stare blankly at the grey worn out cobblestones on the ground and then am startled with a tap on my shoulder. It is as though only seconds have passed but I have likely been daydreaming for some time.

Josh asks, "Babes what is with you? Every time I leave you, I seem to find you off daydreaming."

"You know me, I can't help it." I shrug.

He shows me a light grey velvet box and says, "To the most imaginative woman that I know." He opens it for me and makes me giggle because of course it is the ring. I pick it out of the box, play along and say, "Oh what a nice surprise. Did you pick this out yourself?"

He winks and answers, "I may have had a little help."

"Well, it is beautiful. I have the nicest husband in the world."

Josh is never one for surprises besides this was so nice of him.

The rest of the day on St. Thomas consists of getting a few trinkets for family back home, a walk and relaxation time at the beach. Soon we are re-boarding the ship. I just want to disappear into my room for the night and not end up in any more drama. We are Wednesday evening and I am now counting down the days to get home and keep my marriage in one piece.

A familiar voice calls out, "Jordan?"

A shiver up my spine, Josh whispers, "I think he is calling you?"

"Please, keep walking, don't look at him." They say you are the one that attracts negativity into your own universe but I didn't ask for this. There is a bit of a crowed on deck as people board the ship, which begins to disperse. I say, "Come on" and lead Josh by the hand but it is of no use, Steven catches up to us.

"Hi Jordan, I was calling you back there."

Disappointed, I put on a fake smile and say, "Oh you know with the crowed things can get pretty muffled."

"Yes, your right. How did you like St. Thomas?" Why is he making small talk with me?

"It was good." I reply while trying desperately to not open up the conversation even further.

He smiles and replies, "I bet and gosh look at that gem on your finger. Wow that is blinding." Instinctively I want to hide it from him. He asks, "Was that some sort of anniversary gift?" He pries.

Josh comes in to save me and says, "It was just a gift from her husband."

Steven says to him, "Well done." He addresses both of us and says, "Well guys I didn't just come here to make small talk I wanted to see where you guys were at in you decision?"

I answer, "Steven we are trying to take as much time as we need to review. I want to look over it again this evening." That's a lie and Steven knows it but is gentleman enough play dumb.

"Well, that is quite alright as long as you are focusing on the contract that means you are steps from a decision." He takes a breath and says, "I know Devon has taken the two of you under his wing. Every author and publisher on board this ship knows that." I have no idea why is Steven doing this, he already told Sara. He continues, "I gave Devon some incentive to help you in making the right decision. This morning my publisher Barb Eaton, I think she introduced herself to the two of you on the first day on board? Well anyway Barb Eaton paid a visit and got to speak to his wife Sara this morning."

What an asshole. I asked Steven not to say anything and so he got Barb Eaton to instead. I can't say anything with Josh around and glare at Steven. He knows I know and I catch that discreet spark in his eye that is only for me to see.

He says to me, "I'll leave you guys be and we can catch up tomorrow?"

I correct him, "I need two full days. We will talk Friday."

"Yes, we shall. See you then." He bows and walks away.

Josh murmurs, "What the fuck is wrong with that guy?"

"I think money talks. He's just persistent, that's all, annoying but persistent."

Josh says, "You told me about him maybe ripping off the bandage may be easier than letting this stuff drag out." I know that he senses that there is something more to it but I can't. I'm not ready to put my marriage through jeopardy. I look into this beautiful man's eyes his soul and see the person that I fell in love with. I see Josh and can't imagine my life without him. Sure, we fight but I need him, love him and can't let him go. I can't and then there is Devon, falling for him so dam hard, the passion in his words, that hot animal desire and it being so easy to open up to him. open my heart and soul and know that he feels the same.

Devon and I are both cowards in that sense but in the other sense we both know that this is a Romeo and Juliet situation except Romeo and Juliet in ours care for more hearts than one and are selfish in wanting both. We are both guilty of it and the hard thing is it's easy for your mind to say it's wrong but when you heart wants it so much, how do you turn that off? You can't, I love Josh and I love Devon, two very different and amazing men.

I say to Josh, "I think before we do anything I should talk to Devon."

"Why, isn't it your choice?"

"It is but Devon knows Steven more than I do and for a certain reason Devon had thought this would be the best thing to do for our situation."

"Okay, well you should talk to him soon so that it's over and done with."

"I agree. Well, I was having a hankering for some chicken strips did you want to have an early supper?"

Josh says, "Sure"

Chapter 46
Opposites

We head back to our room after dinner. Today was a busy day of swimming with the sea lions, shopping and being active has tuckered us out completely. It is only 8:00 PM but we lie down like two old people and pass out.

The room is dark when I wake from rest. I roll onto my back, stare into the darkness and wonder did I wake on my own? What time is it? I glance over at the side table it is 9:45PM. How did I manage to wake up? Whenever I am just beyond tired and go down early, I can never just sleep through the night. It is always that I end up waking and now I feel rested enough that I am wide-awake.

What a day, I look around our dark room as things start to come into focus. Tomorrow will be a full day at sea and then Friday is the Bahamas. Friday will be the day that I will need to give Steven the answer and hope that Josh won't believe what he sees in the photos or a thing that comes out of Steven's mouth.

I notice light in the corner of my eye and glance over to the side table. My phone's screen is flashing with a message it is from Devon.

It reads, "Hey Jordan, sorry about not talking to you today. Things happened. Is it okay to talk now?"

I respond, "Yes I can talk. Josh is just sleeping."

"I want to meet in person. Can we meet in the lobby?"

"I'll be there in five minutes."

I carefully change into some pants and a t-shirt and tiptoe around not to disturb his sleep. I leave a note on Josh's nightstand should he wake. I slip out.

I see him as I leave the elevator and enter the lobby. What a handsome man. Devon is in jeans and a blue golf shirt. His brown eyes spot me. The sad look in those handsome eyes says it all as I walk up to him, I whisper, "I am so sorry, I know, Sara confronted me today. Are you okay?"

"I would like to go somewhere private to talk."

"Okay, sure whatever you want."

He takes my hand in his, leading me. I know where we are going, to our room. We are safe, I think. I ask, "Does Sara know about this room now?"

He has a solemn expression and shakes his head no. I continue, "Well Devon say something to me."

He unlocks the door to our secret room. We both shuffle through the threshold and he says, "Sit down"

"Okay" I murmur.

He sits next to me on the bed. He is quiet, sad and he just looks at me with emptiness. He is never this quiet. His head down and he reaches for me.

Touching my chin with his finger and he leans in and kisses me. It is full of love, want and desire. Tender he holds me in his arms and finally says, "Oh Jordan, my want that I can never truly have." He kisses me on the forehead and touches my lips gently with his fingers.

I know that he is all messed up inside. He is heartbroken and without having Sara to confide in at this very moment, he is turning to me. I whisper to him, "You may want me but you want Sara more. I know my love; I see it in your eyes. You are hurting. It's okay if you want this to stop."

He shakes his head and admits, "But I don't and I won't let it. "

"Devon, I don't understand. Sara knows, I thought you wanted to talk to me about that?" It is as though he doesn't want me to acknowledge it. I persist, "Devon please, this affects my life too. Sara spoke to me today. She told me she knows. I don't mean to sound insensitive but Josh doesn't know. Is she going to tell him?"

"No Jordan, Sara won't get between the two of you. It is none of her business and she is not that kind of person."

"How do you know?"

He raises his voice a level, "Jordan don't question me I know my wife."

I get up and blurt out; "fine" I won't let Devon talk to me like that.

He demands, "Where are you going?"

I turn to face him, resting my hands on my hips. I say, "Devon, I don't need you snapping at me. This isn't only my fault. You aren't telling me why we are here so I don't see a point in staying. I know that our fun is over." I take a step towards the door.

"Jordan, sit down."

"Why?" My hand is touching the door handle as I glance over my shoulder at him.

His voice becomes calm, "Just sit with me please."

He is drunk with pain and I wait for him to talk as we sit in silence. It is like he needs a friend with him and finally he admits, "Sara is not talking to me. I don't blame her; well, she talks to me but it's only if something is required. It's cold, robotic. She has told me that she isn't going to come between you and Josh as much as Josh is her friend, she doesn't want to be the one to bring pain into his life. As for Sara and I, we need each other. She is dependent on me and at the end of the day, I know that you hate when I say this but I do love her and our friendship even though we are in a sexless marriage. I can't leave her and I can't come in between you and Josh and this family that you two are starting."

I don't know what to say without coming across as a complete bitch. It is somewhat good news that she is staying with Devon. It means that he has a chance to mend things between them. We are both married and our partners come first.

I don't say a thing but just snuggle up to him in a defeated embrace. I'm his friend in this moment even though everything is so messed up. I am okay with it and want him to be okay too. I think the reason why I accept this is that my heart aches, emotionally and mentally. I love him but it hurts having that reminder constantly nagging at your heart that what you want most is just out of reach. It weighs heavy on your heart and soul and I am tired of fighting off that pain.

I'm not sure how late it is but we both stay on top of the covers but lie back next to each other on the bed and soon the silence turns to talking. Devon says, "Did I ever tell you the first time that I met Sara?"

"No"

"We had a mutual friend who hosted an oyster roast. We met there, I have never so much as seen her before and well we hit it off. We couldn't stop talking to one another. We flirted, laughed and played and as we consumed more oysters, things led on and fourteen years later, we are still together. Our friends never thought it would last but they say opposites attract. I believe it and not to mention our fifteen-year age gap. It's been so long and she is my friend."

"Time will heal, I think. I know that you will make it right. She will see that you are trying. You are a good man and I don't think either of us had meant for any of it to happen. It just sort of did."

He faces my direction and says, "Jordan you know we are the best of friends and wow if we had only met before either of us were in a relationship everything would be so much easier."

"Yah well this is life and I am learning the hard way that some things no matter how much you want just can't happen. Devon, I love you, I do and I know that you love me too but I also know that you love Sara and I love Josh. I don't want you and Sara to break it off. It hurts to see you hurt. We both are in love with two people and that's it. I know and you don't need to explain it to me."

"Thanks Jordan I just repeat stuff because I don't want either of us to lose sight of reality."

"I know"

We lay there in each other's company for a few moments when finally, I say, "It's late and I should head back to my room. Are you staying here tonight?"

"Yes, Sara needs her space and it is only fair that I give it to her."

I start to get up when the touch of his hand gets my attention. I ask, "What's up?"

"Jordan, I know it is wrong to even think this especially now but I need you. Just for a bit longer."

I know what it is that he wants. I see it in his eyes. It's hard to explain he is sad but he needs my company and feel the love that he is missing in his own relationship. I ask him, "Are you sure that you want to do this?"

"Yes, I need you as a friend." He says as a friend but we both know it is more than that. Friend is just a boundary word that means that we will never be boyfriend and girlfriend or husband and wife.

This situation is all wrong but I need it too. We both crave the release.

I remove my clothes down to my panties, the color, ivory and the material, silk with laced trim. They are soaked because I want him and the mild scent of it is in the air. My curvy body, tight, little warm lips with that cherry red button wanting it.

Devon is rock hard for me and I lie down inviting him to push into me. I moan upon entry. He pushes in deep, letting me feel every inch. My juices are hot from the fire within and my secret sexy man conquers me. I beg with my body to kiss his lips as he thrusts faster and harder. Devon is not playing nice. He is hungry and I know, I am his and with that, he makes me spill. I close my eyes as it throbs. I moan and cream all over the base of Devon's thick shaft, clear, yummy juice. I was trying to hold out a little longer but he knew how to take it from me and he did it because he is greedy for his own.

I want to please him and lick and play and bite, cup and stroke it to the motions that he showed me. Devon is getting close but he says nothing to help me. He wants me to figure it out and I play a little longer as he holds out. Devon doesn't warn me about how close he is. He keeps his sighs quiet and then he surprises me by spilling into my mouth. I swallow his yummy pleasure and lick my lips.

I return to Josh and open the door to our room. A lamp is on and in a quiet voice I say, "Josh are you up?"

He gets up from the bed and meets me at the door, "Keep your shoes on."

I freeze with my foot raised as I was about to take off my flat and glance up at him, "Why, where are we going?"

"I'm not going to be taken for a fool." He says and holds out an envelope with pictures of Devon and me.

"Josh I, I... you know that Steven will do anything. He has nothing to lose and it's his way of trying to get to us."

He shakes his head saying, "Jordan just shut up. Save yourself the lies and leave."

A tear runs down my cheek. I protest, "Can't we talk about this?"

He takes my arm, turns me around and pushes me out into the hallway. He says, "There is nothing to talk about." Coolness in his voice and he shuts the door.

Chapter 47
The Man to Stay

Here we are Thursday morning and the ship is out at sea today. I didn't sleep much last night but had no choice but to go back to Devon's secret room and tap on the door. The two millionaires kicked out of our own rooms.

I stare vacantly at the big window; all I see is deep blue water with wisps of sunlight that break through the depths. This room is below the water. I have no idea if it is nice out or overcast all I know is that morning has come.

I have never spent the night with Devon but it is far from meeting my expectations. I lay there next to the window and under the sheets with my back to Devon. Wanting to sleep or at least try for another hour but it is to no use. I know without looking at him that Devon is up too.

I feel him rustle and I turn to face him. I didn't realize but he had the television on but on silent.

Sounding groggy he says, "Hey girl, I thought you were sleeping."

"Tried to but I can't."

"That's two of us." He says in a sigh.

I stretch under the sheets and say with a tired voice what is on my mind, "I don't get how Steven could do that. I thought he was holding out for a deal with me. Well, the man has played his cards. He is not getting a deal with me now."

Devon admits, "As much as I hate him, Steven is a smart man. He must have picked up that your reluctance was leading to a decline."

"Are you blaming me for this?" I glare at him.

Devon explains, "No, I'm not blaming you. That is not what I meant. Something tipped him off. We may never know. What we do know is he did want a deal with you, so there must have been no doubt in his mind that you were going to back out."

"I don't even know where to begin? At least you have a chance with Sara. I think that this is it for Josh and me."

Devon rolls over to face me, "Jordan don't say that. It's a new day and you are going to fight to save your marriage. I need you to do that for me."

"How, Josh knows about us and he is not the man to stay with a cheater." My voice breaks as tears start to water.

"Trust me, Jordan. We will set this right okay." He takes his thumb and dabs the tear that is running down my cheek.

"Devon why do you want me to try, I mean I know that we love each other. Why are you so determined to do this and not let things run its course?"

"Jordan, I know you well enough to know that you still love him. You're a fighter, you are and it would be a shame for you not to try. You need to at least do that and give yourself the chance. You have a baby on the way. You need to fix this or at least try."

I correct him, "Your baby."

He draws me in for a hug and holds me, "Yes, my gift to you and to Josh. Please Jordan will you listen to me?"

I sniff and try to regain my composure, "I'll listen."

"Okay, I think that I have a plan to make this right."

"Okay." I give it my all to focus on him and not the sadness.

"Do you know if Steven spoke to Josh at all?"

I shake my head, "I don't know. He just had the photos in hand."

"Okay well whether Steven was there or not makes no big difference. We need to downplay those photos and I have been thinking all night for you. I think that I will go with you back to Josh and your room and explain myself."

"No Devon, that won't work."

"Give me the chance. I need to have a man to man with him."

"Devon, maybe you don't know Josh as well as I thought you did. You are asking for a fight. He literally shoved me out of the room last night. Josh was hardly civil with me; he's not going to be with you. I can promise you that."

"That is my choice." He gets up from the bed. He was only in an undershirt and boxers, drops them to the floor and steps into the shower. I lie there for a moment. I can feel it. This is not going to be good. I am only in my panties and I follow him into the shower.

Despite being, two caught cheaters we have not changed our behaviors. We are what we are and it is a stress release.

He gets dressed into his and I get back into my clothes from the night before. We do take a moment to exit the room separately.

I go first and walk down the hall to the elevator. No one is lurking in the hall, no Steven, no Barb, no one and a moment later Devon exits the room and we take the elevator up to see Josh.

Chapter 48
Cute When Mad

I tap on the door gently, no answer and tap again and wait a moment.

I whisper to Devon, "You don't have a chance. He's not going to answer."

"Let me." Devon taps on the door and says, "Josh, it's Devon." We wait a moment in silence. Devon is about to tap again but doesn't because Josh opens it with force.

Josh seems to take no notice of me, glares at Devon and says, "You have some fucking nerve to come face to face with me." He shoves Devon into the hallway wall.

Devon's hands are up in defense, "Look man, I am here to talk to you, a man to man, please."

"Get out of my fucking face." Josh is about to slam the door on us but with taking little notice of me I slipped in behind him.

"Jordan, what the fuck do you think you're doing?"

"Josh, let us in for at least a few minutes. Allow me to at least get my stuff."

His eyes are cold. His face mean, hurt, angry he says, "Get your stuff and leave."

Josh lets his guard down just enough to take no notice of Devon following him into our room. Devon gently closes the door.

I start to gather my things. I do this to buy time and allow Devon to do whatever it is that he had in mind.

Devon is careful in his approach, "Josh I just want to talk to you." Josh says nothing to him and I know that he is trying his hardest not to murder Devon. The silence is a way of restraining himself from throwing a punch. Devon continues, "Look, Jordan said that you had some pictures of us in your hands last night of the two of us making out at the Author's ball."

Josh snaps at him, rushing forward, putting no space between them and locking eyes with Devon, Josh hisses, "Devon I don't need to hear this."

Devon doesn't acknowledge Josh's attempt to intimidate him. He looks back into Josh's eyes and replies, "You do, if you love your wife you need to." Devon takes a breath and I pause for a moment to gauge each of them. Devon continues, "I'm not here to tell you that those are fabricated images or they aren't us. I am not here to lie to your face."

What is he thinking? How does Devon think that confirming the pictures are real will help?

Josh glares at him and takes a step closer to Devon and I hold my breath in fear that punches are going to start to fly. Devon says, "That was the two of us at the Author's ball but what you didn't know is that I was drunk. I know that it's not an excuse but please I need you to know that. The kiss was all on me, not your wife." Devon looks into Josh's eyes before continuing. I think I catch a tiny glimpse of hope in Josh. He stands still with his full attention to Devon who continues, "Josh look I am sorry, drinking is no excuse to how I acted and if you were there you would have seen that after that kiss, Jordan slapped me across the face." He chuckles nervously and continues, "Your wife has a firm hand. Please if this means anything, I know that your wife is hurting big time for you. This wasn't her fault it was just me being a giant douche bag of a man. She loves you and my hiccup from the other night shouldn't be the reason for your split."

My jaw is to the floor as Josh stares Devon down.

Josh repeats to him, "You made out with my wife?"

Devon's voice is but a murmur, "Yes, I kissed..." Josh punches him in the face. Devon stumbles back. The wall keeps Devon from falling.

Josh spits out as if it is a bad taste on his tongue, "Fucker"

Devon knew that was coming and knows to let it be. My southern man knows how to throw punches but that wasn't what he came here to do. He dabs the blood off his lip with his fingers, regains his footing and backs out of the room, grabbing the door handle and letting himself out. Josh's knuckles are red from the one punch. He is still furious but now it is not so much at me but instead at Devon. I stand there in silence waiting for him to cool off.

Josh says, "What the fuck Jordan?"

A tear runs down my face, "I didn't say anything because it was nothing and that was the end of it, nothing more. I didn't want to tell you and have you become worked up over nothing."

"Jordan, I am your fucking husband. You hear me?" He grips my shoulders and says, "I have every right to know if someone as much as lays a finger on my wife. Do you understand?"

I can't look him in the eye and instead fixate on the carpet as I talk, "Josh, I handled it the night it happened."

One of his hands rubs the back of his neck now as he says, "Jordan, dammit please just listen to me as your husband I have every right to know. I rather you tell me then waking up to a knock at the door in the middle of the night then finding you not in bed next to me and photos slipped under the door of you and Devon. Like seriously, what else was I supposed to think? You were gone."

I look up into his eyes, "Josh I'm sorry."

"I wish you would think for a second. If you had told me maybe all of this wouldn't have happened."

I say, "You would have gotten into it with Devon."

Josh is still fuming but a slight smirk crosses his face, "Yes I would have had my moment with him but really Jordan, this blackmail crap with Steven

Peach and all of that bullshit would have never happened. If you and Devon didn't return in time, I was about to pay a visit to tell Sara."

Josh doesn't know that Sara already knows. I sigh and say, "Can we put this behind us?"

He loosens his grip and rubs my arms gently, "Yes, just talk to me that's all that I ask."

"Okay" He is still on edge but his nerves are starting to settle. We are sleep deprived. Bags are under his eyes and I have been nothing but a ball of nerves since he had kicked me out last night.

He says, "What now, do we grab breakfast?"

"I'm not hungry could I just lie in your arms for a bit?" I strip down to my panties and slip in under the sheets he follows me and I snuggle into his arms. Much needed sleep comes quickly.

We wake up around noon. The day it is not wasted, we both needed the rest. We lie there for a few moments and it is like reconnecting all over again. Big fights seem to do that.

I ask, "How's your hand?"

"Probably better than Devon's face" Josh smiles and I roll my eyes and he sees. "Don't give me that. The man deserved it."

I ask, "Will you be able to get along with Devon moving forward?"

"Why do I need to?"

I glare at him, "It's not healthy to hold grudges."

"I'm not I just don't like him that's all."

"Josh, I slapped him, you punched him, isn't that enough? You are forgetting all the good that he has done for us."

This time he rolls his eyes at me, "I'll be good." I glare at him. Sometimes the amount of testosterone that runs through his veins is too much. When Josh gets mad, he sees red. He explains, "I just need time to cool off that's all."

"Okay"

We get up and I peek out the balcony window to check what the weather is like to help me decide on what to wear. The sky is grey and there is a bit of a mist coming down. The chairs on the balcony are wet. I decide to put on some black yoga pants and a hoodie and Josh gets into some light blue plaid shorts and a light blue golf shirt.

The restaurant is quite busy, which I think the rain is the reason. Looking around I see familiar faces and I think I spot Steven a couple of seats over and focus in on the man.

Josh asks, "What's on your mind?"

"Is that Steven Peach over there?" Josh turns his body to look in the direction and I say, "Josh, don't make it look so obvious."

He turns back, "Jordan what does it matter who I decide to stare at. I'm allowed to look." I say nothing and he glances back at the man to get another good look and finally says, "Yes that's him."

"He makes me sick. I'm not hungry anymore."

Josh chuckles, "Oh you are cute when you're mad."

I stare at Steven and catch his eye. He glares at me before the waiter returns to his table. I watch as he pays his bill and then gets up and approaches our table.

He stands over us, "I am surprised to see the two of you here together."

I say, "Steven you're a dick to think that your stupid games would work on us. I asked for a couple of days to think things over and you couldn't even do that for me. I have already accepted another offer."

He looks at the ceiling and laughs before saying, "I thought you had. Well consider my actions a repercussion to stringing me on."

I spit back, "What did you expect me to do? You backed me into a corner." My hands are starting to shake. I hate confrontations. My heart is pounding and I know that my cheeks are flush as Steven just towers over the table.

Josh knows this is making me upset, stands up and says to Steven, "My wife and I would like to eat in peace, this conversation is over. You can leave."

Steven forces a laugh, "Is that so? Well, what if I'm not ready to leave?"

A waiter approaches our table and asks, "Is everything alright?"

Josh, in a low voice tells Steven, "We are done, leave."

I answer the waiter in a raised voice, loud enough so that the tables around us can hear, "Yes everything is fine. This man is just leaving."

Steven smiles, nods his chin to the waiter and then murmurs to Josh before leaving, "You are a fucking idiot to stay with your slut of a wife."

Josh stops him. Placing his hand on Steven's shoulder and forcing Steven to turn around and face him. Josh says to him, "Want to say that to me again. I thought I heard you say something but want to make sure."

The restaurant is quiet; people are holding forks in midair. The servers have stopped serving and everyone's attention is on our table.

Steven says to Josh, "Your wife is a slut."

"Josh No!" It's too late. He clips him in the eye, breaking the skin on his cheek.

Steven addresses the entire restaurant, "Did you see what that man did to me? That's assault and I have a restaurant full of witnesses. Do you think that I won't press charges?"

Josh says, "Whatever, that's not how I see it you were verbally abusing my pregnant wife. We are just trying to eat."

A few of the cooks have come over to escort Steven out and he raises his hands in protest to them and says, "It's okay, like she said, I was just leaving." Steven looks down at me and growls the words, "Don't worry this isn't over."

Luckily, Josh didn't catch that last comment because I'm sure that he would have also been escorted out.

Our waiter comes to our table and asks, "Are you guys, okay?"

I am close to tears, I hate confrontations but I manage to keep the tears in check and say with a shaky voice, "I'm a little rattled but am happy that he is gone."

The waiter smiles and says, "You handled yourself well and he is band from this restaurant. You guys came here to eat and I am here to take your orders."

"Can I have the club sandwich with a diet cola?" I ask.

The waiter nods and glances down at Josh and asks, "For you sir?"

"I'll have what she is having."

The waiter replies, "Coming right up you two." I am surprised that Josh wasn't asked to leave either since he was the one that threw the punch but I guess with a pregnant woman by his side and a restaurant full of people that saw that Steven had instigated the restaurant staff were lenient on us and let us stay.

Josh's fists rest on the table still clenched. Josh says, "I am ready to beat the shit out of that fucker." He is still on edge from what had just happened.

"Please don't. I don't want to get kicked off this cruise. We have a couple days left."

"Yes dear, just saying I won't actually do it. Well maybe give him a warning, stupid fucker."

I roll my eyes. Well at least his mind is off the entire Devon situation but mine is not. Devon, what am I going to do with Josh and Devon? Well, I guess technically Josh and Devon don't need to be in each other's company for the rest of this cruise although I would hope that Josh could leave this cruise without a chip on his shoulder.

We finish lunch and Josh asks, "What do you want to do now?"

"Oh, I don't know, well the rain has stopped did you want to go for a swim on deck?"

He answers, "Meh I don't feel like swimming. Well, I have to make a stop at the drug store and pick up a razor want to do that now?"

"Sure"

We head down and I am not sure what has gotten into each of us. Maybe it was the broad scope of emotions, the high and low or the serge of adrenaline. We are in a good place right now given the circumstances that today has delivered so far. To the onlookers we look relaxed and maybe a little tired but that's okay I rather that than appearing angry or sad.

Am I sad on the inside right now? No, I can't say that I am. I am forever grateful that Devon came to the rescue and ultimately saved my marriage but I am disappointed in myself for not being as clever and feeding Sara a white lie in order to save Devon from the heartache he is going through.

Josh says, "You got that look on you. What's going on in that pretty little head of yours?"

"I'm just re-living the stuff that has happened to us in the last twenty-four hours."

He scoops me into his arms, "Dear, why do you have to torture yourself like that. It's done, let's get passed that. I am okay with it."

"I know. I blame it on my overactive brain."

We walk the aisles of the ship's drug store and follow Josh through the aisles until we find where the razors are."

Josh has a favorite brand that he always buys and they have them. I look at the price on the shelf and Josh grumbles, "Duty free my ass."

I pick up the package, wondering if it is a value pack or something and say, "It can't be that much more."

"Jordan, they are charging eighteen dollars Canadian for two fucking razors!"

Maybe it is the fact that Josh reminds me of an angry cartoon character when he is mad or it is just the fact that he is so bothered over a few extra bucks but I start to giggle.

Defensively he says, "What?"

"Nothing, you're just funny that's all."

He spits out, "Well come on, that's ridiculous, eighteen dollars and it probably costs pennies to make." He huffs.

"Maybe you can look for another brand that's cheaper?"

He grumbles, "I'm going to have too."

"Josh, you know that we are millionaires now, right?"

He glances sideways at me, "That's not the point. The point is I am being screwed over; its robbery is what that is."

He turns to the shelves and starts looking for a cheaper alternative and I decide to smell the men's antiperspirant on the shelf across from the razors. Side tracked for the time being I pop the lids and take a whiff. This one has a flowery scent; the next one has that cheap cologne sent. Oh, that hurts my nose.

Josh turns to me, "What the hell are you doing?"

"Smelling the antiperspirant" I know I just got caught doing something weird. I know that I am tired.

"You are ridiculous."

I pop the cap and bring the antiperspirant closer to Josh, "Here, smell this one. It smells like grandpa."

He waves me off, "I'm not smelling it come on I'm taking these ones."

Josh ends up with the brand that he wanted all along, the eighteen fucking dollar one. It is funny, he is not happy with the fact that back home it is cheaper by a few dollars. I think even after he gets used to the idea of us being rich, he will still make a stink if he feels like he is paying too much for something. The afternoon the clouds clear and the sun comes out after leaving the ship store.

"Josh I'm going to head up for a swim, did you want to come?"

"I think I'm going to head to the gym. I may stop by the pool after."

I head up on deck by myself, sporting a bikini and putting my bump on display. I have a sarong wrapped around my waist and I have my e-reader ready for me to be lazy for the afternoon. I find a nice spot by the poolside and put my things down. I think that I'll go in now.

It is quiet there are a few others in the surrounding chairs and I am the only one in the water. My guess is the other passengers on the cruise are doing rainy day activities like the theatre, movies, casino since that is how the day had started.

I dunk my head and allow my hair to flow behind me. I am weightless in the water and dive with my eyes open into the sparkly blue pool. The chemicals in the pool are not that strong, my eyes don't sting. After a while my fingers and toes begin to wrinkle and I find myself resting on the side of the pool looking at the others relaxing poolside and then I see her.

Sara is by herself on one of the recliners facing the pool. She has a couple of magazines and a fancy looking cocktail on the side table and appears to have a magazine in her lap. At this point, I don't think that she realizes I am here. My guess is that if she did, she would have moved to one of the other pools.

I watch her for a bit. It is clear that she is sad. The skin under her eyes appears puffy and the color in her face is more faded. The strong woman that she projects herself to be unbreakable and very tough. Devon had said that she had a bit of Italian in her. She comes off as one tough cookie but right now her vulnerability. Sara is not crying now but you can just see it in the worn out look of her eyes. Her posture looks broken, sunken and introverted. I watch Devon's beautiful older woman from the poolside and I contemplate on if I should make my presence known. Would it help? I just feel terrible about it.

I am going to regret it more if I leave without saying anything to her.

I get out of the pool and relocate to a chair next to Sara and she glances up to me.

"What do you think you are doing?" She growls at me in a low voice.

"Sara I'm not asking for your forgiveness but I do want to say a few things."

"You really have a lot of nerve." She lays the magazine on her legs and glares at me."

"Sara, I spoke with Devon this morning and know that you two are not separating which I see is good news and a sign of hope. I wanted to say to you that despite everything, Devon loves you. It's not his fault, it's mine. Those pictures that you saw, yes we kissed but what you don't know is how it happened."

Sara snaps, "I think I know dam well how it happened."

"I kissed him after he had a few drinks. I knew and took the opportunity. I have no excuse and I am not asking you to forgive me. I am asking for you to give Devon a chance to show that he truly loves you."

She straightens her back, leans forward in her chair like a cat ready to attack her prey and blurts, "Get out of my face bitch."

I don't waste another breath on her. For an old woman Sara can get mean. Sometimes I can't see how these opposites attract works in Devon and Sara's relationship and its times like these I wonder how he can hold onto a relationship with a cougar.

That was my failed attempt of peace with her. Devon has his work cut out. Women have a strong intuition and I know that Sara is trusting hers and I don't blame her. I tried for Devon's sake and for the sake of our long-term business relationship but it is of no use. I can't fool Sara but maybe my words will bring some sort of closure that straying won't happen.

I gather my things and leave the pool area. I don't want to deal with her glares.

I head over to the gym to see if Josh is still there. I pause, mid step when I see him. Josh is on the treadmill at a brisk walk and he's talking to Devon, who is on the treadmill next to him.

Chapter 49
Different Creatures

I know Devon likes to cycle but I had no idea that he was one for working out in a gym. I stand there from afar watching as the two talk to one another.

They both appear to be calm. They look like two old friends catching up on things. I cannot believe it. Sometimes I wish I were a man. Seriously, when they are mad, they fight, throw a few punches and afterwards they are friends again. Why can't women be like that?

I stand there just far enough for them not to notice but close enough to ease drop.

Devon says to Josh, "The first thing you need once you get back is a good security system. Sara and I invested in one. When more money rolled in, we relocated to a gated community. It's crazy because I never thought that I would need all the security but seriously there are some whack jobs out there and man to man you need to keep your wife and family safe. You know what I mean?"

Josh replies between breaths, "I hear you. We do have a security system at our house now."

Devon interrupts, "It may help in the beginning but trust me the crazy ones will come out of the wood work."

I am dumb founded that they are getting along. I am not complaining but wow. I envy the relationships men have with their friends. I know that moving forward at least for a while being in the same vicinity as Sara will be rough. Women are completely different creatures. It is hard to tell what the future will bring but hoping that time mends that wound for her sake and for Devon's sake.

I approach Devon and Josh who are still moving at a steady walk on the treadmills and say to them, "I am happy to see you two getting along."

Josh says, "Devon's a good guy. It was just a slip up."

I blurt out, "Well I'm impressed." I am shocked actually at how quickly the dust is settling.

Josh rolls his eyes, "Yes Jordan. Devon got what he deserved and we can move passed it."

I glance over to Devon. With some effort, his lips curve up to make a faint smile and a nod to confirm to me that he and Josh are good now. He has the beginnings of a black eye forming. It is bruising below his eye and his eyelid is puffy but his eye is luckily unharmed.

I say, "Well that makes me happy. I have a great husband and a great author friend. Josh I'm going to head back to our room and wash up. You can take your time."

"Okay will do." He pants out.

I wave bye to Devon and Josh and depart for my room.

I feel like I am in the twilight zone or something because what I just witnessed was something that I thought would never happen. I am still confused by it all, well enough of that, Devon and Josh are on friendly terms again which is wonderful.

I check my phone after my shower and notice a few texts from Hailey she says, "Hey Jordan, hope your vacation is going well. Are you famous yet?"

I lay on the bed with my towel wrapped around my mid-section and text her back, "Hi Hailey, vacation has been very interesting! I don't believe that I am famous yet but need you to keep a secret for me until I get back."

I place the phone down for a second to brush my hair and the screen soon flashes. She writes, "I can keep a secret. What's up?"

"I may not be famous yet but want you to know that you are talking to a millionaire. I signed a publishing contract this week."

"Wow Jordan!"

"Yes, tell me about it."

"Do your parents know? Does anyone else know?"

"You are the only other one that knows besides Josh and Devon Chambers. Devon actually helped in me getting this contract. It was with his publisher."

"Well, congratulations!"

"Thanks! I will need to tell you more about it once I am home."

She writes, "Sounds good Jordan."

"Okay talk to you later."

I put my phone down as Josh strolls on into the room. He is glistening from his workout and it is as if he is a new man in comparison to this morning.

I say, "Hey how was your workout?"

"It was great." He kicks his running shoes off near the door and walks into the room.

I don't care that he is damp with sweat and put my arms around him, resting my arms on his shoulders. I ask, "Honestly, are you and Devon good? You're not holding any grudges?"

"We are good." He gives me a kiss on the cheek and strips out of his clothes. I believe him it is just that little voice in the back of my head just wanted to hear it again.

He says, "Come keep me company while I rinse off."

I follow Josh into the bathroom and the pervert in me loves the view of his backside. It is something about a man's butt that drives me nuts.

He says, "You know, Devon and I were talking and that prick Steven had some nerve. I get people will sink to certain lows if they think that they will get somewhere." The shower is already on to let the water warm up. He lays a towel on the floor just outside the shower.

I lean against the vanity, watching him step into the shower and ask, "What are you two up too?"

He peeks around the shower curtain, there are some soap bubbles over his brow and says, "Jordan don't get upset all we talked about is now we are in a whole other playing field where people will pull stunts to try to take their opposition out. What Steven did wasn't much. I mean photos are photos but Jordan you know that our world was so close to crashing down. If he is going to pull shit like that than he, has it coming to him. That is all that I am trying to say."

"Babes what are you doing to him?"

He turns the shower off and opens the curtain. His body dripping and the fresh clean scent is just so yummy. It is hard to stay focused.

He answers while wrapping a towel around his torso. "We aren't doing anything to him."

"Josh come on, what's that supposed to mean?"

"It means Devon is going to have a payback done to Steven, neither of us needs to lift a finger because Devon has others that will take care of it."

"What sort of payback? He's not going to get hurt or anything, right?"

"Nobody is going to get hurt."

"You promise. Josh if something happens to Steven, I don't want this coming back to us."

He touches my shoulders with his damp hands and assures, "You worry too much. Steven is not going to get hurt. It's just an eye for an eye, something that will piss him off, that's all."

"Will you tell me?"

He smirks, "It will be more fun as it happens. You will know by the end of the day tomorrow."

I leave the bathroom and Josh follows me in his towel. I say, "You guys are terrible to sink to his level."

"It's just an eye for and eye. If we do this to him and it becomes news, it will serve as a deterrent for any other people who were thinking of pulling similar crap. It won't interfere with tomorrow, I promise."

Friday is here. The ship has pulled into port and Josh and I are taking a taxi to Atlantis resort in the Bahamas. The morning has been quiet. I think that we are both tired from the entire week. I always wanted to visit this resort and now the opportunity is here.

Josh pays the cab driver, steps out of the taxi and holds the door open for me. The cab behind us is Sara and Devon. Devon is putting on a cheerful appearance while Sara is clearly withdrawn. I know that this is hard on both of them but at least Devon and Sara are together. Devon tries to make the best of the situation. I feel for him. I see he is trying but perhaps it is just that Sara knows that she no longer has his entire heart to herself.

Devon hollers, "Josh, Jordan, what a gorgeous day. We couldn't ask for anything better."

Josh replies, "Agreed, so are you and Sara coming with us today."

Sara, remaining friendly in front of Josh answers, "Oh I'm going to do a bit of shopping and meet up with a couple of friends from the cruise ship later." She forces a smile. Sara knows that Josh does not truly know the extent of it. I appreciate her act of kindness to Josh for caring enough not to hurt him.

Devon asks her, "Is this just a women only thing?"

"Yes dear." She gives him a kiss on the cheek for show and smiles at all of us before continuing on to her own excursion.

I tell Devon, "I had my heart set on swimming with the dolphins today and wanted to go to the aquariums. Apparently, they have a manta ray here and I would love to see it."

Devon smiles and says, "Yah that sounds great Jordan."

I ask the both of them, "Do you mind if we do that today."

Josh says, "It's your day dear."

Devon says, "I am game." Sara leaving him for the day is hurting him. I see it with catching his subtle longing glimpse at Sara as she walked away. I gather that her decision to do something without him came as a surprise to Devon. He keeps his true feelings concealed and I act as though I didn't notice.

I already know the answer but ask just to be polite, "Is Sara meeting you at any point later?"

"No this is strictly a girl's day for her. I'll see her when we are back on the ship this evening."

We walk through the resort and make reservations for the activities. The first is the dolphin swim. Josh and Devon start a conversation that leads to laughing and kidding with each other while we make our way to the first activity. That little voice inside me wants to ask what is going to happen to Steven. I haven't forgotten what Josh said earlier. I decide to leave it be just as Josh has hinted and continue to listen to their chat in hopes that something will give me a glimpse as to what exactly is planned.

Josh says to Devon, "So your friend has got everything covered?"

Devon says, "You bet. I just wish I could be at the dock to wave goodbye when his boat leaves. From what I understand they are leaving now."

I bite my tongue and pretend not to be paying attention and look at the gardens as we walk. Devon says, "Jordan you are too quiet. What is going on in that pretty little head of yours?"

"Oh, I'm just thinking that one day is not enough to do everything here."

"Well, my dear you know what your next vacation is."

"That's true." I can always return to the Bahamas.

Josh asks, "You must be a little bit homesick by now?"

I say, "Yes and no. I would like to sleep in my own bed but as for all the things that we have seen and done I'm not ready to go back."

Devon doesn't come into the dolphin pool. He says, "Guys I'm not feeling the water right now. I'll stand on the side lines and snap a few pictures."

I say, "Devon, I don't want you to feel like a third wheel."

He puts his hands in the pockets of his shorts and shrugs, saying, "I don't feel that way at all, besides it's a nice break from catering to the guests and doing all the author promotional stuff."

I don't push it anymore and let Devon do what he wants. Josh and I are soon in our wet suits and are in the shallow pools ready to meet the dolphins. Josh is funny he plays it cool but I know that he is just as excited as I am to be able to swim with the dolphins. We get used to the water and dunk our bodies in. I glance over at the pools edge and spot Devon standing but he isn't watching us. He is on his cell with his body turned away from us.

Josh swims up to me, touching my shoulder and asks, "What's got you distracted?"

I turn to face him, "Oh I spotted Devon that's all."

He hugs me, "Babes you're in a pool full of dolphins. This is something that you won't get to do every day whereas Devon, you can see him anytime."

A dauphin swims over to us and the trainer says, "Bring your head down. He wants to give you a kiss."

I giggle, "Josh, are you going to get a kiss too?"

"Oh, I don't know?"

The trainer says to Josh, "Go on bring your head down."

The dolphin wades in the water around us with his belly turned to the surface. I reach out and touch the creature's smooth skin.

The trainer explains, "He likes his belly rubbed go on."

We both touch the creature and he swims away doing a flip and swims over to the next family.

A second one approaches us and this is when the experience starts to get a little commercially. It is photo time and Josh and I get some photos with the cute creature. These animals are all play and given their size, they are so gentle.

The time that we paid for in swimming with the dauphins wraps up. Josh and I exit the pool and change back into our clothes but Devon is gone. Devon knows what we were doing next and Josh and I make the choice to move on to the aquariums.

As we walk Josh asks, "What do you think about Sara and Devon."

"I think they're good friends and nice people."

"No that's not what I meant. Don't you think that it's odd that Sara went off and did her own thing?"

He can tell when I am lying most of the time and I am going to answer truthfully, "I thought it was strange."

"Do you think something is going on between those two?"

"I have a feeling something is up." I am careful with my words. I rather not speculate with him any further.

"Yah I got that impression too. Sara seemed to be in such good spirits and now it's just strange, distant."

I exhale and say, "I think it had something to do with what Steven Peach did. I think she is a little rattled by the photos."

"Does she believe otherwise?" He stops to grab a hold of my response and I am careful to answer. I say, "I mean, we know what those photos were and we know that people can get bold when they are drinking. You know that I would never stray but I think she views it as there was some underlying truth to his actions." He glances at me concerned and I continue to explain, "Drunken people can be very honest and I think she sees it as Devon likes me more than he should and maybe on the reverse doesn't desire her?" I gulp and continue, "I think that I am reaching here. I mean you and Devon had the chance to talk and you know Devon was being honest."

Josh says, "Do I?" His voice has risen.

I confirm, "You do. I was just a pretty woman all dressed up and he got confused. I think that she is upset with him allowing it to get to that point." Josh has that look where he is starting to question further and I need to straighten this one out. I explain, "I could easily put myself in her shoes. I would be hurt in finding out that you were attracted to another. We know that it was just one of those moments and I am sure whatever it is that she is going through, the dust will settle. I think it is just that initial shock of it. They have been together for over fourteen years and I think this is the first instance of something like that happening."

Josh says, "Yes that's a hard situation. It was a bit different with me finding out you slapped him across the face and that it was his first move and not yours. It makes a difference."

"Josh when you found out I nearly died. I didn't think you would forgive me and I especially didn't think that you would forgive Devon."

"You I could forgive. It wasn't your fault but Devon you are right. Normally I wouldn't have let it go but I am glad I could listen and hear him out because this business relationship is everything that you worked to achieving. If you ask me about how I feel about what happened at the Authors Ball, yes I am still pissed off but at the same time Devon got what he deserved and it can be put to rest." He sighs, "Here we are talking about it again but I guess that it sort of had to come up with talking about Sara."

I smile, "Yes, well changing topics I can't wait to see that Manta ray."

There is no denying that this place is a touristy area. All of the places that we have been are tourist spots but this one tops them all. It is the resort of resorts and Josh and I visit the aquarium. It is like no other that I have seen. It is as if you are at the floor of the ocean and their tanks are full of large and small fish, sharks and even divers who are feeding them. You can't help but stop and stare in wonder of everything that you see. The tanks have the theme of peering into an underwater ancient ruin site with these beautiful status and pillars along the floor.

There is a tunnel that we walk through where the ceiling is glass and overtop is water and fish swimming overhead. You can hear a pin drop in this dome. Everyone in here is gazing at the sights.

We arrive to the area where the manta ray is and it is just amazing. He is not as big as they can get in the wild. He is a younger one I suppose. He moves like an underwater bird, quick through the water and with little effort. He is beautiful. Even though this place is an attraction there has been many articles published on the manta program they have here. The mantas are on display but they don't live here forever. Eventually this giant beauty will be helicopter carried to the ocean in a giant net. It is nice to know that he won't be in captivity forever but if he was, this has got to be one of the most amazing aquariums that I have seen. It would have been a good alternative to the ocean.

I see Josh's eyes look on in amazement as the creature swims by.

He says, "How is that babes?"

"It's beautiful. We have to come back here again for a full week."

"I would be good with that."

"Really?"

"Yes really. You worked hard and deserve it."

I smile, "Wow thanks babes. Will you come with me?"

Josh takes my hand as we continue on our way to the next exhibit he says, "Honey I have an idea of what will happen when we get back to our lives but I am not sure if I will quit right away. Devon spoke to me about all of it. As long as I have time available to book it off, I will be right by your side."

I say nothing but smile. Sometimes the things that come out of Josh's mouth are so sweet. Josh and I explore for the rest of the day and enjoy the accommodations on the resort. The beach, the water park, the shopping, it is a nice ending to a life changing week. The only thing that feels weird is that unsettling feeling of the damage that I have caused to Sara and Devon. We didn't run into Devon or Sara for the rest of the time at the resort.

It is time to board our ship and tomorrow we will be back in Florida and soon boarding our plane back home.

It is now evening and for a change to the end of the week, Josh has made a reservation for us at a posh steakhouse restaurant on board the cruise ship.

He wears a nice blue-collar shirt and khaki pant and I wear the same cocktail dress that I wore earlier in the week.

A server in a clean pressed shirt and pant greats us.

"Reservation?"

Josh says, "It should be under Josh."

She asks, "For two?"

He confirms, "Yes"

"Okay right this way."

We walk through the restaurant and she seats us at a table for two along an oak finished wall with a giant oil painting.

A waiter comes to our table as the greater shows us our seats. She asks, "What would you like to drink?"

I say, "Can I have an iced tea?"

Josh says, "Make that two please."

The waiter says, "I'll be right back."

Josh says, "So I can't remember the last time I spent this much time with you."

"Yes, tell me about it. It's been a nice change to you being gone and working all of the time."

The waiter comes back with our drinks and we place our orders before they leave again.

He holds up his glass and I copy him Josh says, "Cheers to a great week and to the start of a new life!"

"Cheers!"

I have to ask because it is just eating me up, "So are you able to tell me what happened to Steven Peach today?"

He starts to chuckle, "You have been thinking about that all day, haven't you?" His cheeks are rosy from his laughing.

"I admit that it has been weighing on my mind. You and Devon haven't said much about anything which kind of concerns me."

He laughs, "Well I guess it is safe to tell you now because it's done. Don't ask me how but Devon found out what Steven had planned for today at the resort. Anyway, he learned that Steven had planned to do a dive and well Devon was kind enough to tip off the organizers of the dive to extend Steven's time out there so that he would miss boarding the ship in the evening."

"Josh that's terrible!"

"He deserved it. It's payback that's all."

"I don't understand how he managed that. I am sure Steven wears a watch or the people would have the time posted somewhere on the dive boat?"

Josh chuckles, "Devon had it all arranged he spoke to the crew beforehand, told them that Steven needed some fun time and told them to make sure that he wasn't aware of what time of the day it was. I'm not positive but I think Devon asked that they set their clocks and hour back. Not sure but whatever it was it worked."

I chuckle, "Geez you guys are awful but honestly that's a great pay back."

Our food arrives to the table. We are each having steak, medium rare with a baked potato and side of Caesar salad.

I have to ask as he cuts into his steak, "How do you know that it all worked? We never saw Devon since the dolphin encounter."

"I checked my phone when you were getting dressed. Devon texted and said everything worked to plan."

"I get it. I wonder what Devon and Sara are up to tonight. I didn't see any messages when I checked my phone earlier."

Josh shrugs, "He never said but then again I never asked."

Dinner was excellent. I ate too much and blamed it on my pregnancy.

When we get back to our room, I am not sure how but my Josh is hungry for dessert. I see it in his eyes. This week has given him rest and he is ready for play.

He comes from behind me and holds me in his arms, nibbling up my shoulder to my neck and then tilting my head so that I face him and we lock lips. His kiss is light little and he only gives me a taste and making me want more.

I try to go for a grab at his goods but he pulls away and instead goes in for a feel at me. His kiss has already made me wet. There are no games with him we know what the other wants and he put himself into me careful but playful and he pretends that his belly is getting in the way. Mine is starting to. A week on vacation proves to pack on a few pounds but whatever. Josh presses into me and he gives me a first one and moments later a second.

He slows for a second and asks, "Have you had enough?"

"I'm good"

He turns me around so that he takes me from behind. That is his favorite position to finish. Efficient but it is always good and as always, I have drained him of his energy. I am wide-awake and he turns in for the night.

Our sleeping patterns no matter what we do never seem to line up. He is sleeping like a baby within minutes.

While Josh sleeps, I sit in bed. I reach for my phone and check things out. I have no messages, there is nothing interesting on social media and I am all out of writing ideas for tonight. It is about twenty after nine. Devon may or may not be up right now. I send him a text and if he doesn't respond so be it. I know that keeping me at arm's length is best given the Sara situation and I won't hold that against him.

I write, "Hey, hoping that things are looking a little more up. Josh and I missed you today but no worries we knew that you had some things happening. Josh told me about the payback. You men are bad! Good for you to pull it off and it was funny as hell. Anyway, if I don't hear from you, have a good night." I click send.

He responds within a moment, "Things are kind of bad. Sara stayed in the Bahamas."

"Why?"

"Sara said that she needs time away from me. She is still pissed. I don't blame her."

"So, what did you do? Did you end up staying behind?"

"Jordan, I wanted to but she insisted that I go and besides I still have the final party that I need to make an appearance. I'm texting you right now from the party and tomorrow morning I was going to say my goodbyes to the guests I brought."

"Oh, Josh and I completely forgot about the party."

"You're not missing much. It's just the same old."

"I am actually in bed right now and Josh has dosed off for the night. All the fresh air I guess."

A moment passes before his next text comes in. "Jordan, I know I shouldn't be asking but this is the last night and I likely won't see you for a while. Could we meet?"

I glance over at Josh who is snoring away. He is out for the night, I glance back at my phone screen and ask where and Devon answers, "The room where I am staying not the secret room."

"When?"

He sends me a smile, "Now is good. I made my appearance for the night. I want to see you."

"I'll be there in ten minutes."

I send Josh a text in case he gets up and I am not here, "Hey was feeling restless so I stepped out for a bit. I have my phone on me so message me back and I'll come get you."

I carefully get out of bed and slip back into the cocktail dress that was left on the floor from earlier and tip toe to the door and let myself out. It is just time with Devon and I feel comfortable with him that I don't bother to do my hair or put any makeup on. I walk down the hall and to the elevator. This feels all too familiar. I feel like Steven Peach will creep out of the shadows and make some threat to me about getting inside Josh's head. Instinctively I look around and then the elevator dings, announcing its arrival.

The doors open, a man and woman are all laughs as they step out. Her upper lip is a little pink. They were making out just now and smile as they walk past and I step into the elevator.

Up to Devon's floor and he has left the door open a crack so that I can let myself in. I close the door behind me and step out of my sandals. They were the only shoes that I could slip into quickly.

I say, "Devon?" He emerges from the bedroom in a fluffy white bathrobe his hair wet from having showered. I say, "Didn't you just get back from that party."

He smirks "I did but it only takes a second to rinse off."

I approach and give him a hug and he demands a kiss. I say, "You know that I still feel terrible about you and Sara. I wish you had told me something better like that she returned to the ship, to you."

He holds my head in his hands smiles and says, "I don't feel terrible. Sara will come around; besides we have more time together and that is priceless to me." I give him a look. I know he is keeping his hurt for Sara inside and he assures, "Really Jordan don't worry about it. She will come around eventually."

I ask, "Is this what you want? I mean, I want you but I don't want to make matters worse."

He plants his lips on mine. He is so commanding yet gentle and it makes me forget. I am his and he is mine.

He pulls the dress over my head, tosses it on a side chair and carries me to the bed.

I am lying down and looking into those handsome brown eyes of his. I glance down at his massive erection. Thick, long and hard he guides himself in and closes his eyes as he pushes in further. My body invites him, craves him and I sigh at the feeling. He feels right. I enjoy every second that I have left with my friend and the father of my child.

"Jordan, I never get tired of fucking you." He says between breaths as he works on mine.

"I love it when you fuck me." I am his and nothing else matters. He kisses, touches, pushes deep and he has me exploding in moments.

I close my eyes and let my sighs leave my lips and each sigh ignites a fire in his eyes as he keeps me pinned with his shaft.

He tucks a pillow under my back and works on his. I love it when he goes for his. Devon is greedy, hungry and my body just gives in to everything he wants. He grunts as his release flows into me. I want him to be happy and after he slows, I see a true smile light up his face.

He asks, "How was I?"

"Amazing as always, why do you ask such an obvious question, can't you tell that I crave you?"

He kisses me on the forehead and replies, "I can tell but I just wanted to hear it from a beautiful woman's lips." He gets up and goes to the shower and I do the same and join him in a quick rinse off.

Still damp from the rinse, I pick up my phone to see if Josh has messaged me and Devon comes up from behind me and pushes his hardness into the crack or my butt cheeks and asks, "What are you looking at?"

"I'm just checking if I had any messages from Josh. By the way you are bad."

"Am I?"

"Yes, you are." I put my phone down onto the bedside table as he reaches around to feel my girl. I already feel weak in the knees. He knows what do and laughs at my shudders that he is causing.

He guides me to the living room this time and lays me on the couch. He tucks some pillows under my butt to lift me up and warns me. "You know I have never done this before. I want to take you from behind."

"Okay"

He smiles, "I long to taste my pie first and don't be surprised when I lick that other spot."

Did he just say what I thought he said? I have had it from behind but never had a man go down and lick me there.

He dives into my muff, being greedy with that talented tongue of his and he makes me twitch turn and convulse. He holds me in place so that I don't budge from his mouth. He laughs in between licks.

He says, "Come on girl. I know you have it in you."

He clamps down and flaps his tongue back and forth over my swollen spot and I squirt into his mouth. He laps me up and then presses his finger inside to feel my vibrations. I gasp.

He grins, "I wish I could take you home."

He pulls his finger out making me moan and licks it clean.

His tongue is heaven. He knows exactly what to do. He knows my body more than I do. I am tired, my muscles clench and relax and I can feel the wetness dripping up my backside and Devon continues to focus on my cherry spot and as he bites and licks, I explode again.

I am a sopping mess. This time he watches me and places two fingers into my girl while I still pulse. I try to sit up. I want to play with him but he won't have it. He says, "Let me enjoy my pie."

I lie back down as he pushes his fingers inside and out and then he surprises me with his thumb as he presses into my other opening.

I jump at the surprise and he whispers to me, "Take it, I want to be in there." I nod and say, "I want you."

He presses in and my eyes roll back. He pulls my ass cheeks apart and licks me down there. He licks up all that has trickled down from my girl and presses his fingers inside. I have given in entirely to his pleasure.

I am so drenched and soon enough he grants me a break and orders me, "Suck my dick girl."

I bend over him and slobber all over his shaft and soon enough he lies back and my knees are at his head and I pleasure him with my mouth.

Devon has his tongue on me and his fingers thrusting into my ass as I deep throat his rock-hard shaft and squeeze his balls. He explodes in my mouth and I explode into his but we don't stop.

We work on each other and soon he stands us up and makes me go on my hands and knees on the couch as he stands behind me and enters my other opening.

He slides in with a bit of force. I reach under and grip his balls as I hear his sigh, "Wow you are tight."

His shaft feels massive inside my back opening. I stay still as he pushes further. He hurts a bit but it is a pleasurable pain and soon he is moaning and I can feel him pulse. Devon stays inside me and guides me down. He sits on the couch and I sit on top with him still deep. My back is to him and he pinches my tits and touches my cherry as we rock back and forth.

I say, "Ah Devon you don't know what you do to me."

"I do babe. Bounce for me."

In his lap, I start to bounce as he keeps his fingers pinching my cherry. This time I feel in control and my body wants him. I am hungry and want more. Up and down and I start to speed up and thrust harder. I let go and whine a little as I throb and he holds me close and says, "I could feel it."

He turns me on my hands and knees and goes slowly this time. I never get tired of his hands on my hips as he gets off.

Devon and I wash up just to keep the affair hidden. Even though back door is pleasurable, it always makes me want to shower after. We both do and it is for the best. It is just a force of habit.

After showering and slipping back into my clothes I pick my phone up off the bedside table. It is approaching midnight and so far, so good, there are no messages from Josh.

Devon has slipped into some athletic shorts and a t-shirt. He looks ready for bed and I think I am in need of some rest also.

He says, "It's times like this that I just want to keep you for my own, steal you and take you away."

I chuckle, "We must have been lovers in another life. I wish I were yours. I think with this contract we will have more opportunities to see each other."

Those cute lips form a smile and he says, "The world is now yours my dear. I know we will see more of each other. You can buy some land for the horses that you were talking about."

"Yes, and move closer to you." I add.

"I like your thinking."

"Well, I better return back to my room." I let the words linger on my tongue for a moment. It is like playing a game of who is going to make the move. Just then my stomach grumbles.

"Holy smokes Jordan are you hungry?"

I smile, "Guess our workout gave me an appetite."

He suggests, "You can say no if you want but seeing that Sara is staying in the Bahamas tonight and Josh is asleep did you want to step out for something to eat?"

"Sure, I was going to grab some pizza on my way back to tell you the truth. Having your company is a bonus."

Chapter 51
Bond of Lovers

Devon and I go to one of the twenty-four-hour cafeterias onboard the ship. Funny thing is that this is my first visit to this cafeteria and will likely be my last since tomorrow or rather later today I will be back in Florida for the flight home.

The place is busy and I guess that this is normal with all of the late-night parties and people who are hungry after an evening of fun. It is an open floor with tables and chairs and booths to accommodate a couple of hundred. Along the back wall is a long buffet that has everything to fulfill any craving for any part of the day. Devon and I grab a tray, plate and some cutlery and we jump ahead to the pizza section. We both grab a slice of Hawaiian and find an empty booth.

Taking a seat, I say to Devon, "I don't mean to be a downer but what are you going to do about the entire Sara situation?" That glimmer in his eyes fade, his lips fall to a straight line. When I say her name, he looks down. I continue, "I am asking as your friend. I do care for your happiness."

"I know you do." He looks up at the ceiling for a second inhales and exhales and says, "Play it day by day I guess."

I know he does not like this but as a friend, I need to know and ask, "Tomorrow when we get to Florida will you take a flight back out to the Bahamas to try and smooth things over?"

He chuckles and shakes his head, "Oh boy, you don't know her. I am returning home. When Sara is upset, it's best to give her space and let her cool off. I do have a plan in mind it sounds mean for me not to chase after her but it's for the best that I just go home."

"What's that?"

"I'll give her a few days. I need the time to work anyway and then I will cut off her allowance. She will either call me to talk or just come home once she takes notice."

"Devon, I know I have already overstepped but I'm your friend and I don't see how you can make this situation any better by doing that?"

He shrugs, "We are not the typical couple. I have never cheated before. We don't love each other the same as we once did. We don't hate each other but for a long time we have been like roommates in a sexless marriage. This isn't new to us. We have separated over the years so I know when she needs her space but we don't hate each other. She will come around." He shakes his head, "I love her and she knows that I have needs too. I need to feel love and intimacy and feel wanted; am I bad for wanting that?"

"No, I think that's fair Devon. That's what I think every human deserves."

He shrugs, "Don't take it the wrong way but if I had the full relationship with Sara meaning the friendship and the intimacy, I don't think I would have strayed. Let me re-phrase that. I wasn't looking to stray to begin with. When I started talking to you it just sort of happened."

"We are in the same boat. I wasn't looking either. I think we were both in need of a friend and then it evolved."

"Exactly, anyway to bring home my point Sara will come around. Fourteen years together we have been through good and bad, she will return. She is feisty but she will come around." He gives me a smile when he says it and I believe him.

We continue to sit and eat and while we do, I think about if I were Sara, I have no idea what I would do. My first instinct would be to leave him but with Sara being older and perhaps she feels the need to stay since Devon can provide a financial security. I don't know. I do think they have more of a friendship bond than a bond of lovers. I guess I can see why she would go back to him.

I ask, "Do you think that she will eventually tell Josh?"

"No, you haven't seen her caring side that I know and fell for. Deep down she has a good soul. I know she is fond of Josh and she knows how important it is for a baby to have their mother and father. She wouldn't want to be the one to hurt Josh and she would not want to be the cause of a demise of someone else's family. There is no doubt that you are her enemy for life and she's not afraid to make that known but she won't bring down your house. She rather you do that yourself."

I take a bite of my pizza and nod, "Well, I get that she is mad. She will eventually forgive you but for you to say I am her enemy for life?"

He puts his hands up, "Hey I am just saying, as her partner I know how she is. She is too proud to blame herself and I am her man. She needs someone to blame and it's you. Besides didn't you kind of say something to her earlier about it being your fault?"

"Yes, I did."

It seems out of place but he chuckles, "I know at the time you probably thought that you didn't help the situation but what you said got to her. You planted a seed. It will help. I know she will come around because in her mind it's your fault."

"I just have to accept that then. I hate that another person in this world hates me but since you tell me that it worked, I am happy, I guess. I just wish Steven Peach didn't mess everything up."

"That makes two of us and besides you think many people hate you now? Once you become the household name, I know you will become a lot more people will hate you, trust me."

I shrug, "Yes but that's not the same, they will be complete strangers. I know Sara."

Devon warns, "It won't be just strangers. I've learned who my true friends are after becoming successful. People who you thought were your friends will grow jealous and will come to hate you.

I know this sounds crazy but this has happened to me and wouldn't be surprised if you experienced it too."

I am chewing on my last mouthful of pizza. I believe him, aside from the affair, Devon has never led me astray. "Okay well in that case I will get used to it. I think this pizza has given me an appetite for bed."

Devon says, "You read my mind."

I glance down and my phone it is approaching 2:00 AM and there are no texts from Josh. I look back up at Devon and ask, "I was going to go back to the buffet and grab a couple of slices for Josh. Do you want to come?"

"Sure, but why not grab some bagels or donuts for the morning. He's probably sleeping if he hasn't texted you by now."

"He would appreciate the pizza more and cold pizza in the morning is amazing."

Devon rolls his eyes, "Silly girl well what's that saying, to each their own?"

Chapter 52
A Good Sore

The next morning is bitter sweet. I am looking forward to really starting on this new journey but at the same time, I don't want to leave the fantasy of this cruise. I am a little sore from last night's romps but it is a good sore, a nice reminder of Devon.

Josh is already up and munching away at the pizza, I had brought back to the room last night. He is sitting on the bed in shorts and a t-shirt just devouring the cold pizza and notices me starting to stir

"Hey babes, did you sleep well last night?"

"Yes, well I ended up waking and stepped out for some food and fresh air."

"I saw your texts this morning and the pizza is good."

I smile, "I went to that twenty-four-hour buffet. I figured you would enjoy it."

Josh is like a grown-up child in a sense that he is always up at the break of dawn where I like to sleep in. I can tell he is ready to get back to civilization. I know that he enjoyed the vacation that Devon was so kind to bring us on but Josh is a homebody and I know he is ready to get back.

I sit up and take a small slice to fill my growing belly. Josh asks, "Have you talked to your parents at all while we have been here?"

"No, only Hailey, mom and dad don't know yet. Have you told yours about my contract?"

"No."

I say, "These coming days will be interesting and I am pretty sure my belly grew another inch this week. My clothes feel tight."

"That's all the junk food you've been eating."

I make a face at him, "don't be rude!"

"I'm not. I'm just stating the facts. Anyways when is our departure?"

I left my purse tucked in the drawer of the side table next to the bed and reach over to get it. All of the travel information is inside.

I pull out the information and read, "It says that we arrive in Florida at noon and our flight leaves at 1:00 PM and we should land at about 4:00 PM which means with the drive home we should be home after 5:00 PM."

I could walk you through our play by play from now until we got home but to be honest it's just a routine. Everything goes to plan. We depart the ship say our goodbyes to Devon and shake hands with my new publisher and business partner, Howard Stem. Josh and I take a short drive to the airport and fly home first class.

The drive home is just the two of us is relaxing, quiet and somehow just driving down that highway it's contorting that this feels right and I already feel at home.

We open the door to our home and it has that familiar smell that I can't truly describe mixed with the faint smell of vanilla candles. The air is a little bit stale from us being away all week. The light on our cordless phones are flashing, alerting us of messages. I will leave it to Josh to listen to the voicemail.

The way this cruise was planned out gives both of us Sunday to rest before starting up with going back to work come Monday morning. It is weird to think about it but the question has been dwindling on both of our minds, do we quit our jobs come Monday? Trust me we went back and forth about it all of Sunday and even into Monday but decided to wait. I laugh just thinking about it because boy did, we want to.

The only thing that we agreed on is that we needed to take Thursday and Friday off because Howard Stem was flying us to New York in order for me to make my first appearances to promote my book.

The dreaded Monday arrives but this morning I have to admit that this isn't as dreaded as the typical Monday morning. It is as if a weight has been lifted and that whatever stresses that the workplace brings, I really don't care because now I have my freedom. I no longer feel bound or obligated to work through the stresses of work.

The office is quiet when I arrive. There are a couple of others in early like me and my co-worker who sits in the cubicle next to me peeks in.

"Hey Jordan, you are tanned. So how was your vacation?"

I swivel around and say, "It was great. That was my first cruise and I would totally do it again." I recap my week with her and tell her about signing on with the publisher and such. She listens intently as I go through the details.

She asks, "That ring, did you get it while you were on vacation?"

"Yes, it was a present from Josh. I typically wouldn't go for a yellow gem but I don't know this one just caught my eye."

"It's beautiful."

"Thank you, so enough about me, what has been going on here?"

She shrugs and exhales before answering, "Oh you know, the same old stuff. Senior management has their heads up each other's asses. We had some more unreasonable deadlines and to add to the stress they have given termination notices to all of the temporary staff. It will overload us with more work. Like we can even handle what we are already managing. I don't know why they thought letting go the temporary staff was a smart move."

I listen and if I didn't have the book contract this would stress me out but know that this doesn't need to be my life anymore. I never told her the extent of my contract. She doesn't know that she is talking to a brand-new millionaire. I answer, "That's really shitty. Wow, so much crap goes on here in a week. It makes you wonder if they are slowly shutting down our program."

She chirps up, "Who knows what they are thinking. I don't think they are shutting us down but if they are all the permanent staff are safe. Whatever happens, we will end up getting absorbed into another area."

I ask, "So anything else going on, any new gossip?"

"No, just the layoffs, I think that's enough drama for one week." She changes topic, "So how is that little baby of yours?"

"Growing and kicking. I am not sure if it was all the food I ate or this baby but I think my stomach grew and inch."

She chuckles, "I see it. I wasn't going to say but yes you are looking a little rounder but it's just in your stomach. I don't think the weight went anywhere else. You look great Jordan."

By mid-morning, the office fills up and soon the humming of phones ringing, people typing away, the printer going and the coffee machine brewing. People stop by my desk to welcome me back and eventually my boss stops in.

"Hey Jordan, can we talk today?" She is in a rush with not bothering on the small talk.

"Sure"

She explains, "It's completely my fault. I forgot about your vacation, your performance review was due last week and I need to get yours done. I have some time now. Would you mind if we chatted now?"

I put on a brave smile these reviews are never fun. It is always you are doing well "but" and that word just screams in the sentence; but you can always do better. To be honest I don't care anymore. Maybe I should just quit.

I follow her down the hall and take a seat in her office as she closes the door for us to have a private discussion. I know that when the door is close it means bad news.

She takes a seat at her desk and starts with small chat as she brings up her notes of me on her computer. "So, I gather that you heard the news about the temporary staff?"

"Yes, that is terrible. What was the reasoning behind it?"

"Senior management is saying that it's because of budget cuts but who knows maybe if they stopped spending their money on office supplies like those three new shredders in the building, we would be able to retain some of the staff. We need them."

"So, they aren't going to be filling the vacant positions with permanent staff?"

She laughs, "No, they don't think we are working hard enough as it is." She rolls her eyes as she explains and continues, "So you have a pretty good idea of what it is that you need to work on this year. We have already chatted about it here and there throughout the past few months. I think that you did start the year a little rocky with joining my team and the good news is I think that you are coming along. We talked about paying closer attention to detail in your work, keeping notes and regularly checking email. I believe that you are on your way.

I do worry sometimes that your mind is elsewhere as if you are distracted. Maybe it's me but I don't know. What are your thoughts?"

This is not a great performance review. Normally I would feel concerned about this and I am well somewhat but not really because this is no longer my life. I clear my throat and answer, "I do have a lot on my mind. There are things that have been going on in my personal life, starting a family, working on my relationships and working on my hobby. I do care about the quality of the work that I do but at the same time, I don't want the biggest regret in my life being that I spent so much time worrying or being occupied with work. I have worried about it for a while and you know what, this place isn't doing it for me anymore. I used to love coming in but with all the cutbacks and having to stay late and work harder because senior management isn't replacing the staff is not doing it for me. Sure, I don't mind putting some extra time in here and there but this is starting to become routine. The tight deadlines, staying late on short notice isn't fair and then I am criticized on not being able to perform my normal duties to high standards.

Maybe we need to take a step back and realize that there is too much being asked. Something has got to give."

I exhale as I spit that all out at her. My publishing contract has given me that little extra confidence. Normally I would have not said what is really on my mind.

She fixes a smile on her face for a brief second. It is more of a wow I wasn't expecting that, this isn't going to go as planned kind of smile.

I explain, "I do like the people that I work with. I like the overall nature of the work but the demands that are being forced on us aren't reasonable and to be honest, yes I am sort of checked out."

She nods, "I do agree but with a different director managing the staff things have changed. I think that we need to find a balance that works for you and I think that with a little more effort we can get you there. I want you to first start with filing and tracking everything, maintaining your notation system and continuing to prioritize your email. You are off to a good start. I am going to approve the two courses that you had suggested but I am going to add a work management course."

I nod, "That's fair."

She says, "Great, I am taking this as a positive step I do think you are on track. Before you sign off on me delivering your review is there anything else that you want to add?"

"I need to finalize my maternity leave and I need to ask for a couple of days off this week."

She says, "Oh sure, go ahead and give finance a call to make the appointment and let me know if you need anything from me. For the time off, I would prefer if you held off for a bit. We have a lot to do right now and I need you caught up."

I let a sigh escape my lips and say, "I will make the appointment with finance this week but the time off needs to happen." I take a breath and explain, "Last week I signed on with Tail Fin Books and my publisher is flying me out to New York City Thursday morning to work on some promotions for my book."

Her eyes go wide with surprise, "Jordan, wow congratulations that's great news. Really, I mean it but I know I can't control what you do but I really can't approve your time off. Senior management will question me doing that especially when it's all hands-on deck. I have to ask, if you're flying out this week for your book contract that's one thing but how much more is this going to interfere? Will this become a regular thing?"

I smile but try to stay composed, "I have no idea how much time it will demand. After returning from the cruise, I really had to debate on if I should quit. I decided to stay. I think I can find a balance and besides I do think that this is just a one off."

She says, "What if it's not?"

I say, "My due date is coming up. I only have months left here until I am off for the year. Is there a possibility of being able to work a shorter schedule, like doing income averaging? Maybe I could take some sort of leave without pay. I don't think it will get to needing a lot of time off. My publisher knows that I am pregnant. I can't do any major book tours or anything. Can we play this by ear?"

"We can but Jordan I can't approve more time off."

This is out of character for me normally I would give in to my bosses demands but my dream is now my reality and I'm not turning my back on my dream, "I won't ask you to approve time off but I will ask for you to approve personal leave. This job here pays sixty thousand a year but my contract with the publisher is worth far more and I have to go."

I hold my ground. We look into each other eyes and she finally gives in. she says, "Okay, I will approve but you need to realize that you also have responsibilities here. You need to either re-think whether this job still works for you and if it does, I need your full commitment and that is even if you only have a few months of work left. I will ask that if you decide to stay and work here that you work with your publisher to schedule these events outside of your work hours."

I answer, "That is reasonable."

She pushes the performance review papers toward me to sign and I quickly sign. The more I think about this the more I think that I am insane to keep this job.

The rest of the day is back to the routine and by Wednesday night, Josh and I are pooped. We arrive home after doing a small grocery, soon eat dinner and are both just relaxing on the recliners in the living room. Josh makes small chat, "Shouldn't you be packing your bags for tomorrow morning?"

I chuckle, "Yes that seems like a good idea."

He gives me the look and says, "Jordan stop putting it off, you need to get to it."

I ask, "I know it's a few nights, are you going to come with me?"

"Jordan, before you ask questions you should think for a second. What did I tell you in the car on the way home Monday night?"

The memory had escaped me, "I remember now you couldn't get the time off. You don't need to be condescending about it I just forgot."

He rolls his eyes at me, "You're always forgetting. If I wasn't around, I have no idea how you would get around."

"Yah yah" I get up and depart to the bedroom to start putting a bag together when Josh reaches over and touches my arm.

I ask, "What?"

He smirks, "Do I get a kiss?"

"Do you deserve a kiss?"

Hey put his arms up and says, "Hey, I am just stating the facts. Didn't your boss mention the same thing? Attention to detail and managing your time."

This time I roll my eyes, "Yes"

"Well don't hate me for saying it."

"It's the way you say it."

He says, "Oh whatever, give me a kiss and I will tell you something."

I lean in and give him a peck on the lips but he pulls me into his lap and makes me giggle.

He says, "There's that smile. Okay well thankfully I am around. I printed out your itinerary for tomorrow morning and I did check the bank accounts this morning and it looks like we received our first installment from the publisher."

"You have been keeping this from me?"

He laughs, "I checked before we sat down for dinner. They transferred twenty-five thousand dollars to the account."

I laugh and say, "Wow well I think that the contract said the transfers will be made weekly. Sure, makes it that much more tempting to quit."

"It does but let's hold on a little longer nothing is forever so let's take our time with deciding our career moves."

"I agree." He lets me up and I get my things ready for New York.

Chapter 53
Thrill for This

Morning comes early and I find myself wanting to get some in before I go since Josh is staying home for the weekend. I wake to hearing the shower running and wait for the sound of the water shutting off before bouncing on him. I creep in to the washroom undetected; the shower curtain is still closed and I quietly wait with a towel in hand. He opens the curtain and jumps a little, "Jeez, have you heard of knocking?"

"I have, but you're my husband and I want to play." I approach him with the towel and start with patting his boys dry.

"Jordan the rest of me is wet, not just my balls." He exaggerates a sigh and roles his eyes.

"Fine, turn around" Josh listens and I pat his ass dry.

"You're bad." He scolds but lets me have my way with him.

I say, "I want to get it in."

"I know you do." He smirks and I follow him into the bedroom. I know that he will give in and let me do what I want because of what I have gotten away with so far.

He lies back for me to play with him first and I start with licking is yummy lollipop. I waste no time and do my best because I do have a plane to catch.

He rises and I'm feeling like I want to ride on top today so I straddle my husband and he has no objection and grabs my ass and pulls me onto him with the tilt of his pelvis he is in deep and I close my eyes for just a second. I rock back and forth, up and down. Josh has an impressive man. He slides his fingers in for a feel as I rock on him like a rocking horse. He knows how to make me come fast and my ride is short lived as I explode all over him.

Out of breath I say, "Babes, what the hell? You stole that from me."

He smirks, "I know but someone has a plane to catch."

"Do you want yours?"

Josh says, "No I'm fine."

I give him a sideways glance, "You're still rock hard. Let me get on my hands and knees for you." He takes the bait and in moments, he is back inside and giving it to me hard. He is determined and focused and I can tell by his breathing that he is getting close fast. I stay still for him and let him have his way. He doesn't want to be teased he just wants to get his and he does. Josh explodes in me. His breathing becomes deep and slow, he stops pumping me hard and instead he pushes into me as far as he can and I can feel his random shivers and I know that he is satisfied.

Fast-forwarding to when I am dressed and, on my way, to leave for New York City, Josh kisses me goodbye at the airport drop off area.

Josh says, "Love you and text me when you land."

"I will, love you too."

The airport is always busy and I rush to get my bag out of the back seat so that Josh can move along to allow the next drop off to pull in.

It is an organized rush to the terminal and in time, I find myself settled in a nice leather seat with a little television in front.

The flight attendant asks, "Can I get you a drink?"

I glance up at her and say, "A diet cola please"

As she leaves my phone beeps with a message. It's Devon. I haven't heard from him all week. After the cruise I thought it best to leave him be and allow him to sort out the mess with Sara.

I open the message, "Hey girl, you are always ordering diet cola."

I look across from me ahead and then behind and there he is sitting three rows back. That brown-eyed cowboy of mine he nods when I spot him.

The flight attendant returns with my drink and asks, "Is everything alright?"

I smile and say, "Yes but can I ask you something?"

"Fire away."

"I know the man sitting three rows behind me. Do you know if the seats next to me or him are vacant?"

"Yes, you can sit next to him or he can come to you. You two both have a row to yourselves."

Great, thank you." I pick up my drink and bag and walk over to him and say, "I didn't think I would run in to anyone I knew today besides Howard Stem who is in New York and here we are."

He slides over and allows me to take his seat. He smiles, "The life of an author. It's a small world. I was actually flying out from Toronto this morning."

I ask, "What was going on in Toronto?"

"Oh, just a crime thriller convention, it was a couple of days and now it's a couple of days in New York before returning home."

"How is Sara? Is she back from the Bahamas?"

He sighs and rolls his eyes, "Yes she returned Monday and then I left for Toronto on Tuesday. We saw each other briefly."

"That doesn't sound good. So did she return on her own or did you end up doing what you had mentioned?"

He shrugs, "It's not good right now but no I didn't need to resort to cutting off the funds to get her to come home. Sara did that on her own and the thing is with such a large house she pretty well said nothing to me and has kept to herself since returning."

"Why didn't you cancel the thing in Toronto or New York just so that you could be available for when she wants to talk?"

"I have stuff to do. I know it sounds harsh but she is a grown woman and I am not going to go chase her. She is doing this as a payback and I don't appreciate her playing games. I try to apologize and she won't listen. I know I was in the wrong. I get that but at the same time if she wants to stay in a relationship with me, she should at least let me try to make things right. Being pushed away constantly, that doesn't work for me."

I cautiously nod and say, "I think I get it. Well, I don't completely get it and I don't think I ever will because Sara's choice to stay with you would not have been mine if I found out my husband was cheating. I don't mean to be disrespectful. I can see how big a decision that was for her."

Devon bravely smiles and looks down. I know he wants to change the subject and I continue, "Dev, do you want us to stop what we have? We can if it brings you closer to Sara. I won't lie I will be devastated but I respect your wishes if that is what you want."

He gazes into my eyes smiles and whispers, "Jordan you know that I won't give you up. I care for you. I care for the child you are carrying. I know that you hate when I use this word but you are my friend and that's as much as I can be but know that you are my special friend and I never want us to grow apart."

I smile I know in another life we had to have been soul mates. If only we had met earlier, it would have been different.

"I don't hate you for saying it. I know what you mean by it and know that we love each other."

Devon says, "Friend is a safe word."

"I know" I look into his eyes and that spark in them makes me shy away.

He asks, "What?"

"Oh, you're just handsome that's all."

He says, "No, that wasn't what you were going to say. Go on spit it out."

"I was going to ask if you ever joined the mile high club but decided that it may be a bad idea."

He chuckles, "To answer your question, no but I would like to and I think it's a great idea."

I smirk and then look down the aisle to see that the light above the washroom is lit up to indicating that it is in use. I say, "The washroom is being used."

"So, what's that got to do with anything?" I give him a questioning look and he continues, "Oh come on silly we have the entire row to ourselves."

I whisper, "What about the flight attendant?"

"She passed with drinks already we should be fine for a while."

Devon gets a thrill for this sort of stuff and reaches into the overhang compartment for a blanket to cover us.

I lift the armrest and get in closer to him and he slips his hand into my pant and feels my slippery opening. He whispers, "You never disappoint. I never get tired of you." He presses his fingers in and out and rubs my cherry. He holds me close and I press up against his palm. He feels so good and now I want my own feel.

Under the cover of the blanket, I unzip his pant and pull out his massive shaft. I hold it in my hand it is hard and warm. I stroke him and I hear Devon inhale and exhale as he enjoys my touch.

I feel the wet of him starting to leak and I don't want to play into his game I want his dick now so I pull down my pant. The seat reclines just a touch and I back myself onto him. If there were anyone watching, it would look as though we were just spooning but not today, he wastes no time and shoves his man into my juicy pocket. He whispers, "I know you like that." He pushes in and admits, "Every thrust I can feel that little kitty of yours purr. You like him, don't you?"

I say in a whisper, "I love your big man."

Just then, another passenger walks bye and Devon and I lie still for a second. I am about to soak the base of his shaft with my happy kitty and when the person passes it is like they intentionally don't look our way. It was a woman who may have been in her early forties.

Devon starts up again and pushes into me some more and says, "Drench me in your juice." I listen and do as he says and I come quickly and hard. I have to bite my bottom lip to keep quiet.

He whispers in my ear, "Good girl, now under the blanket."

I pull up my pant and dive under the blanket. His shaft is glistening with my juice and I lick it off, my sweetness that I enjoy concealed under the blanket I suck on his shaft and lick his balls. I don't care at this point at getting caught because I feel like I am hidden away. He is quiet. The plane is quiet. All I can hear is the hum of the jets and he never stops me just every now and then I feel his hand rest on my back as I lick him clean. I stroke him firmly and grab his balls for my pleasure. I love the feeling of him in my hands and suck him faster and he thrusts up into my mouth and goes off, coating the back of my throat with his hot juice. I swallow and lightly suck as he gives it all to me. I wait a moment before coming up.

I smirk at him and he is grinning from ear to ear. "Girl, you are good."

"Ditto and you're welcome." I tuck a loose strand of hair behind my ear.

He admits, "I think this is the best flight I have ever been on."

We still have the blanket over us and I lean into him and give him a hug and say, "Me too and you're bad I can't believe that you get me to do things that I normally wouldn't do."

"Hey, no one was forcing you." He chuckles.

"Oh, I know it's me, I just want it that badly that I give in."

Devon asks, "Do you regret joining the mile high club?"

I shake my head no and he smiles and says, "Well stop the complaining silly."

The rest of the flight is relaxing and stress free and I close my eyes for a bit, snuggling up to my cowboy and wake when the intercom comes on warning of the landing at JFK.

New York is an organized bustle of people and the terminal is a zoo. I am happy that I have Devon here with me who knows his way around and in no time, we spot Howard Stem waiting for us. Howard leads us to a black limo parked in the rental car lot.

During the drive, Howard explains the day's events. We are to drive to a radio station. Howard was able to get a small slot on some popular talk radio show.

I cringe and get nervous to the thought that thousands of New Yorkers will hear my voice. I feel sick.

Devon notices, "Hey what's wrong?"

"I didn't know we were going to be on the radio."

Howard ignores my reaction and says, "It's great isn't it. I would have told you about it but I only received the call last night that the time slot opened up."

"I don't think I can do this." I admit.

Howard pretends not to hear it and explains, "It's just a short ten-minute spot and then you are done. To be honest I will be answering most of the questions. The host may ask you one or two questions but that's all. It will be easy."

Devon coaches, "You are going to be fine."

I try to put on a brave smile. I am going to have to get used to this. I just thought that I would only need to worry about meeting people in the bookstore not having my voice heard by thousands.

The limo drops us off at the station and the driver lets us out with holding the door open for us. A greeter at the door to the station welcomes and escorts us to the receptionist. She is a tiny thing very skinny with just a little shape to her and her hair is a rich brown color and cut in a bob.

She confirms, "Mr. Stem, Mr. Chambers and Mrs. Connor?"

Howard confirms, "Yes"

She smiles, "Please follow me." She leads us down a light grey hallway. Along the hallway, there is a window, which allows us to see into a cozy room. I see some computers, microphones, and electronics. There is a man in the room in front of a microphone and a bunch of controls. He has an olive complexion with a salt and pepper beard lining his jaw. He is in jeans, a white golf shirt and white ball cap.

The receptionist opens the door to the room, escorts us in and introduces everyone, "Jim this is Howard Stem, the publisher for Tail Fin Books."

Jim smiles and shakes Howard's hand firmly, "Nice to meet you, Howard."

"Thank you and I appreciate you accommodating to have us on."

The receptionist continues, "This is bestselling author D. Chambers."

Devon extends his arm out, "Please call me Devon."

"You got it." Jim replies.

The receptionist smiles at me and looks over at Jim, "This is Jordan Connor, soon to be bestselling author."

Jim's eyes go wide as he smiles, "Really, well it's nice to meet you to Jordan."

I say, "Thank you and it's nice to meet you too." My palms are sweaty and the host pretends not to take notice of my wet hands. I am so nervous.

Jim's instructs everyone to take a seat. We all find a spot, taking a seat on these tall stools that have backrests.

A staff member from the station adjusts a mic for each of us and they give us each a set of headphones.

Jim explains, "This is going to be a live show. Howard has already approved the majority of the questions I have a couple of my own if that's okay with you guys?"

Devon and Howard seem okay with it and Jim continues, "We may or may not get to them. I added them in case we can't fill the ten minutes. The mics will be set to on so please keep that in mind. They will pick up the slightest sound and your head set will be set to on so you can hear yourselves during the broadcast. I will introduce you all and then get right into the questions. Do you guys have any questions before we start?"

Howard and Devon say no and that leaves me. My hands are still sweaty and I can hear my heartbeat in my head as my shyness takes control. I nod because I can't say no.

Jim says, "Okay great." He gets to work on us confirming that our headsets and mics are on and then we begin not missing a beat.

"Good morning, New York, this is The Morning Heat with Jim Ricard hosting live from the studio in the heart of the city. Today I have three very interesting guests who have stopped by the studio.

Just months ago, he worked for a high-tech company down in Austin, Texas and now he is traveling the world and promoting his bestselling novel. His name is D. Chambers author of the Alexis Fallon thriller series.

Sitting next to Mr. D Chambers is an up-and-coming new Author, she is from Canada. You may or may not have heard of her but you are learning of her today and it is my pleasure to introduce Jordan Connor. She has written published her first book to her new romance series, Breaking Lines, which has hit bookshelves this week.

Next to Jordan is the man who discovered these two very talented individuals. He works here in New York for Tail Fin Books and his name is Howard Stem. How are you all today?"

"Good" Devon answers. Devon is comfortable and I can tell that he is enjoying this.

I smile and reply, "Great" it's a lie. I am shaking in my skin.

Howard says, "Fantastic"

Jim answers "Great, well let's start with you Devon. I understand you have been writing for over five years. What do you think it is about your most recent works that grabbed the attention of the world?"

Devon has answered this question before. I can tell because he doesn't miss a beat and answers smoothly, "I think it was the combination of writing about a dynamic, beautiful young woman Alexis and the mixture of writing a story with layers. That is what draws people in. For me, Alexis is my dream girl and made her into everything I love about women."

Jim asks, "What does Mrs. Chamber's think about Alexis?"

I muffle my laugh but my giggling gets picked up by the mic and Jim chuckles with me.

Devon looks at the ceiling smiles and sighs, "I walked in to that one. Well Mrs. Chamber's knows of Alexis but she has yet to read my books. It is a desire and what better way to add to the story with creating a desirable, relatable and likable character. I create fictional characters but those characters personalities are drawn up by the people I have come across in my life and there is a little bit of Mrs. Chamber's in Alexis." I sigh in relief for Devon. He made a great save. I am not sure if Sara will ever listen to this interview but if she does, I think she would appreciate his answer.

Jim says, "She must be flattered that part of her is in Alexis?"

"I think so."

Jim asks, "I have asked other celebrities this and I'll ask you. How has life changed since being thrown into the limelight?"

Devon answers, "It's amazing. To see something that you have worked so hard on and then to see it take off and the characters that you have created become loved by complete strangers is humbling. I am truly thankful to everyone that has believed in me and to the fans that have made my dreams come true."

Jim says, "Speaking of your fans I understand that you recently took some on a cruise?"

"Yes, I had some book signings across the United States and Canada and we did draws at the signings and a fan from each signing came with me to a cruise in the Caribbean last week."

"Wow, that's amazing."

Devon adds, "It was fun. The group that went was a lively bunch and it was great to give them that as a thank you for supporting me."

Jim turns his attention to me, "It is my understanding that you were also on the cruise?"

I clear my throat and reply, "Yes"

Jim knows at this point he is going to have to work to get me to talk, he has touched my clammy hands and I am sure that I am now a shade whiter.

He asks, "Was it a coincidence that you were on the same cruise because from the research I have done it is my understanding that you signed your contract with Tail Fin Books on that cruise."

I answer carefully, "It's a long story. Devon and I knew each other before the cruise. I have read his books and recognized him at a water park in Ottawa before one of his book signings. We had ended up chatting. I told him about my own writing and I guess that he saw something in me and extended a cruise invitation to my husband and me. That cruise has changed my life. That's how I met Howard Stem and the rest is history."

I smile timidly and look up at Devon who gives his approval in me answering this question and just when I think, I am finished, Jim digs more, "So you two hit it off immediately?"

I don't like where this is going but answer anyways, "Yes, we have lots in common and our personalities mix well."

Jim comments, "I have read parts of your book Jordan and have been online to see what your fans have said and they seem to speculate that the man that your main character is having an affair with is based on Devon."

I nearly choke, oh dear I answer, "I don't know what to say to that. I wrote the book prior to meeting Devon." That is a half-truth. The truth is I had talked to him online for months.

Devon saves the day, "Jordan is a gifted author and I was lucky enough to see it in her and honored that I was the one to discover her and give her the opportunity of success. She knows how to take her own fantasies and make them real in her writing and she has a gift of creating great characters."

Jim looks down at his question sheet. Somehow, Devon's response is enough for Jim to change focus and he has moved on to Howard. The palms of my hands are soaked in sweat and I am starting to feel tired with my nerves in full swing. I take a breath while Howard answers Jim's questions, "So you have two talented authors here. Do you consider yourself lucky? Is the way Jordan was discovered a normal method to getting your work discovered for the aspiring authors who are listening to this show?"

Howard answers, "Yes it's not every day you get a great like Devon in your portfolio let alone finding a hidden gem such as Jordan. To the aspiring authors I would recommend using the resources that you have available to you. It was pure luck that Jordan recognized Devon, they became friends and the rest is history. I think if you have friends that are writers or publishers, follow up with them. Let them know of the works you are doing. They may provide you that boost that you need to get in but at the same time, I recommend not to rely on them. I would say to those aspiring to work hard at your writing. Use online resources such as social media. Send in query letters to the publishers that interest them. Make yourself known and never give up, especially if writing is something that makes you happy."

Jim nods and replies, "That is great advice and for those listening. Is Tail Fin Books accepting any queries at this time?"

Howard answers, "Yes, we are looking for more romance authors to branch out into that genre."

Jim says, "Great and please let us know where Jordan and Devon's book signing will be?"

"They will be at Pages Book Store this afternoon from 1:00PM until 3:00 PM."

Jim replies, "Great well that wraps things up. Thank you so much for dropping by the show and be sure to check out Jordan Connor and Devon Chambers books that are available now."

I hear a commercial being played on the headphones, follow Jim's lead and remove my headphones.

Jim shakes each of our hands, "Great work guys and Jordan I hope that you didn't take the questions too personal. I ask the questions that everyone wants to know."

"Sure, I get it, no worries." I pretend like this interview was a breeze but my nerves are shot.

The three of us get back into the limo. Our next stop is the bookstore. Devon and Howard are chatting away across from me and I am brooding in silence. Devon is the first to take notice. He asks, "What is up Jordan?"

"The questions that the radio host asked, he said that he asks the questions that everyone wants to know. Why would my fans or the blog sites or whatever think that my story was based on an affair with you?"

Chapter 54
For Her

I forget how lonely it can be without her. I know when I was doing all the overtime, she wasn't happy. I can see why. She has only been gone since this morning and I miss her like crazy. I couldn't fly down with her because her flight left during a week day and I still need to work, but I'm not doing much of it now.

I'm a software developer and I also manage the database here at work. My desk is in a cubicle jungle of grays and most of the people here have dull personalities probably because they rather be elsewhere. I don't blame them.

I look over my cubicle wall for a moment to get an idea of who is here. It is still early so the office isn't full. I spot the lamp light a few cubicles away and on the far wall, I see that my boss's office door is open and the light is on.

I miss Jordan, my fun, creative and beautiful wife. I don't even want to be here. When I got to work this morning, I saw on my phone that she had sent me a message letting me know that she found her seat on the plane okay. It sounds like she is having fun and in the same breath, I know she wants me there.

I want to be there for her. I am so proud of her but sometimes I don't think she sees how much I feel for her. I have always been hard on her but I did it to push her although at times she was convinced it was to hurt her. I think she knows now that I meant well.

My work email is open in the background and for some reason even though I know Jordan is off in New York City I somehow expect a good morning email from her. She usually sends me a hello message to my work email. I'm used to it but I know that won't be the case today. What am I going to do with myself this weekend? I sigh.

My computer beeps to alert the completion of a scan I was running on the department's database. I start a second scan and minimize it while it runs its course. This weekend is going to be boring like it is here. It doesn't make sense to stay the weekend at home. It's not like we are broke and I suppose that habits die-hard. I'm decided. I'm going to find a flight to New York City that leaves after work. I open up a browser and search for flights and sure enough, I find a departure time that works for me. Before I book the flight, I text Devon. He gave me his number at some point on the cruise. I want my arrival to be a surprise.

"Hey Devon"

Devon replies, "Hey Josh. Are you trying to get in touch with Jordan?"

"No, that's why I'm texting you. I'll be flying to New York tonight. I want to surprise Jordan."

Chapter 55
Added Publicity

The two men look at each other as though they already know across from me in the limo. I say, "Seriously guys, tell me what's going on."

Howard sighs, "It comes down to your good old friend Steven Peach. He had copies of the photos and he posted them online."

"When were you guys going to tell me this?" I cross my arms and look back and forth from Devon to Howard, waiting for one of them to answer.

Devon shrugs and says, "Relax, you had to know something like this would happen."

"Devon, I thought..."

"You thought those pictures would go away?" I am shaking and Devon continues, "Jordan, I didn't try to keep it from you. I told you what becoming famous was like."

"Devon, if you knew than why did you allow it to happen?"

"It was an accident. You know that."

"I don't know what to say. I mean, it's one thing to have to explain this to Josh and it's sorted with him but my family, my friends, the people that I work with."

Devon looks at me and says, "Listen, I am sorry that you have to go through this and so early into your fame. On the up side of things you are dealing with heavy matters now and to be honest, this photo leak is giving us some added publicity." He takes a moment to shuffle over in the limo and takes a seat next to me. He puts his arm around my shoulders and continues, "Jordan, these things happen. There will always be some Steven Peach out there looking to take you down. I say let them try. We will go to the book signing. You will meet your fans, shake hands and sign books. It is as simple as that."

Devon's words as simple as they are has a calming effect and I look into those brown eyes that say it is okay, I got you. I say, "Okay, you're right. I'm over reacting." The most important person in my life has already seen the photos. If my friends or family finds out it is not the end of the world.

Howard adds, "You will do just fine Jordan. It will be an hour maybe two hours, tops."

The limo pulls up in front of Pages Book Store and the driver comes around to let us out. The front steps are a sea of people who are mostly here for Devon. I know this because they are calling his name and holding up copies of his books. This morning I am simply riding Devon's coat tails on this journey to fame.

The outside of the building is deceiving because when we walk in its huge, large open floors that open up so that you can see the second and third level and the ceiling is painted to look like a blue cloudy day.

If this were a concert, I would be Devon's opening band. People are just going wild for him more so than the crowds would back home. New York's people are vibrant.

Howard, Devon and I make our way to the podium, shaking a sea of held out hands along the way. Howard is first to speak at the podium and begins by saying a quick thank you for coming speech and thank you for supporting the authors of Tail Fin. I whisper in Devon's ear as Howard talks, "I am not good at public speaking like you. I just want to say a quick hello. Could you lead?"

He smiles, "Sure."

All I hear next is Howard saying, "Mister D. Chambers!" The crowed erupts with applause.

Devon takes a step forward to the podium. He was good at speaking to crowds even before his fame. Devon is a natural and people hang on to his every word, unlike me. I can be introverted and I know I am not as likable a person.

I stand there just a step behind him like a little fawn hiding behind its parent's legs. The crowd laughs at his jokes and cheer to his mentioned accomplishments. I watch, not listening to his words but watching the reactions and then I hear my name, "Jordan Connor!" I startle out of my daydream and Devon glances back at me motions me up to the podium with the slightest nod.

The crowd is clapping. I couldn't have a more welcoming crowd than this one. Devon stands with me at the podium he has his hand on my back a sign that he is with me.

The clapping quiets down and I clear my throat, force a smile and say, "This is my very first book signing today." The crowd claps; cheers and I let out a breath of relief, look up into Devon's eyes and he smiles and rubs my back with his one hand. The cheers quiet down again and I say, "Devon has such an amazing group of fans and I am humbled and touched that I have been able to experience the energy in this room." More claps and cheers erupt. I chuckle and start to find myself. I begin to take control of my nervousness. "My book, Breaking Lines is on sale today and I look forward to meeting and signing your copies." I sigh; my short speech is behind me at last. The crowed is amazing and supporting.

I questioned Howard Stem's decision to have me do a book signing so soon after my book hit the shelves but I see why he did. Devon's fans are a passionate bunch. Having passionate readers to gobble books is every Author's dream and at the same time, this is a good introduction for me to get my feet wet.

Devon is the star of today's signing and I forget the anger I felt from earlier about the photo leak. It is humbling to witness Devon's fans up close as they meet him. All are smiles, some are a pile of nerves, some speechless, others are chatterboxes. I sit next to Devon and watch them approach and interact with him.

Devon is a wonderful role model to look up to and he is the kind of Author that I want to become. He greets each of his fans with a warm smile and it carries into those beautiful warm brown eyes of his. Devon has a charisma that you can't really train someone to have. It is natural for him and he gives each one of his fans who have been standing in line for hours that feeling when they approach the table that they are the only ones in the room and that they matter to Devon. I know that I don't have charisma and am envious of this natural skill that Devon has.

Devon is the headliner who is getting all of the action with signing books and posing for photos. Here and there, some of Devon's fans ask me into their photo. I step in and smile with them. Some just ask me to help take their photo with Devon and I am okay with that too.

The first hour passes and I have signed a few from the pile of books that were stacked up in front of me at the desk. Some of Devon's fans had picked up my book while Devon was signing their copy of his novel and like a two for one deal, they would ask for my autograph.

In the second hour of the signing things start to pick up for me and now fans are approaching the table with my book as well as Devon's in hand and soon I am being asked to pose for photos and I start to feel like I am no longer an afterthought.

Towards the end of the scheduled signing people tend to become more relaxed and I find that the fans are asking more questions as the signing progresses. Most are questions about the next book release, next event or what it feels like to see your book in print.

I received some other not so fun questions. One man asked me if I plan to name my baby after his father Devon. I almost choked on my water when he asked. Devon steps in, "Her husband's name is Josh." The man smirks and I hand the signed copy of my book back to him. The bold man realizes his time is up and allows the next fan to approach the table. I glance at Devon as the man leaves. I know the skin on my neck has turned a shade of pink. Devon murmurs, "It's just a heckler and you are almost done. You are doing great."

I try my best to shake the sting of that question and work through a few more meets and this time a woman asks, "Is your husband Josh not here with you today because you left him for Devon?" Devon overhears the comment and this time I answer, "Josh had to work today. He wanted to be here." I force a smile and hand her back the signed book. I am sure that this woman would not think to ask questions like this to her own friends.

Devon gives me an assuring smile. I handled it well. Another approaches the table but they don't have Devon or my book in hand instead he has a paper and he positions himself so that he is standing at the center of the table between Devon and me. We both look up at him and he smiles and lays his paper down before us.

It is a photo from the cruise of us locking lips at the Authors ball. I stop breathing. This stranger smirks because he gets the reaction that he was hoping for and Devon steps in, "You are just too funny. Do you want us to sign your photo?"

"Yes" he says completely amused with himself.

Devon says, "very well" and he takes the photo and writes, 'To a very amusing fan, all the best D. Chambers'

Devon hands the photo over to me and I scribble below Devon's signature, 'and Jordan Connor' I hand the photo back to the prick.

He says, "I do have one question for you Jordan. Was sleeping your way to fame worth it?"

My hands are shaking and I keep them under the desk, "You are mistaken." I say through my teeth. He stares at me as though he is expecting more. I am doing my very best not to run away. Devon calls for the next in line up to the table and it forces the prick to move along.

Before he leaves, he says, "I got my answer good luck Jordan." I am not sure what he meant by that comment and I am not going to lie it is still weighing on my mind as I force myself to smile and welcome my last fans to the table.

The signing wraps up with a short speech from Howard, thanking everyone who came. I couldn't be more excited to have it be over with but remain on my toes and shake hands of the lingerers in the store while on our way out to the limo.

The limo drops us off at the hotel. Howard has booked rooms for Devon and me. I look at the reception desk and I know that I can't stay here. The marble floors, the mahogany tables in the lobby the gold door elevators. The rooms have to be in the hundreds per night. This isn't me. This isn't home. I turn to Howard and say, "I can't do this."

He looks at me, "Don't worry Tail Fin Books is covering the expenses for the weekend."

"No, it's not that. I can't stay here in New York for another day. I want to go home."

"You have another book signing tomorrow."

"I'm sorry but I want to go home."

Devon steps in, "Jordan look at me" He puts his hands on my shoulders and looks into my eyes as they start to tear up.

My voice cracks from trying to contain emotions. I say, "I just want to go home."

"Why just because you had a few hecklers at the signing?"

I look down at the floor for a moment and he says, "Jordan you can't let that stuff get to you."

I finally look back up and him and sigh, "I know, I hear you it's just that I'm tired, this baby is doing flips in my stomach and I miss Josh."

"If Josh were here, would that change your mind on leaving suddenly?" I nod and he explains, "Josh was going to surprise you at tomorrow's book signing."

My tears stop and I look up again and ask, "He is coming to New York?"

"He is flying in tonight on a red eye and was planning to surprise you tomorrow. He didn't want us telling you. He wanted to surprise you."

"I had no clue." I feel bad now for putting Devon in the spot of ruining the surprise.

Devon chuckles, "That is the point of a surprise right."

"I suppose."

We check in and I hang out with Devon in his suite but tonight it is tame. I am just not in the mood and instead need him as a friend and not a lover.

The mood is relaxing and we do what two friends do and sprawl out and watch our favorite shows. It is nice and I think that we both needed that.

Reading this you can predict what happens the next day. Howard, Devon and I attend another signing and Josh arrives to the event. I needed Josh, my husband and my love. After the signing, Josh and I say goodbye to Howard and Devon and take some leisure time of our own to see the sites while we are here. We visit Central Park, watch a show and touch the bull statue. We even take a helicopter tour around the Statue of Liberty. We stay the weekend and come Monday morning it is back to work.

This is where it starts to get weird. I pull into the work parking lot and there is a crowd of reporters and camera crews standing at the front entrance. I drive in slowly and find a spot to park. Did I miss something while I was in New York? I put the car in park, turn off the car, step out, and approach the building.

I get the feeling that they are waiting for something or someone as I walk up.

A lady in a matching red blazer and skirt approaches me, "You are Jordan Connor."

"Yes, what's going on?"

"We would like to ask you a few questions about your book."

"Are all the reporters here for something else initially?"

"No, they were all here in hopes to get an interview with you."

I get shy, "Oh, I wasn't expecting this." I take a step back and start to worry about how I am going to get passed these reporters and into the building.

"It's okay." She smiles and the camera man steps in closer aiming the camera to my face.

"I have to admit I am a little nervous. I don't mind answering questions but now isn't a good time. I have to go to work. Do you have a business card and maybe we can set a date to talk?"

The reporter is smooth and she says with a smile, "I agree completely. Here is my business card. Thank you."

I walk up the steps to my office building. Other reporters are shuffling to get my attention like wolves on a lamb and it is hard to hear the individual questions through the shouting. The camera crews hold out mics on metal sticks over my head and cameras jockeying for a good picture and I just say to the general crowed, "Good morning, I have to go into work this morning. Have a great day guys." I swipe my card; the door unlocks and I quickly enter the building. I have never been so happy and relieved to be at work and on a Monday of all days.

I approach my cubicle and my co-worker tilts her head out of her own and says, "Did you see your welcome show?"

I smile at her, "Yes I saw them."

"They stopped me this morning to ask questions about you."

"I hope that you only mentioned nice things."

She says, "Yes, didn't say anything about our fights." She winks at me and continues, "So now that your work is getting recognized how long are you going to keep this up?"

"What do you mean?"

She rolls her eyes and explains, "Jordan I read online that you signed a million-dollar contract with Tail Fin Books. I don't know why you haven't said a thing."

I shrug, "I didn't want it to get weird in the office."

"It's weird already with all of these reporters standing out front."

I let a sigh escape my lips before saying, "I know, it's just I didn't want to give my notice so soon or anything. This doesn't feel real and I just wanted to wait and see if this would all work out."

I get to my desk and call Josh to tell him what had happened. I don't know what to do and Josh left it to me to decide. I have worked over five years here and had planned to stay here for the rest if my career and now what?

The morning progresses and by mid-morning an email is sent to the entire office. It is at general message, not referencing anyone specific but the message is advising everyone not to the media about people who work in the building and such. This is about me and surprisingly management has not pulled me into a private meeting to discuss the media that is camped out front.

I spoke too soon the boss peeks in, "Jordan we need to talk."

I follow her to her office where a senior manager and the director are already sitting.

"Have a seat, Jordan." I take the only spot available, which is across from them.

The director speaks first, "You are aware of the media zoo out front. They are all there because of you."

"Yes, I saw them." I already feel like this meeting is not going to go well.

The director says, "We have already asked them to leave and they have. I need to make it clear to you that whatever you accomplish in your personal life must not interfere with this workplace."

I speak up, "Sir, it's not my fault. I don't even know how they found out that I work here."

"It is your responsibility for your co-workers sake and the sake of this business."

My boss steps in, "Jordan, we know that you signed an amazing contract with Tail Fin Books. You would have to live under a rock not to know. The thing that is concerning is you didn't tell us this and give us the heads up and now we have had to deal with a zoo this morning."

"I'm sorry, it's just I didn't think that something like this would happen."

My boss speaks up, "Management has talked together before calling you into this meeting and we think that it is best that you take some vacation time now to allow for all of the attention to cool down."

I sigh, "I don't have a lot of vacation time left. I just came back from the cruise and I took some time last week to head to New York."

The director says, "You have the one-time vacation entitlement." He is referring to the extra week set aside for marriage and such. It is a one-time entitlement.

I object, "I don't understand why I need to leave; the media is gone and I am here to work."

The director has already made up his mind. I see the look in his eyes. He is already ignoring my pleas. Both my boss and the director give each other some knowing glance. This time my boss speaks, "Jordan, this is for the best."

I don't know what to think. What is wrong with these people? Seriously, do they want me to quit? Just last week my boss was giving me a hard time about taking time off for New York City. I know that I don't need to do what they are asking, I have done nothing wrong but, on another note, do I really want to keep my job? Everything that Howard forecasted is happening and besides the deal with Tail Fin Books, I know that my book is starting to take notice because it is starting to make sales. Hypothetically, if I quit today, I will lose the entitlement that I had been saving for years. I know that the time off is silly but on the other side I did put in all those years of work and do feel entitled to having the time off.

Picking and choosing battles may be the best option. I have a fair fight but decide to give in to their request and take time off.

I return to my desk, gather my things and depart. It is nearing lunchtime so I send Josh a text and meet him.

We stop in at our favorite coffee shop, get some sandwiches, iced cappuccinos and a donut each and take a seat in a corner booth to eat and talk. He explains between chews, "Maybe it is for the best."

I take my sandwich out of the wrapper and say, "Maybe, I just don't get how they found out where I worked."

"Jordan don't be ridiculous. Your work has a public directory."

"Oh my god, yes I completely forgot. Okay well that is a relief. I thought that we would need to worry about the reporters showing up at our home address first."

Josh takes a sip of his drink then says, "Well we do need to worry about that but as long as our home address isn't listed anywhere public, we should be okay."

"I don't think it is." I reply.

After lunch, I drop Josh off at his work and I stay in town and make use of my time. I do a grocery since I can't return to my work and soon enough, I pick up Josh and we are on route home.

We pull into the driveway and thankfully, there are no news reporters but when Josh makes a run across the street to check our mailbox that is when a white SUV with a television news logo pulls up in front of our home.

I don't want to deal with this again and just enter into the home. They followed us and I feel disgusted that they did that. I watch through the curtains of our front window and I see Josh speaking to them across the street in front of the community mailboxes. I can tell that he is asking them to leave and thankfully, they do.

Josh comes inside, "Can you believe that? They followed us all the way home."

"This isn't good." I sigh.

"No, it's not." He affirms.

"Well, they are gone."

The baby gives me an energetic kick and I rub my stomach.

Chapter 56
Safe Haven

The days get strange after that news van followed Josh and me home. I didn't think that things would pick up so quickly. I can understand and appreciate the term, overnight sensation because that is how it all happened. A little bit of promotion, a renowned Publisher to support your work and immediately you become popular.

I took all the vacation days that I had and sick time I had accrued from work. Josh and I decided that it was time to make the change that Devon had explained on the cruise. Our home had become the go to place to camp out for media vans and it was starting to bother our neighbors. This baby was on its way. We loved our home but now with the lack of privacy I needed the security and a safe haven for us to start our family.

I looked for homes by searching the online listings in my time off and when Josh was off work, we would make appointments to see them. Eventually we settled on a larger home. The process was quick and our realtor was the best. This new home was closer to the airport but still out of the city. The home came with a hundred acres, a horse barn and pool. It was gaited, private and hidden from the road by many mature trees.

I had over two months of accrued sick days to use because I rarely called in sick in the years of work but after the success with this book and the attention that I was getting from the media I ended up using them all. My doctor wrote me a note to provide to my workplace that explained I needed early time off for the pregnancy. Her concern was that the media attention was stressing me and she wanted me staying off to relax. I could have just quit but for me it was the security of having a job that I could fall back on if this author career didn't work out. It was the principle too. I earned that time and it was mine for the taking and I used it to change my life, settle in a nicer, more private and secure home and I used the time to make my ultimate decision.

A couple of months gave me the much-needed time off and my belly grew. There was no way of me ever returning to work at this point and it is time to move on and accept that my dream has come to life.

I accompany Josh on the drive to town on a crisp clear November morning.

Josh is in the driver's seat and makes small chat, "So are you having second thoughts?"

I chuckle, "No, don't make me second guess myself."

"I don't make you do anything. You do that on your own."

After dropping Josh off at work, I take the familiar route to work. I turn into my work's parking lot and find the furthest spot from the building. I don't want the smokers outside to see that I am here or get spotted by anyone else. I take my time in leaving the car. For a few minutes, I just sit in the driver's seat with the keys out of the ignition and stare out at the lawn. This is it, all of these years in working here, dreaming about my writing career taking off and leaving and finally the day is here. I don't want to make a scene with people wishing me good luck and such. To be honest no one at work knows that I have come to this decision and the plan is to go in and clear my desk of all my things after giving my notice.

I step out of the car, lock the car door and then walk to the building. My plan fails. The smokers having a break outside see, wave and holler, "Hey Jordan, welcome back!"

I wave to them, holler a, "good morning" and enter the building. By this time of morning, almost everyone is here. The hallway is a hum of people talking, the sound of fingers moving on keyboards and the electronic beeps followed by the shuffling of paper from the printer. I approach my cubicle and there isn't much there. The desk looks bare. I did take some of my personal belonging before I took my extended leave. I have a few cloth grocery bags in hand that I grabbed before locking the car and I pack my two mugs, makeup and headphones. I throw out my notebooks and the notes that I pinned up to the cubicle wall. It is amazing how good this feels, it's freeing.

One of my co-workers' peeks in, "Hey girl I thought that was you."

She gives me a hug and continues, "My you look like you are ready to pop."

I laugh, "I feel like I am about to pop."

"So, you are packing up your things?" She asks in a whisper.

I make a forced sad face and answer, "Yes, with this baby on the way I am starting to get uncomfortable and besides it was just a matter of time."

She whispers, "I had a feeling, Jordan. If I were in your shoes, I would be doing the same. The advice that I have for you is to enjoy it." She gives me another hug.

"Thanks, you're a good friend."

She asks, "So have you told them yet?"

"Not yet, I was going to drop my stuff in the car and then come back in to tell them."

"Let me help you to your car."

We walk out together and she explained that a few of the women in the office wanted to throw me a baby shower but now it will have to be that and a going away party. I tell her to let them know that I thought it was so kind. I tell her that I would be in touch and they should come over to my new home.

I think that my boss was expecting me to make the choice that I had because she already had all of the paperwork completed when I stopped by her office to give my formal notice. All that I needed to do was sign on the dotted line.

Often when people give, their notices it is like a custom for them to send a fair well email to everyone and it is always something to the toon of, leaving is bitter sweet, I will miss everyone and that this was such an amazing place to work, blah blah blah. I didn't send out that traditional email and I didn't allow for my peers to do up some going away lunch. I didn't even go from office to office to say a personal goodbye to everyone. I just shook my boss's hand and walked out of there with my head held high. The feeling wasn't bitter sweet it was just sweet, amazing actually and I didn't regret not doing any of that because at the end of the day, the people who truly care for you will keep in touch and there will never be a goodbye with the ones that you consider friends.

I get into my car, take one look at the building where I had put in so many hours of my life and know that this is the end of a chapter in my life.

Chapter 57
The Kiss

I start on my drive home for the day until the evening when I have to drive back to town to pick up Josh. While on route for home, my friend Hailey sends me a text and my phone lights up "Hey, long time no see. Did you want to meet for lunch?"

I pull over to the side of the road and text her back, "Sure, when and where?"

She gives me the co-ordinates and I change my course and meet her for lunch at the same Texan Grill that we ate at before. I park the car in the restaurant parking lot and walk into the restaurant. Hailey is sitting at a table near the entrance.

"Jordan!" She waves me over to her table as soon as she spots me in the doorway.

"Hey Hailey, it's been too long." I take a seat across from her.

"That's your fault. You were supposed to text me when you got back from the cruise."

"That's right, I am so sorry I didn't mean to put you off."

"Don't worry. I know you have had a lot on the go."

The waiter comes with drinks. Hailey ordered them for us just before I arrived and we place our food orders and then continue.

Hailey says, "How are things?"

"Crazy, I just quit my job this morning."

"Wow, well I guess it was coming now that you are making more as an author."

"Yes, well I was planning to wait a little longer to make sure that I spread my roots with this writing career but with the media knowing that I work there has sort of changed things and now with this baby nearly here there was no point on going back."

Hailey says, "I think that you made the best choice. I mean I have read some of the articles and reviews of your book and you are getting some good press. People love your book."

"Thanks, I feel good now but Hailey every day I was weighing the pros and cons with deciding on if I should quit the job."

Hailey nods and continues to ask, "Anyway, how are things at home?"

"Oh, things are great. We are almost unpacked and the baby's nursery is complete."

"That's great Jordan but what I meant was how are things going with you and Josh?"

The waiter sets down our food and we are quiet for a moment. When he leaves is when I respond. "You have been reading the tabloids?"

"Jordan how can you not. When your best friend is plastered all over the pages you can't help it."

I sigh and say, "Things are good. I mean there was a bit of a blip on the ship but Josh and I worked it out and things are better."

She looks at me with concern in her eyes, "The media seems to think that there is something going on between you and Devon."

There was an appetizer on the table for us to snack on while we wait for our orders and I nearly choke on the nacho in my mouth and quickly take a sip of water to clear my throat, "One picture and that is all it takes."

"Jordan it's more than just one picture. There is that picture of the two of you kissing on that cruise ship. There are photos of you and Devon getting into a limo in New York City that implies you went on some secret date. There are even pictures of you at a book signing that show Devon rubbing your back and the expression on your face when some guy came to your table to ask you both to sign the picture of the two of you making out."

"Hailey, it's not like that. The limo was the car we used with our publisher Howard Stem. That's how we got to all the book signings in New York City. There were actually three of us in that limo."

She regards the information I just explained, "The media makes it look like something else."

I say, "Yes well, I don't like it but Howard and Devon assured me that all publicity is good publicity."

We pause for a moment as the waiter refills our glasses and asks if everything is what we expected then Hailey continues, "Can't you complain to the news outlets or something?"

"What's the point? Besides, there are always going to be something for them to blow out of proportion. I mean I don't like it but I just need to weather the storm for a bit."

Hailey has a background in criminology and I can tell that she has more questions and being her friend for many years I can tell that she wants to believe me but I know that she is not convinced.

She says, "Look I am not trying to start a fight. This isn't why I wanted to have lunch with you. I'm just concerned that's all and they always say there is some truth to what the media puts out. Those photos at the signing the look on your face in some of the images as that person was asking you to sign that photo, your eyes looked ashamed. Honest people I think would have more surprise or shock not shame."

I admit, "The kiss happened on the ship but honestly, Devon had a few too much to drink and it was a little mishap. Josh knows that."

She gathers her thoughts then asks, "Did you like it?"

"What do you mean?"

"Did you like the kiss Jordan?"

I know she will be able to tell if I lie to her so I admit, "I liked it. I am ashamed that I do."

Hailey stays the course and doesn't change her mood to anger. She looks concerned. "Devon knows that you liked it?"

I look down at the table and answer, "Yes he knows but we both know that we have our own families and our own lives."

"Jordan, you need to make sure that you keep on track. You are about to bring another life into the world. You know that I am your friend and I think for the sake of the baby it is best to distance yourself from Devon."

I sigh with relief that she isn't questioning the other tabloids hinting at the fact that Devon is the real father. "You are right."

Hailey asks, "Is there any way for you to not go to the same signings and author events?"

"Yes, but I am bound to see him from time to time. I can avoid some but not all. Anyway, in the coming weeks my baby will be born and I won't be going out as much."

"That's a good thing. Stay home, take care of your newborn and stay out of the media for a while."

"I will have to make an appearance from time to time but yes, I get what you are saying. I have some questions for you. What do the other girls think with all of the media?"

"Jordan I'm not going to lie but they think you have gone over the Boundary line in your marriage and you are lucky that the gossip that is going on in our circle of friends hasn't gotten back to Josh."

"Are they really my friends if they are talking behind my back?" I lean back in my seat.

"You admitted to me here, they know you and with what we have seen and read, we know when you are keeping something. I am your friend and will always be and as your friend I urge you to make Josh the center of your world until you love him the way that you once did."

"I do love him."

"You also love Devon and that needs to stop."

The waiter returns and asks how our food is at the most awkward time. It is about time to leave and we ask for the bill.

Hailey continues, "Let's keep it at that. I am your friend and as your friend that's all that I wanted to say on that note."

The rest of the time, we talk about Hailey and her family, my new house, our husbands and careers. I cover the bill for the both of us; not that I had to it is just that I wanted to. I needed the girl talk and Hailey is a great friend.

Chapter 58
You Already Know

This is it. I am not ending this on some crazy cliff-hanger or anything like that. I got to go on an amazing vacation, get the book contract of my dreams, make love to my cowboy, buy my dream home and I am about to become a mother in the next few weeks.

Devon is still going strong with promoting his work. His marriage to Sara isn't the greatest but it is better than it was before. Devon and I have both agreed to cool off for the moment so that he can focus on Sara and so that I can focus on bringing a child into the world.

It is a Saturday morning and I forgot to tell you Josh hasn't yet let go of his day job but he has quit his part-time work and now has the weekends to spend with me. Our new home is coming together quite nicely.

I'm in the kitchen having a toast and Nutella and he comes to join me.

"Good morning" His deep voice make me jump a little.

"Josh I can't believe that you slept in."

"I didn't, I was in the office just doing a bit of work on the computer and speaking to my parents."

"Oh, what's new with them?" I lick a bit of Nutella off of my finger.

He sighs, "Jordan, they told me that they read something about you and Devon."

It is always about Devon and me. Why can't they just write about our books? I say, "What's wrong?"

"They read an article that speculated this baby is actually Devon's baby."

"Josh, you know that is not true. How would that have been possible when we only ran into Devon in late summer? I was pregnant in the spring."

I see him thinking this through and the rationale behind my words. He asks, "Do you still love me?" There is doubt and sadness in his eyes as he looks into mine as the words leave his lips.

I put my unfinished piece of toast back on the plate and assure him, "Yes of course. Please don't let those strangers dictate our happiness." I say and extend my hand over the kitchen table to touch his hand.

Josh says, "There was something else that I was doing in the office."

I stop breathing. Was he trying to log into my accounts, my social media, what? I have to coach him and ask, "What were you looking at?"

"The donor we picked for this child. The donor is blonde haired and blue eyed."

"Yes?"

Josh continues, "The donor's family tree is all either brown or blonde haired but all of them have blue eyes. You come from a family of blue and green eyes."

"What are you implying?"

"It would be next to impossible for this baby to be born with brown eyes is what I am trying to say."

"Josh, what are you talking about, the donor's family tree only goes back three generations. There is a chance for brown eyes. What's wrong if our baby has brown eyes?"

"Devon has brown eyes."

I look at him for a moment. Is he joking? No, his face is ice cold, his eyes don't waver and his lips are closed in a frown. Whatever his parents said, they put something in his ear to make him doubt. I say, "What does that mean?"

"I think you know what it means." He's not joking.

"Josh this isn't funny. Do you suspect that I slept with Devon and somehow this child is his when I told you that I first met him after I was well into my pregnancy?" Only Sara knows after putting the pieces together and seeing the look in my eye when she confronted me on it. I know that she never told Josh because Josh would have confronted me earlier as he is doing now.

Josh says, "You better cross your fingers that this baby is either blue eyed or green eyed."

I spit back, "What if they are brown eyes then what?"

He says without missing a beat, "I think you already know."

About the Author

C.R. Misty, is an accomplished author who has been enchanting readers with her captivating romance novels. Misty finds solace in both the written word and the silver screen, where she delights in witnessing tales come alive. When she's not crafting extraordinary stories, Misty channels her creativity into the vibrant strokes of a paintbrush, nurturing beautiful blooms in her garden, and embarking on thrilling adventures in unexplored destinations. Sharing her life's journey with her ruggedly handsome husband and a devoted German Shepherd fur baby, she calls Ottawa, Canada, home. You can track her progress on book retailer sites and social media.

If you enjoyed this novel, please show your support for this book by writing a review online.